D0971561

Dark Souls

Also by Paula Morris

Ruined: A Novel

Dark Souls

A NOVEL

PAULA MORRIS

Point

Library of Congress Cataloging-in-Publication Data

Morris, Paula.
    Dark souls : a novel / Paula Morris. — 1st ed.
        p. cm.
    Summary: Sixteen-year-old Miranda Tennant arrives in York, England, with
her parents and brother, trying to recover from the terrible accident that killed
her best friend, and while in the haunted city she falls in love for the first time
as two boys, one also suffering from a great loss and the other a ghost, fight for
her attentions.
    ISBN 978-0-545-25132-7
    [1. Ghosts — Fiction.   2. Interpersonal relations — Fiction.   3. Grief —
Fiction.   4. Loss (Psychology) — Fiction.   5. York (England) — Fiction.
6. England — Fiction.]   I. Title.
    PZ7.M82845Dar 2011
    [Fic] — dc22

                                                          2010033871

      12 11 10 9 8 7 6 5 4 3 2 1   11 12 13 14 15/0

                        Printed in the U.S.A.   23
                        First edition, August 2011
                        Book design by Becky Terhune

For Agatha and Matilda Devlin

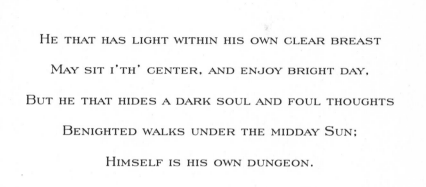

He that has light within his own clear breast

May sit i'th' center, and enjoy bright day,

But he that hides a dark soul and foul thoughts

Benighted walks under the midday Sun;

Himself is his own dungeon.

John Milton, *Comus*

PROLOGUE

At night, cornfields looked like the ocean. When clouds covered the moon, the vast darkness on either side of the road could be glassy bodies of water stretching into the distance. All they could see, driving home that night from the party in the farmhouse, was the road ahead, narrow and straight.

This was a game Miranda liked to play sometimes, even though she was sixteen and old enough to know better. She imagined that the country road was really following a rocky shoreline, that if they stopped the car and opened the windows, they'd hear nothing but lapping waves. They'd be in a different state — one that gazed out onto the Pacific or the Atlantic — not stuck in the middle of the country, in the sticky center of a dead-hot summer.

Maybe Rob, her older brother, liked to play the game as well. Maybe that night he'd forgotten that the darkness surrounding them wasn't the black water of a quiet bay. It was a forest of tall corn, brown and wilting during the day, rustling in a late-night hint of breeze. He couldn't see through that dark thicket. He couldn't see the other car speeding along another road. He couldn't hear it, either: Miranda and Jenna had turned up the radio because they'd finally found a song they liked. Jenna was in the front seat. She always liked sitting next to Rob, though she was Miranda's friend — the only real friend Miranda had made since their parents dragged them, a year earlier, to live in a small college town surrounded by cornfields.

Jenna turned her head to say something to Miranda. She'd bent forward, reaching to turn down the radio. The song had ended. Jenna was laughing.

There was a brightness, what seemed to be a spotlight piercing the passenger window. And then something slammed into them: The sound was like iron jaws crushing the car, crunching it. Everything was spinning, blurry. They were tumbling in the air — bumping, then tumbling again. Miranda remembered closing her eyes. She didn't remember screaming. She didn't remember the glass of her window cracking.

When Miranda opened her eyes, she was curled upside down, the seat belt barely holding her in place. Her face was stinging. Her neck, pressed hard against the roof of the car, ached. She didn't know how to breathe, let alone speak. Her shaking hands and legs felt so feeble, so useless, she wasn't sure if she could unfasten the seat belt.

But somehow she did. She stabbed at the seat belt lock until it clicked open, grabbing at the strap so she wouldn't drop onto her head. And somehow she managed to shimmy out of the shattered window and onto the hard ground. Even the guys in the sheriff's car, when they eventually got there, were impressed. They told her she'd done good. It took them much, much longer to cut Rob out of the driver's seat. They had to send for a man with a truck. They kept telling Rob to hang in there because help was on its way. Any minute now, they said: You just have to hang in there, buddy.

It was a hot night, but Miranda was cold. She sat in the dust, a deputy's jacket over her shoulders, the corn whispering around her. There was another car, a red car, upside down in the intersection. Men talked on radios. One of them gave her a half-empty plastic bottle of water. They said her brother was going to be okay, once they got him out of there. They said that when they got them to a hospital, someone would pick all the pieces of glass out of Miranda's face. They said the red car must have flown through the stop sign. They said they were real sorry to tell her this, but the other girl in her car was dead.

Miranda knew this even before they told her. She could see Jenna, small and squashed, upside down in the front seat, her fair hair illuminated by headlights. Jenna's eyes were closed, and her mouth was open. She had been about to say something, Miranda wanted to tell them. They'd been singing along to the song on the radio, mainly to annoy Rob, and then Jenna was about to say something. Now there she was, hanging in the front seat, the door smashed in around her.

Miranda shivered: The breeze had turned cold. She hung her head, blinking back tears. Someone was walking toward her, footsteps scuffing the dirt. When Miranda opened her eyes, she could see right away that it wasn't one of the deputies. It was Jenna, in jean shorts and blood-smeared Blondie T-shirt, her charm bracelet glinting at her wrist. She didn't have any shoes on: She'd taken them off in the car, Miranda remembered, because the straps were hurting her.

Miranda opened her mouth to cry out: She could still see the Jenna in the car, buckled and squashed and bloodied. But here was this other Jenna walking toward her, smiling. She drifted her fingers across Miranda's scalp, brushing Miranda's hair back from her stinging forehead. Jenna's touch was gentle, but it felt like the iciest winter wind.

Jenna took another few steps into the field and disappeared, dissolving into the darkness. Miranda called out her name. She staggered to her feet, the jacket falling off her shoulders, calling Jenna's name over and over again. The corn rustled back at her, keeping its secrets. One of the deputies got her to sit down again, and to drink some water. Miranda heard them saying that it would be better if she sat with her back to the car so she wouldn't have to stare at her friend's body trapped there in the front seat.

That night was the last time Miranda saw her friend alive. The last time Rob could sit in a car — or any confined space — without having a panic attack.

The first time Miranda realized she could see ghosts.

4

CHAPTER ONE

Miranda and her mother caught a taxi from York station, with three suitcases stuffed into the trunk, and the extra luggage piled between them in the backseat. Even though the sky was an ominous gray, Rob and her father said they'd walk.

Miranda's mother opened her mouth to object, but then she changed her mind and said nothing. Miranda knew what her mother was thinking. It was a frigid cold winter's day. The mist looked close enough to touch. They were in a foreign country, and a strange city — built on the ruins of an old Roman fort, an old Viking capital, a medieval stronghold. Its thick stone walls loomed over the station's parking lot. The streets were narrow and winding; there was a river to cross.

"They're sure to get lost," her mother murmured, tugging the hem of her coat so it wouldn't get slammed in the door. "But . . ."

She didn't need to finish her sentence. Rob hated sitting in cars, especially small European cars where someone tall like him had to hunch. The only way they'd managed to drag him to the airport back in Iowa was because one of the neighbors drove a school bus. Rob spent the flight roaming the aisles or standing around the back of the plane, looking out the window at the endless clouds. On the train across the Pennines, Rob paced the entire length — eight carriages — multiple times, until Miranda complained he was acting like a demented polar bear.

Ever since the accident, Rob couldn't stand small, confined spaces. Whenever he felt trapped or surrounded, he got dizzy and sick.

"He'll be okay, Mom." Miranda would have squeezed her mother's hand, but there were too many bags in the way. She did this kind of thing a lot these days — trying to reassure her parents that everything was okay, really, even when nothing was okay anymore. But she was tired of talking to doctors and listening to people ask how she *felt*.

There was nothing anybody could do about it. Nobody could bring Jenna back. And nobody could take away the guilt. Why was Jenna gone, and why was Miranda still here? And why had Miranda staggered around the smashed-up car like a dizzy fool when she could have tried to help Jenna, to save her? The only useful thing she'd done was dial 911.

Miranda and Rob's doctor thought a family vacation

far, far away was just what Rob and Miranda needed. Far, far away — those were his exact words. As though they'd be staying in a castle in a fairy-tale land, not a rented apartment in some wintry English city.

They were here in York because their parents wanted to be here. Jeff, their father, was a history professor, and he was giving a paper at a conference on Richard III, one of his scholarly obsessions. He was planning to come alone until Peggy, their mother, was invited last-minute to fill in as a guest conductor at the music festival held each December in York Minster.

"It's on a street called the Shambles," Peggy was telling the taxi driver, fumbling in her bag for her reading glasses and the directions she'd printed out. "Do you know it? It's near something called . . . Coppergate. Is that one of the city gates?"

"Don't worry, love," said the driver. "I know where the Shambles is. And a 'gate' is what we call a street here — it's an old Viking word. Coppergate, Petergate, Stonegate."

The river Ouse — a name that once upon a time would have made Miranda snicker — was a steely gray, glazed with patches of ice. Bare trees lined the riverbank. Even the geese taking shelter beneath them looked cold, their feathers bristling in the wind. A garish tourist boat, with an open top deck of red plastic seats, was moored on the far side. The chalkboard propped on the deck read *No Tours Today*.

"You see," the driver went on, "what you're calling a gate, we call a bar."

"A bar?" Peggy echoed.

"Bootham Bar, Monk Bar. Some of the old entryways to the city. And what you'd call a bar, we call a pub. Plenty of those in York." The driver shot them a grin over his shoulder. "Just remember — streets are gates, gates are bars, bars are pubs."

"That's funny." Peggy's laugh was nervous. She bent toward Miranda and lowered her voice. "Your father will never find it."

They passed one of these bars — sand-colored stone, with a gaping archway. A stairway led to another chunk of city wall, a couple of stories high. Miranda gazed up at the bobbing heads of people walking along it. Behind them, she could just make out the ivory peaks of the huge medieval cathedral.

"Look, Mom," she said. "That must be York Minster."

Peggy wriggled and ducked, but Miranda realized it was impossible for her to see over the hillock of bags.

"One week from Sunday," sighed Peggy, talking about the concert. "For better or worse."

The orchestra would be performing in the Minster, a building that was almost a thousand years old but still taller and more imposing than any other in York. Miranda's mother had been breathing, eating, and sleeping the concert ever since she got the gig.

The taxi turned: A long stretch of wall was visible now, sitting high above a green gully. Miranda was hoping to spend a day, at least, exploring the medieval walls. When she was little, she had dreamed about living in a castle. Her doll's house — pink, plastic, fake colonial — looked so generic compared with the sprawling stone edifices, with their moats and drawbridges and arrow slits, that she read about in books. She never saw herself as a princess, never bought into what her father jokingly referred to as the Disney Industrial Complex. When she'd thought about living in a castle, it didn't involve fluttering around in a gauzy dress, waiting to be kissed or rescued.

Instead — not that she would have admitted this to anyone, especially Rob — Miranda had imagined herself scampering along lofty battlements, dodging the raining arrows of marauders, or seated at a feast in the Great Hall, watching acrobats tumble and bears dance, warmed by a roaring fire and the heady taste of mead (whatever that was) in a pewter goblet. Silly fantasies, she knew, especially as she learned more about history. The past had its darkness, its nasty secrets. Castles were drafty and cold in winter, smelly in summer. People starved to death in them during sieges. Belowground, where they never saw the light, prisoners were kept chained.

Still, it was the sinister parts of the past that made it interesting. According to Miranda's father, Richard III had supposedly murdered the two young princes, his own young nephews, to grab the crown for himself. They didn't come much more sinister than that.

"Problem for you ladies is them bags," the driver was saying. "Cars can't drive along the Shambles. I'll get you as close as I can, but then you'll have to walk."

"Great." Peggy sighed again. She looked tired, Miranda thought, after two flights and the train ride. In fact, both of their parents had looked tired for months.

"We'll manage," Miranda told her, though she didn't know how they would, exactly. It was too cold to stand around on the curb, waiting for Rob and her father to turn up. And the place they were staying was "a quaint upstairs flat, with old-world ambience," according to her mother, who could recite the website. In other words, no doorman, no concierge, no porters — and no elevator. The Shambles: not a bad description for day one of the Tennant family's vacation.

Climbing out of the taxi, Miranda could see right away that the street was too narrow for cars. It was lined with old, half-timbered houses, some leaning so far forward it looked as though you could pass things from one upstairs room to another, right across the street. Even though it was a dank and miserable Friday afternoon, the street was thronged with tourists.

Miranda followed her mother up the street, wishing people would get out of her way. Couldn't they see she was dragging two suitcases, wearing Rob's messenger bag, and trying to keep a grip on her own purse? She didn't know what Rob had packed in his bag — concrete and bricks and industrial-size boxes of Xanax, maybe.

"It's just like Harry Potter, isn't it? Like Diagon Alley!" said Peggy, sounding overly cheerful. Miranda tried to muster an enthusiastic smile. Sometimes her parents forgot that she was sixteen now, not six. Though

she had to admit: It did kind of resemble Diagon Alley —
quaint and rustic. Every house in the street looked
hundreds of years old. Throw in a thatched roof and a
wand store or two, and the picture would be complete.

Most of the lower floors of the buildings along the
Shambles were stores selling expensive souvenirs or
chocolate or watercolor views of the Minster. A group of
young Japanese tourists, wearing Burberry scarves and
transparent rain ponchos, stood in a clump outside a
tiny art gallery, taking photographs of each other with
their cell phones. A middle-aged woman carrying a bulging plastic bag of groceries bumped into Miranda and
apologized: She seemed to have materialized out of
nowhere, until Miranda noticed the slivers of alleys that
connected the Shambles with what looked like an open-
air market.

Miranda paused to readjust her cargo. Her mother,
farther up the street, had stopped underneath a hanging
painted sign that read DEVLIN'S PIES AND FANCIES.

"I'm just going in to get the key!" Peggy waved the
crumpled booking sheet she was clutching. She mouthed
the words *the key* again while stabbing her finger at the
ground-floor shop — as though Miranda were deaf or
stupid — and then disappeared through the door, aban-
doning two suitcases outside.

Miranda had to scramble up the street as best she
could, suitcases bumping along the cobblestones, to stand
guard. Her father and Rob were taking their time getting there. They'd probably dropped into a bar — sorry,

pub — on the way so her father could try a pint of Ye Olde Warm Ale.

Miranda stood with her back to the shop window. Hopefully, this flat wouldn't be too bad. Her mother said they were the first visitors to stay there, ever. The upper floors had been used for years as storage space for Devlin's, and the renovations were completed only a month ago.

The building directly across the street looked as though it could use some renovations as well. Miranda was amazed that its slumping top two stories managed to stay up. Unlike its neighbors, which were either scrubbed brick or freshly painted, this house was peeling and derelict. All but one of its windows were boarded up. It looked completely out of place in such a picturesque historic street.

When the swarm of camera-toting tourists in front of her moved on, Miranda noticed someone leaning against the house's boarded-up doorway. He was a young guy, a couple of years older than Rob, maybe. He wore a long black coat — grubby, worn leather, with buttons missing — and he was gazing into space. He was tall and gaunt, and he had the most ferocious dark eyes Miranda had ever seen, though maybe they just seemed intense because his face was so white. He was as pale as a vampire.

Miranda didn't mean to stare, but there was something interesting and "off" about him. Boys at home didn't look like him — not even the college students. He wasn't good-looking in any sort of conventional way. He was too thin, too pale, too sullen.

He turned his head and caught Miranda looking. She shrank back against the shop window, her face sizzling, wishing she could disappear into the ground or at least behind her luggage. Before she glanced away, Miranda glimpsed the look on his face. Not interest, not indignation. Suspicion.

The store's doorbell chimed, and Miranda's mother stuck her head outside.

"Miranda! Lord Poole is here — you know, your father's friend."

"Oh," said Miranda, though she only vaguely recognized the name. The guy across the street caught her eye again, his expression even more intense, and then he stalked off down the street, his open coat billowing behind him like a cape.

Miranda's mother emerged from the shop, brandishing the keys and breathless with excitement. Miranda wasn't sure if it was because they'd managed to find the right place, or because she'd just met a member of the British aristocracy. Lord Poole himself was smiling and snowy-haired, with a V-shaped beard, red cheeks, and wild silver eyebrows. He wore a waxy, dark green jacket and mud-splashed rain boots. He should have a gun cocked over his arm, Miranda thought, and a Labrador trotting at his heels.

"I come into York so rarely these days," he said, after Peggy finished her effusive introductions and Miranda had submitted to his iron-grip handshake. "I tend to keep to myself in the country. Very crowded here, isn't it? Tourists, you know. Present company excepted, of course."

"I hoped Jeff would be here by now," Peggy said, frowning. "I'm sure he and Rob are lost."

"Distracted, probably," said Lord Poole. "York is an early modernist's paradise."

"Miranda's very interested in history as well," Peggy told him.

"Glad to hear it," Lord Poole beamed. "Like father, like daughter — yes? You know, I have a very old book that may be of interest to you," he added, patting the pockets of his jacket as though he were looking for it. "I'll drop it off this weekend."

Miranda tried to smile, but she was starting to feel chilled to the bone, not to mention very tired. It was almost sixteen hours since they'd left home, and she hadn't got much sleep on the plane. Her father should be the one standing here in the freezing street chatting with his BFF, Lord Poole. All Miranda wanted to do was find her bed and collapse on it.

"That's really very kind of you," said Peggy, darting a fierce look at Miranda. Evidently, her mother didn't think she was being polite enough. "Miranda is a little tired right now — the flight, you know . . ."

"Of course, of course!" Lord Poole looked embarrassed. "Please, let me help you carry these bags upstairs. Miranda will have plenty of time to read up on all the local history and mystery. Lots of strange, dark secrets here."

"Really?" Peggy fumbled with the key.

"Oh yes — a lot of old ghosts walking the streets of York, you know. This is the most haunted place on earth."

Miranda's stomach clenched, as though she'd just been punched. She didn't want to hear this. She really, really did not want to hear this.

"Ghosts everywhere," said Lord Poole, warming to the subject. "Viking pillagers and Roman soldiers, Catholic martyrs, plague victims, hanged highwaymen . . ."

"Well!" said Peggy, her smile a little too bright. They were getting into the danger zone of Talking About Death, which tended to be off-limits these days in the Tennant household.

"Haunted tours are very popular, I hear," Lord Poole blithely continued. "Fun rather than factual, I think. Actors in costume leaping about in the snickelways."

"Snickelways?" Miranda was surprised to hear herself speak, because her throat was so dry.

"Ah . . . alleys, I suppose you'd call them. Passages. York's a labyrinth of secret places."

Secret places. Ghosts. Miranda couldn't listen to anything else Lord Poole and her mother were saying. All she could hear was the agitated thudding of her own heart.

Miranda had never told anyone about seeing ghosts — not the doctors, not her friends, not Rob, and certainly not her parents. She hadn't told them about watching Jenna get up and walk away from the crushed car, and she hadn't told them about the other ghosts she'd spotted since.

Late in the summer, driving along a country road with her father, she'd seen a farmer with an ugly wound spread across his chest, leaning against the route marker at the crossroads. Miranda had cried out in horror before she realized that all her father could see was the cloudless blue sky and a hawk circling the field.

And sitting by the river once, watching the university team row, Miranda had suddenly felt an eerie, unseasonal cold that shivered up her body from her toes. The gray face of a woman, insubstantial as mist, stared at her from just below the water's surface, one ghostly hand reaching up through the ripples. Miranda had screamed, leaping to her feet. The girls she was with — Bea and Cami, who were doing all they could to help her miss Jenna a little less — didn't know what had upset her. They thought she'd been stung by a bee or that she'd spotted a snake slithering up onto the bank. They couldn't see anything bobbing under the gentle waves of the river.

Sometimes, Miranda wondered if she'd seen more ghosts and not even realized. But it wasn't a subject she could exactly discuss. Bea and Cami and the other girls at school had been sweet, but sometimes Miranda saw them exchanging glances. Since the accident, they thought she was messed-up, fragile, kind of unhinged. If

Miranda told them she could see ghosts, they would think she was a freak.

So if York was even more haunted — "ghosts everywhere," as Lord Poole had said — than Iowa, Miranda didn't want to think about it. Not yet, anyway, until ghosts started showing up. This much she'd learned in the months since the accident: Ghosts *were* everywhere, whether Miranda wanted to see them or not.

CHAPTER TWO

"Miranda — you have to wake up."

Someone was calling her name, and Miranda wanted whoever it was to be quiet. She didn't want to be shaken, stirred, or moved in any way from the soft nest of her bed.

"Wake up, you idiot." The voice belonged to Rob. The hand that had just turned on the brightest light in the room probably belonged to Rob as well. "You've been asleep for three hours, and Mom says if you don't get up you won't —"

"Sleep tonight — I know," croaked Miranda. Her eyes were practically gummed shut, but the light was still too strong. She didn't care if she couldn't sleep tonight. All she wanted to do was sleep *now*.

"It's *already* tonight." Rob sounded smug. "It's dark outside. We're going to dinner in an hour. Get up, Dormouse."

Dormouse was the name Rob used to call Miranda when they were little, because she was always curled up somewhere in the house reading a book, unwilling to play basketball with him on the driveway or join some frenetic game of tag.

"Whatever," she said, sitting up and rubbing her eyes. Rob was standing in the doorway, flicking the light switch on and off to annoy her. The room was small, with black rafters striping the low white ceiling. Rob's tall frame filled the door. "You should be thanking me for taking the smaller room."

"You should be thanking *me* for bothering to wake you up in time," said Rob. "You have total bed head and your face is all creased. You look like a fool, as usual."

He thumped away down the narrow hall before Miranda had a chance to throw her pillow at him. Rob was eighteen, two years older than she was. Bea and Cami and some of the other girls at school thought he was really cute, but they were wrong: He was just her goofy, vain, bossy older brother, who treated her as an occasional accomplice, servant, and general inferior being. Still, they looked so much alike that people often mistook them for twins.

Miranda stood in front of the small mirror tacked none-too-securely to the bedroom wall. Peggy said Miranda's hair was auburn, which meant it was something between red and brown, and everybody else thought it was dyed. Her eyes were brown and ordinary when they should have been green and exotic, but there wasn't much she could do about that. Jenna used to tease her about her stilt legs and unnaturally white teeth — "Next to you I look like a midget with tooth jaundice," she'd complain — when they were wasting time on the Internet deciding which celebrities they resembled. Miranda didn't do that anymore. Sometimes it felt as though she didn't do *anything* anymore.

She'd never been someone who had tons of friends and a big social life. Not in Bloomington, Indiana, when she was a little kid, or in the suburbs of Chicago, where they'd lived for almost ten years before her parents got jobs at a new university and moved the family to Iowa. Sometimes she'd felt that she'd never fit in anywhere. Nobody else ever had classical music playing at their house every day. Nobody else had a cat called Bosworth — named for the battlefield where Richard III was killed, as Miranda had had to explain so many mortifying times. In seventh grade, her class had to write letters to some kids in Nigeria, talking about life in America, sports teams they liked, how they spent their free time. When they got to what their teacher called "hobbies and interests," Miranda wrote that she liked reading and writing. "Those aren't hobbies, freak," said the mean girl who sat next to her. "They're schoolwork. What is *wrong* with you?"

Jenna was the first real best friend Miranda had ever had — someone who didn't think there was anything wrong with her. Someone who didn't think she was too nerdy or too quiet or too tall. Jenna got her out of the house and made her go to parties, and once she'd even talked Miranda into a double date. Miranda's guy-for-the-night was on the school debate team and — according to Jenna — a genius. "Dude, he is your only intellectual equal in this school," Jenna had promised. "And he could totally be the younger brother of Daniel Craig — you know, if Daniel Craig had brown hair and was tall and came from Norwegian-American farming stock."

The guy from the debate team might have been tall and brainy, but during dinner he talked on and on, in a loud voice, about which colleges he was considering and how they'd be lucky to have him, and when he kissed Miranda good night, it felt as though a baby was slobbering on her cheek. Even Jenna, who always tried to give everything a positive spin, had to agree that the evening was a disappointment: *Her* date knew nothing about Jenna's obsessions — *Archie* comics, New Wave music (strictly 1979–1984), and soccer. "I can't believe he's never even heard of David Beckham," she muttered to Miranda on the way out of the restaurant. "From now on, we're only dating Europeans."

Unfortunately, there were no Europeans at their school, only Americans. But then someone knew someone else who was hosting a Spanish exchange student, and Jenna managed to wrangle a party invitation. The party was way out of town, at a farmhouse, so Jenna sweet-talked Rob into driving her and Miranda. The Spanish student, a cute guy named Alejandro, knew all about soccer, and he told Jenna that if she came to visit him in

Spain, he'd take her to see Barcelona play Real Madrid. "Tonight," Jenna announced when they climbed back into the car, "was the Best. Night. Ever. I demand to be in control of the radio on the way home."

That was the night of the accident.

Miranda shook her head, turning away from the mirror. If she kept thinking about Jenna, and what happened at that crossroads deep in the cornfields, then she was going to feel sad and guilty and angry all over again.

At least Rob seemed to be in better spirits these days, she thought, tying her hair into a loose ponytail. For months, he'd moped around the house, too preoccupied to even bother to tease her. Though he *could* be a tiny bit grateful to her now for taking the smaller room. When she stretched, her arms practically brushed the rafters, and there was hardly anywhere to stand: The bed, a nightstand, and her suitcase, sprawled open on the floor, took up all the space. The one bare piece of wall was consumed by a clanking radiator and the mirror.

Rob had a better view as well: His room overlooked the market with its canopied stands, the backs of the big stores on Parliament Street, even a church spire. In Miranda's room, the two dormer windows overlooked the street, but it was impossible to see much apart from the house opposite, the scruffy one with boarded-up windows.

Miranda pulled back the flimsy white curtains. Rob was right: It was very dark outside, even though her cell phone — no good for calls or texts over here, but useful as a clock — said it was just after five P.M. People were still shopping and sightseeing below — Miranda could hear them, though she'd only be able to see them if she opened the latticed window and leaned out. It was too cold for that, she decided. She wished they didn't have to go out tonight to eat.

The crumbling house across the street looked almost close enough to touch. Its sole unboarded window faced into Miranda's room, but its attic was in total darkness.

Miranda caught her breath; it was beginning to snow. Soft white flakes fell onto the sill and down into the street. Snow wasn't exactly a novelty — they got a ton of it in Iowa, deposited in intense blasts every winter. But watching it fall onto the eaves of these gingerbread houses made the snow seem like something out of a fairy tale. It was only a light dusting, the kind that would be gone by the morning, she knew. Still, it was pretty.

In the attic across the street, a light flickered. A tiny light — the stub of a candle, Miranda could see now, sitting in some kind of dish and placed just inside the window. The rest of the attic was still dark, the candle illuminating nothing but the snowflakes as they hit the pane and dissolved into smears of sugary ice.

The candle flickered and surged, its flame a long streak of liquid gold. That was when Miranda saw him — not move into place, exactly, or sit down, but just appear, as though he'd been there all along. A young guy, older than Rob but not by much, his pale skin luminous in the candlelight. His brown hair was short and thick, disheveled in a way that suggested he'd been running his hands through it. His dark eyes stared straight at her. He was looking at her and through her at the same time, and it was too late to lean away from the window, to close the curtains and pretend she hadn't been peering into his room. It was a gaze that pinned her down, in a way that Miranda would think about over and over the next day and still not be able to explain.

Through the blur of snowflakes, Miranda could see that his was an imperious face, with a long, thin nose and high cheekbones. Despite the pallor of his skin and the tired purple shadows under his eyes, he was beautiful. The most beautiful guy she'd ever seen. She didn't know how else to describe him.

That was a word Jenna used to use, talking about the guys she thought were supremely good-looking. "He's just so *beautiful*," she would say of a dead rock star like Jim Morrison, or someone alive but unobtainable like her favorite celebrity crush, David Beckham. None of the boys at their school were beautiful, of course. They might be cute, or hunky, but never beautiful.

This guy in the window, Miranda thought, would impress Jenna, even. He was so beautiful, she couldn't take her eyes off him. She didn't even feel embarrassed when he stared right back at her. This was the second time today she'd been caught staring at a guy — what was up with that? She'd never behave like this back home. Around the boys at school, she always felt shy and dorky.

"Dormouse — bathroom's free!" Rob shouted from the hall. "Don't take all night. Nobody here knows you, so it doesn't matter if you look ugly."

"Okay!" she called nervously. She turned her head toward the door in case her brother came in and caught her staring at some random guy. But Rob didn't come in, and when Miranda looked back outside, all she saw was a window smeared with snow. The light in the other attic had gone out. The dark-haired guy had moved away from the window. If it had been later at night, Miranda might have thought she'd dreamed the whole thing up.

Lord Poole took them to dinner at a cozy place on nearby Fossgate because the streets were too slippery to walk far. Miranda skidded on the cobbles, not paying enough attention. She was preoccupied with the guy in the attic window, wondering if maybe she'd see him walking down the Shambles tomorrow. Would he speak to her? Would he even recognize her?

Halfway down the street, a tiny stone bridge humped over a stagnant-looking canal that was, apparently, the river Foss.

"Dammed by William the Conqueror," Lord Poole explained when they paused to peer at the narrow black ribbon of water.

"Why?" asked Rob, pulling up the collar of his jacket. "Didn't he like it?"

Jeff and Lord Poole started laughing. Miranda rolled her eyes, though she doubted that Rob could see in the dark. "He means William the Conqueror *built* a dam."

"So the city's walls wouldn't need to go all the way around," Lord Poole continued. "Part of it was protected by the river."

"Can we eat now?" asked Rob. He wasn't interested in history the way Miranda was. She had no idea how he was planning to occupy himself while he was in York, but she hoped he wasn't going to tag along with her everywhere, complaining when he couldn't find an Apple store or moaning about the rain.

By the end of the meal, the rest of her family looked as tired as Miranda had felt earlier that afternoon. Peggy kept taking her red-framed glasses off and rubbing the bridge of her nose. Because a non-family member was present, Peggy had slathered on more lipstick than she usually wore at home, Miranda noticed, a vivid pink imprint visible every time she tilted back her glass. She was excited about this trip to England: It was a great opportunity, a big break, getting to conduct the orchestra. And she was relieved, too, Miranda could tell — relieved that they were all together, on a family vacation, everyone pretending that everything was fine again.

Her father was excited to be here, too, so absorbed in the conversation that he was oblivious to the fish-pie gravy dribbling onto his zip-up fleece. He was tall like

Rob, and endearingly awkward with his knees and elbows, even though he was old, Miranda thought, and should be more together by now. Actually, they were a tall family — "You Americans are so strapping!" Lord Poole declared — and York seemed like some kind of quaint toy-town. They lumbered away from the restaurant that night like sleepy giants, walking under the twinkling Christmas lights, disoriented by everything Lord Poole was pointing out.

Just before they reached their flat, Lord Poole asked them if they wanted to step through another doorway, into what he described as a shrine to a local saint, Margaret Clitherow. A secret chapel, he said.

"This vacation is already way too educational," Rob muttered to Miranda. He stepped up into the shrine's doorway and instantly backed out again. Too small a room — he didn't need to say it. Even Lord Poole seemed to understand.

"You okay out here, buddy?" Their father grasped Rob's arm, and Rob nodded. The rest of the group filed past him into a small, wood-paneled room. But it wasn't *that* small, Miranda thought. In fact, it was bigger than Rob's bedroom in the flat. She couldn't believe he was using his claustrophobia as an excuse to get out of what he had instantly decided was a boring tourist stop. She made a mental note to call him out on this later.

Aside from the not-so-smallness of the room, there wasn't anything too surprising or unusual in the shrine. Not that Miranda had ever visited a shrine before. She wasn't sure what she'd expected to see. It was just a quiet space, dimly lit, with a plain altar and paneled walls. They all sat along a creaky bench in the back row while Lord Poole — whispering, though nobody else was there — told them the story of St. Margaret Clitherow.

"She was the wife of a butcher here in the Shambles," he said, "during the reign of Elizabeth I. She married very young — younger than you are now, Miranda — and she converted to Catholicism while she was still a teenager."

Miranda grimaced at the thought of getting married that young. She couldn't imagine anyone she knew at school doing something so adult.

"The religion was outlawed then," Lord Poole went on, "and it was very dangerous to be harboring priests, as she was, and allowing them to conduct mass in her home. She was imprisoned several times, and finally the authorities had enough of her. This was 1586, a very volatile and nervous time in Elizabeth's reign."

"Catholic plots against the queen," nodded Jeff. "Not a good time for Margaret Clitherow to be caught smuggling priests."

"What's this about *peine forte et dure*?" Miranda pointed to a typed biography of the saint, posted on the wall next to the bench.

"Strong and hard punishment," said Lord Poole, and Miranda noticed her parents exchange uneasy looks. "Margaret Clitherow chose to remain mute at her trial, refusing to enter a plea of guilty or not guilty. Wouldn't say a word, possibly to avoid implicating her husband — he wasn't a Catholic. Possibly to ensure her children and servants wouldn't be called as witnesses against her. And the penalty for this was a very cruel punishment, *peine forte et dure*. Devised in medieval England, despite the French name, to persuade prisoners to speak. Or to kill them, of course."

"Used once during the Salem witch trials as well," said Jeff quietly, looking down.

"Margaret was taken to Ouse Bridge," continued Lord Poole, "and made to lie on the ground. A sharp rock, the size of a fist, was placed under her back, and a large door was laid on top of her. And then, one by one, rocks were piled onto the door. Sometimes this process took a long time — hours, even days. But they were merciful with Margaret, and piled all the weight on quickly. She only took fifteen minutes to die."

"Well — we should be thinking about getting back." Peggy stood up, flashing a significant look at Jeff.

"So — she suffocated?" Miranda asked Lord Poole quickly. There wasn't any point in hearing such a sad and creepy story, she thought, unless you got all the details. And after what she'd seen with her own eyes, nothing much could disturb her anymore.

"Crushed to death," Lord Poole whispered, leaning close. As he stood up, he murmured, "Ribs break, then you start bleeding. And your organs . . ."

"So now she's a saint," Jeff mused in the loud summing-up voice he used in the lectures Miranda had attended. "With a shrine in the house where she hid the priests."

"Well . . ." Lord Poole began, but Peggy interrupted him, worrying aloud about Rob waiting outside in the cold, and then apologizing to Lord Poole. "No, no — you're quite right," he said. "We should be on our way. Plenty of time for history."

They all walked slowly up the snow-dusted Shambles, Rob telling his parents about two people who'd walked by dressed up as reindeer. Miranda and Lord Poole ambled along behind them. She couldn't stop thinking about Margaret Clitherow's decision to remain silent, even though it meant such a terrible punishment.

"Some people say," Lord Poole confided, his voice low, "that they experience some kind of serene presence in Margaret Clitherow's shrine. That they sense her spirit."

Miranda hadn't felt anything when they were in the shrine — nothing but pity, anyway, for Margaret and the barbarous way she had to die. But no ghostly presence, either serene or creepy. Maybe Miranda could see ghosts only in Iowa. That would make this week much more bearable, she thought, if York's centuries of ghosts were completely invisible to her.

They stopped outside their flat, and Jeff asked Lord Poole about arrangements for the following week. Rob wandered over to a store on the other side of the Shambles, a few houses down, and stood gazing in the window. It was one of those places — lame, in Miranda's opinion —

where you could get your photo taken in medieval garb, outfitted like the Sheriff of Nottingham and Robin Hood. Her mother was sure to suggest they go there and get dressed up like extras from *The Other Boleyn Girl* for some corny sepia-tone family picture.

Rob stood with his hands in his pockets, oblivious to the couple in matching fleeces who were staggering out of the store, laughing uproariously about whatever photo they'd just been posing for.

Oblivious even to the woman who seemed to emerge out of nowhere — from the window, though that wasn't possible — and appeared to hover there just above the pavement, looking directly at Miranda.

Miranda was transfixed, so surprised by this strange sight that she was holding her breath. How did this woman materialize so suddenly? She hadn't stepped out of the shop, like the laughing couple: She'd floated into the street. Her face was sweet and angular, and her dark hair hung over her shoulders. All she wore was a loose, off-white sack of a garment, like some kind of coarse nightgown. It was torn across the chest, streaked with dark stains. Dark stains like blood.

Even though the night was cold, and her pale arms were bare, the woman was smiling. She reached out her hand, and a sharp, tingling cold passed through Miranda — an electric jolt of ice. Miranda's heart was beating fast now: She knew what this meant. She remembered the wintry breeze that was Jenna's hand, brushing over her hair one last time. The icy fingers reaching up from the river in Iowa, sending surges of cold up her leg. Rob and everyone else in the street couldn't feel these cold darts. They couldn't feel or see the woman in white at all. She was a ghost.

"Time to go in, Verandah," her father was saying, using his old pet name for her. Saying it in public, in front of strangers, was strictly forbidden, and usually she would have scowled at him or at least rolled her eyes. But tonight Miranda didn't move — couldn't move. This was what it meant, she thought, when people talked about being frozen to the spot. She felt like an ice sculpture. This ghost didn't scare her the way the woman in the river had scared her, but that didn't mean Miranda felt calm. The ghosts in England could see her, just like the ghosts in Iowa. But what did they want?

"Ah!" said Lord Poole, walking over to stand next to her. She could sense his presence rather than see him, because she couldn't take her eyes off the apparition. "You and your brother have good instincts."

Miranda opened her mouth to speak, but only a stifled squeak came out.

"That's the thing I was about to tell you in the shrine," said Lord Poole. "The irony of it. The shrine, you see — they got it wrong. The Clitherows never lived in that house. The house where Margaret Clitherow lived is the one you're looking at right now."

"So all the people who say they've felt her presence in the shrine were . . . deluded?" Jeff was standing on the other side of Miranda now, laughing. Miranda reached out a hand, each finger seized by bracing cold. The woman in white was close enough to touch, but Miranda's hand passed through her. The woman was as insubstantial as air.

"Well, you never know," said Lord Poole. "It may be that —"

"What was she wearing?" Miranda interrupted, disoriented by the sound of her own voice, high-pitched and breathless. "Margaret — when she died?"

"Er . . . her shift, I imagine." Lord Poole sounded bemused.

"That's a sort of all-purpose undergarment," her father explained. "Like a petticoat, say."

"A nightgown?" The woman in white smiled at her, and Miranda's entire body surged with an icy liquid jet.

"That kind of thing, yes."

The ribs broken first: That was what Lord Poole had said. The blood on her shift — was that from the smashed ribs?

Everyone was saying good night now, and the woman in white was fading rather than walking away, her sweet smile evaporating into the night. In a moment she was gone. Miranda blinked, trying to focus her eyes, the cold jets seeping from her body. Maybe she was so tired she was hallucinating.

People strolled by, talking and laughing; some wandered over to the shop window to look at the absurd staged photographs. They wanted to pretend to live in the good old days, Miranda thought. Not so good for some people.

"Well, Miranda." Lord Poole was standing in front of her now, smiling. "At least you know the right place to look for her ghost now."

It might have been her imagination, but Miranda could have sworn Lord Poole was giving her a long look.

"Do ghosts only come out at night?" Rob asked, scratching his head like a sleepy child.

"Not always," said Lord Poole, and then he seemed to change his mind. He gave a formal little bow and took a step back. "I mean, I really have no idea. I've never seen one myself. At least, I don't think I've seen one. Who can say who's a ghost and who's real?"

He looked at Miranda and smiled, but she didn't smile back. She was thinking about how many ghosts she might have seen without realizing it. The farmer at the crossroads had looked completely alive. It was only his wound that gave him away — that and the fact that Jeff obviously couldn't see him at all. Maybe half the people walking down the Shambles right now were ghosts. Miranda wasn't sure. As Lord Poole said, how could she possibly tell?

CHAPTER THREE

So, what are our plans for today?" Peggy asked. It was Saturday morning. She stood at the kitchen sink, squirting orange dishwashing liquid into the frying pan.

"Finish reading *Northanger Abbey*," said Miranda, pointing at the book lying facedown on the dining room table. She felt exhausted, and the sighting of St. Margaret Clitherow last night had unnerved her. If more ghosts were lying in wait for her out on the streets of York, Miranda wasn't in any hurry to see them.

"Watch English soccer on TV," said Rob, his mouth full of scrambled eggs.

Peggy gave an exaggerated sigh.

"Guess again," she said, drying her hands on a dish towel.

"Today and tomorrow are the only days your mother has free." In an armchair by the window, Jeff was struggling with what looked like dozens of newspaper sections, bought first thing that morning, when he ventured out in the drizzle for groceries. The snow was gone, but the sky was the color of lead.

"You and Mom go out, then," Rob suggested. He was sitting at the table, his duvet wrapped around his middle like some kind of inflated sarong. Miranda could barely squeeze past him to take her own plate back to the compact kitchen. "Have some quality adult time. Like a date night, but during the day."

"We thought we'd all do some fun things *together*," Peggy said. "As a family."

"It's phrases like 'fun things' that make me want to go back to bed," said Rob, taking swift, greedy bites of a toasted English muffin. He waved its remains in Miranda's direction, gesturing at the toaster. He wanted another one, she guessed, and he wanted her to make it for him.

As if, she mouthed at him.

"Where's your sense of adventure?" called their father, wrestling with another newspaper section. "You've got all week to mope around alone, acting like disaffected youths. Today and tomorrow we're all going to do things your mother and I want to do."

"So — no fun at all," Miranda muttered. She poured herself another glass of orange juice and slid the carton back into the fridge before Rob noticed and demanded she pour him one as well.

"We've got a lot to fit in," her mother said, breezily ignoring any signs of mutiny. "Your father wants to go to Micklegate Bar . . ."

"Where the heads of traitors were impaled on spikes," Jeff said, oblivious to Peggy's pained expression.

"And there are several churches I want to see, including one nearby called Holy Trinity — someone in the orchestra told me about it."

"And Clifford's Tower, which is that medieval castle keep on top of the grassy knoll you and I saw yesterday, Rob." Jeff picked up one of his newspapers and various inserts slithered out onto the carpet.

"And Bettys Tea Rooms, for a traditional Yorkshire afternoon tea. Someone told me there's a cute branch called Little Bettys right on Stonegate."

"Let the games begin," drawled Rob, scowling at Miranda. She'd toasted herself another English muffin and was eating it, standing up at the kitchen counter.

"It's starting to rain again," she pointed out. Through the small kitchen window, all she could see were slick rooftops. "Maybe we should stay in."

"And they say we never take them anywhere," Jeff remarked drily to Peggy. They both looked pained, Miranda thought, despite their determination to act all cheery. They were right, she had to admit. There'd be plenty of time this week for lying around. Two days of family activities, however dull, would make her parents happy.

"But could we do some shopping today?" Miranda couldn't resist asking. The stores here had to be better than the ones in Iowa. Cami, whose aunt lived in London, had told her she had to go to H&M and Topshop at least.

"Sounds like a deal," said her father, jumping to his feet and managing to dislodge the stack of newspaper sections he'd piled onto the coffee table. Like it or not, thought Miranda, family fun was under way. For her parents' sake, she'd make an effort. Even if she'd much rather be snuggled up in bed with her book, lost in another place and time — somewhere far away from a city of tourist sites, and tea shops, and ghosts.

Saturday was market day in York. The cobbled square they could see from Rob's bedroom window, with its market stalls under green-and-white striped awnings, was thronged with shoppers. Mostly, people were buying food — glistening fresh fish banked on shores of ice, or paper bags bulging with vegetables, or pungent cheeses — but there were clothes on sale as well, like winter socks and woolen scarves, and the flower seller was doing a big trade in vibrant pots of purple heather.

The real action, Miranda discovered, was on pedestrian-only Coney Street, which curved to follow the river. This was fashion central, the store windows decorated with tinsel and baubles, and crammed with sassy party dresses — the kind, Miranda thought, that she wouldn't mind buying but would never wear. Holiday parties did not feature big in her plans this year. Her mother tried to talk her into a gilt-edged minidress, and Miranda finally opted for a black beaded cardigan and some high-heeled suede ankle boots that would make her look about ten feet tall. Jenna would approve, she thought. Not of the cardigan, maybe, because Jenna thought Miranda wore too much black, but she'd have liked the boots. "Embrace the height, sister," she used to tell Miranda. "Celebrate those stilt legs of yours." Going shopping without Jenna felt weird and wrong. Too normal, in a way, when nothing should be normal anymore.

It was hard not to get swept up in the buzz of it all, though. York wasn't that much bigger than the college town where they lived, but it was somewhere new for Miranda, and the streets were much livelier than the small grid of student bars, diners, and half-empty stores back home. Even her father, hardly the world's most enthusiastic shopper, seemed to be reveling in the good-natured bustle: He had to be dragged away from a rack of CDs ("Look, Peggy — they still have record stores here!") when everyone else, weighed down with plastic shopping bags, was ready to go back to the flat.

After they dropped off the bags, they stopped in King's Square to watch a juggler — dressed as a jester — juggle bowling pins in the air.

"Beyond corny," Miranda muttered to Rob, taking a giant step away from her father: He was embarrassing them, as usual, by taking too many photographs. The bare trees shivered in the breeze; people in the small crowd were stamping their feet to keep warm. Peggy wriggled onto the end of a long bench seat, and Rob and Miranda managed to get a spot near the man roasting chestnuts on an open brazier.

Right away, Miranda spotted something more interesting than the juggler. Just a few feet away, a surly group of Goth kids huddled close enough to the brazier to catch some of the warmth of its fire. Jugglers she could see any day in the pedestrian mall back home, but genuine English Goths were a more unusual sight in Iowa.

All of them, guys and girls, wore the same heavy workman's boots, and they were all in black, of course. Some of them were smoking, the lit embers of the cigarettes the only spot of color against their dark clothes and wan faces.

"Oi — Nick!" shouted one of the guys, and Miranda followed his gaze. On the far side of the square, stomping toward Petergate, was another youth-in-black, raising a pale hand when he saw his friends. Miranda realized, with a strange thrill of recognition, that she'd seen him before. He was the guy who'd been lurking in the doorway of the boarded-up house in the Shambles.

He started walking over, weaving through the crowd. The panels of his long leather coat flapped like bat wings, and Miranda wondered why he didn't fasten it, when the day was so cold. As he got closer, she noticed he was half carrying, half dragging some kind of trash bag. And as he got closer, he spotted her looking.

Miranda glanced away, pretending to be watching the

juggler's antics with his silly jingling hat. But she knew that this guy Nick had seen her — worse, that he'd *known* she was staring. Miranda felt stupid, like a gawping tourist. By the time she had the courage to dart a quick look over at the Goths again, Nick was nowhere to be seen. He'd come and gone, and his friends were still standing there. One of them was mock juggling with a couple of charred chestnuts, ignoring the glares of the chestnut roaster.

Little Bettys Tea Rooms — known, according to Peggy's guidebook, for its bizarre Yorkshire specialties like fruitcake served with a slab of cheese — was housed in a small black-painted shop, the sign above the door shaped like a teapot. Its window was stacked with tea canisters, holiday chocolates wrapped in gold and red foil, and bowls of glazed buns. The line for the tearooms upstairs was long, so they got only as far as the tiny downstairs shop, buying a selection of fluffy scones and jam tarts to take back to the flat. Rob said he'd wait outside, until he spotted a pretty blond girl behind the counter. He loped over, asking inane and unnecessary questions about why their shortbread was so long and why they sold coffee when Bettys called itself a tearoom.

"So much for the claustrophobia," Miranda teased him on the way out. White Christmas lights sparkled above her head, strung across narrow, stone-paved Stonegate. Ahead of them, York Minster soared into the bleak winter sky. It was massive, built on a much larger scale than any of these twee shops and low-ceilinged pubs.

"What do you mean?" Rob looked innocent.

"I mean, that place is way smaller than Margaret Clitherow's chapel."

"I'm just interested in the local cuisine," he said breezily. "Unlike you, I'm intellectually curious."

"Curiouser and curiouser," Miranda retorted. "And pathetically transparent."

"Stonegate, you know," said Jeff, falling back to walk alongside them when Peggy paused outside another shop, "was once the Via Praetoria, a major Roman road that led to the river — and to the main entrance to the city."

"You should tell Rob all this," Miranda said. "Apparently, he's intellectually curious."

They made a few more stops in other stores, then returned to the flat. As Miranda was unwinding her scarf from around her neck, she realized that she didn't have her gloves.

"I remember taking them off in the National Trust shop," she told her mother. "I must have left them on the counter or something."

She was annoyed with herself about doing something so stupid. The gloves were suede, a gift from her grandparents.

"After we eat, we can walk back over," Jeff suggested, but half an hour later it was obvious that nobody felt like doing much of anything. Rob had found a soccer match to watch on TV, Jeff was falling asleep reading the newspaper, and Peggy had already dozed off on the sofa.

"I'll go," Miranda whispered to Rob, who was slumped in an armchair. "I won't be long."

"I'll go with you," Rob said. "You might have left them in Little Bettys."

"No — I know I had them when we walked out of there. They aren't being held for ransom by the object of your affection, if that's what you're thinking."

He grinned, then looked back at the television. "Okay. Then you don't mind going out by yourself?"

Miranda shook her head. She hadn't seen Margaret Clitherow on the Shambles today. But maybe — just maybe — she'd spot the guy from the attic. Though she'd wondered, on the way back today, how he'd managed to get in and out of what looked like a boarded-up house. Not to mention what he was doing living in an almost derelict building.

All of yesterday's snow had melted, yet it felt colder now — much colder. There seemed to be no ghosts (or guys) along the Shambles, so Miranda marched down Goodramgate, hoping it was the quickest way to get back to the shop. To her relief, the woman in the floral smock behind the counter remembered her, and handed over the gloves.

Back on Goodramgate, Miranda almost collided with a group of people — laughing, swinging shopping bags — emerging from one of the many little lanes wending away from the street. Maybe this was a shortcut to the Shambles.

A snickelway, as Lord Poole said. Without stopping to think, Miranda turned into a very narrow alley, with high brick walls on either side and a low arch, where the lane passed under — or maybe through — a building, like a tunnel through a mountain.

When she emerged from the snickelway into another street, nothing looked familiar. Miranda couldn't see any street signs, and there was nobody around to point her in the right direction. In front of her were several modern redbrick town houses, the most recently built things Miranda had seen in York. They looked very ordinary, almost suburban. The street through them was pedestrian-only, traffic blocked by shiny black bollards. There was just one streetlight, and someone had twisted a skimpy string of Christmas lights up the trunk of the small lone tree. It was so quiet here — hard to believe she was just a short walk from busy streets and stores.

Something tugged at the hem of her jacket. Once, twice, three times. Miranda reached down to brush whatever it was away and searing cold shot through her hand. She looked down, straight into the face of a child.

"What?" Miranda heard herself gasp. Her heart was thudding. The little girl, her pinched face blue-white with cold, her eyes a cloudy gray, stared up at her. One small clenched hand still grasped the hem of Miranda's wool jacket.

"You startled me — I didn't see you," Miranda burbled. The child said nothing. She just stared up at Miranda. Her hollowed cheeks looked bruised almost.

The little girl held Miranda's gaze but shuffled away a little, still holding on to the jacket. Miranda could see her more clearly now. Her hair was a soft brown, dank and dirty and plastered against her head. Her eyes were wide and scared. She wore no shoes. Hanging loose on her thin frame was a blue dress, worn through in places, its long sleeves ragged. Miranda had never seen a begging child before. Is this what beggars looked like?

"What?" Miranda whispered again, transfixed by the girl's pale moon of a face.

"I'll show you," said the girl, her high voice so faint that Miranda could barely hear her. "Come with me."

"Come where?" Miranda asked. When she'd tried to brush the girl off, she'd felt nothing. Nothing but cold. Nothing but that intense, piercing cold.

"The place," the girl said. "I'll show you where he locked them up."

"No!" The word erupted from Miranda's mouth. She was scared now — scared of this strange girl and her cold touch, scared of where she might be led. Miranda took a step back, and then another. She didn't want the girl touching her anymore. She didn't want to see where anyone was locked up. "Go . . . go away!"

The girl's arm was still outstretched, but Miranda was free of her. She took another step away, too afraid to turn her back. She shouldn't have wandered down here by herself. Just a few more steps, and then she'd run. Run back down the alley or snickelway or whatever it was, to the safety of lights and cars and other people.

"She won't hurt you," said a raspy voice behind her. A boy's voice, with an English accent. Miranda spun around — her heart throbbing in her throat, practically choking her.

The guy in the black leather coat stood there, blocking the path to the alley. The expression on his face was part incredulous, part amused. He pulled a single match from a pack in his pocket and chewed on it as though it were a toothpick. Miranda stood dead still, not daring to move.

"How do *you* know?" she managed to say. He shrugged, throwing the gnawed match into the shadows.

"Stands to reason," he said, his voice softer now. "After all, she's only a ghost."

"How do you know that?" Miranda asked him, trying to swallow down her nerves. A gust of wind blew a piece of litter along the ground. In the distance, there were car horns sounding and the Minster bell tolling the half hour. Even in the semidarkness, the eyes of the pale Goth seemed to bore right through her.

"How do I know she won't hurt you? Or how do I know she's a ghost?"

"Both." Miranda shot a nervous glance to her left. The girl had disappeared.

"Well, I know that ghosts can't hurt anyone. Spook us, maybe." His mouth curled into a sardonic smile. "What's she going to do — hit you? Her hand would just pass right through you."

With his left arm he mimicked a slow-motion punch into the air.

"But I *felt* her," argued Miranda. The guy looked surprised. And maybe, thought Miranda, a little impressed.

"Aren't you special?" he said, his tone mocking.

"So maybe you're wrong about her being a ghost." Miranda wasn't going to let him patronize her. "If I shouldn't be able to *feel* anything."

"Oh, you can feel things," he said. There was only one button left on his coat, Miranda noticed for the first time. It was clear glass, and it was hanging by a thread: That was why the coat was always flapping open. "You'll feel cold, for a start. Drawn in, maybe. But they need our help if they want to do any harm, to other people or to ourselves. Mary there, though, she's not a troublesome one."

"How do you know her name?" Miranda was still suspicious.

"I know *your* name," he said. "Miranda, isn't it?"

Miranda's mind raced: Knowing about the icy touch of a ghost was one thing, but how could he possibly know *this*? Then she thought of the first time she saw him, when he was lurking in that doorway along the Shambles. Her mother had called for her, telling her to come in and meet Lord Poole. . . .

"And I know *your* name," she retorted. Two could play at this game. "It's Nick."

For the briefest of moments he looked rattled. Then he grinned at her and gave a sweeping theatrical bow.

"Nick Gant. At your service, milady."

"Miranda Tennant," she said. "But how do you know this . . . Mary's name?"

"Asked her, didn't I? When I was about fourteen, mucking around here with a spray can, looking for some trouble. Lots of people know about her. The ghost tours come this way every night. If you stand here long enough, you'll hear one of the guides spinning a tale about her and the other kids. Rubbish, mostly. Some of the guides know what they're talking about, but most of them are just actors. It's all top hats and terror with them. Wouldn't know a ghost if one tugged on their coats."

"What?" Miranda was startled. Nick had heard her mother call her name in the street: That, she understood. But how did he know that Mary had tugged on the hem of her jacket? Miranda hadn't told him that.

"It's what Mary does," he said, looking surprised that she was even asking. "And then she offers to show you where the bodies were left. No point in following her, though. I've tried it, and she just disappears."

"Who is she?" Miranda asked.

"Went to a ragged school here," he told her. "That's what they called them — ragged schools for poor kids. Late 1840s, I think. It was a slum then. Bedern. That's the street's name."

"Oh." Miranda nodded. She must have looked as confused as she felt.

"I say 'here,' but the building's gone. It was a place for kids nobody else wanted — you know, orphans or

48

runaways. The destitute. They'd get lessons and something to eat. People gave money to support it — the church, rich people. Some say the kids in this one were farmed out as slave labor around town as well, to clean chimneys, that kind of thing. I tried to ask Mary once about it, but she's not much of a talker."

"I didn't know ghosts *could* talk."

"Some can, some can't. Some you see only once in your life, and others'll be hanging around every day."

Miranda thought of Jenna. Miranda had been back to the cornfield dozens of times, but she'd never seen, or even sensed, Jenna ever again. No matter how hard she willed it, Miranda couldn't make her best friend reappear.

"And why does Mary keep coming back to this street?" she asked.

"Why does she haunt it? The usual reasons." Nick looked at her as though she were stupid. "Violent or unnatural death. Unfinished business, you know."

Miranda shrugged, as though she knew all this already, when really she knew absolutely nothing about the ghost world. Meeting someone who understood all this, who could explain things to her — it was more than a relief. It was exciting.

"When any of the kids died, the man who was running the place didn't report it. Didn't want to lose the money for them, I've heard. Just piled up the bodies in some kind of cupboard, hoping the winter cold would keep the corpses from stinking."

"Horrible." Miranda shuddered. "And Mary was one of those poor kids?"

"Sounds like it," said Nick. He pulled his coat tightly around him. His hands were bare. He had to be cold. "You hear all sorts of wild tales from the tour guides about how the stench of it finally drove him mad, and how he stabbed all the other children and got carted off to an asylum. But then this place would be crawling with ghosts, I reckon."

"And it's not?"

"Just Mary and a few others. There's one over there, by the drainpipe — see him? The little boy?"

Miranda peered, but she couldn't see a thing except the drain and the brick wall. She shook her head in frustration.

"Interesting," said Nick. "You can see Mary, but not him. I expect he doesn't want you to see him, or need you to see him. They're funny things, ghosts. Temperamental."

"So you're saying . . . I can't see *all* ghosts," Miranda said, struggling to understand. "Just the ones who want me to see them?"

"Want you to see them, or don't care one way or the other who does. There are some famous ghosts in York I've never seen, like the girl who's supposed to wander down Stonegate in the middle of the night, looking for the lover who abandoned her. Women are the only ones who've ever seen her. People say she doesn't trust men."

"And this little boy doesn't want me to see him."
Miranda kept staring at the blank patch of wall, not sure
whether to believe Nick or not.

"Don't take it personally," he said, his tone mocking.
"You got Mary to talk to you. She doesn't talk to many
people, you know. Maybe you *are* special."

"I don't know," Miranda said, feeling as stupid as
she sounded. Something about Nick's gaze made her awkward and shy. "I don't really understand much about
seeing ghosts yet. It's only . . . it's only been the last six
months," she blurted. "Since my friend died. I saw her —
once. Just the one time. But never again. I don't know
why. I mean, I don't know why I saw her the night
she died, and why I never saw her again. I've seen some
other ghosts. Since then, I mean. But nobody I know.
It's weird."

Miranda didn't know why she was saying all this to a
complete stranger. She never talked about ghosts; she
hardly ever mentioned the accident. And now here she
was, standing in a dark street in a foreign country, blab-
bing all her personal business to a weird guy. A weird guy
with a cool accent — but still.

"World's full of unhappy souls," Nick observed.
"People wanting to be seen, or heard, or helped. Think
of it this way — you should be glad you've never seen your
friend again. Maybe she doesn't need to haunt anyone or
anywhere. Perhaps she appeared to you that one time
because she wanted to say good-bye. That was *her* unfinished business."

Miranda bowed her head. She was glad it was dark so Nick wouldn't be able to see that she was blinking back tears.

"I should be going," she said, sniffing, trying to get a grip. "I should be getting back."

"Are you . . . are you around tomorrow?" Nick's tone had changed, and he was looking at her in a different way, as though he felt sorry for her. He'd seen her crying, Miranda realized. How embarrassing.

"Well, I'll be doing some stuff with my family. . . ."

"Monday?"

"I guess. . . . Sure. Monday's fine," Miranda said slowly. What was she getting herself into? Was he . . . asking her out?

"I'll take you to hear something, okay?"

"A concert?" she asked, puzzled. Nick smiled, shaking his head.

"Not a concert. Something much more interesting. Meet me on High Petergate, by the city walls. Bootham Bar. Outside the green front door. You can't miss it."

Nick spun on his heel, his coat flapping open. Like a night bird about to take flight, Miranda thought, and disappearing into the darkness. Disappearing down the snickelway, at any rate.

"What time?" she called at his back.

"Dusk!" he shouted, without turning around. Miranda stood for a moment, talking herself through the confusing instructions. High Petergate. Bootham Bar. The green front door. And what did "dusk" mean?

"Dusk isn't a time," Miranda complained aloud, and then she remembered that Mary might still be hanging around. She'd had enough encounters with ghost children for one night. She took off, running down the snickelway back to the reassuring bustle of Goodramgate. Although Nick had walked that way less than a minute earlier, he was nowhere to be seen.

CHAPTER FOUR

The Sunday afternoon walk to Clifford's Tower was longer than Miranda thought it would be, but maybe her father's confusing and circuitous route was to blame. Luckily, they could see the tower from a distance, because they ended up wandering through a packed, mazelike parking lot for the last ten minutes.

Everything seemed smaller here, Miranda thought — the cars, the parking spaces, the lanes the cars were expected to squeeze down. It was just as well that they hadn't rented a car for their stay: They'd never manage to negotiate a Legoland parking lot like this.

"Day-trippers," joked her father, with a dismissive wave, as they rounded the line of parked tour buses.

" 'York is . . . the second most visited city in England,' " her mother read from her guidebook, promptly bumping into a car's side-view mirror. "After London, I guess."

"Does the book say how we get up to *that*?" Rob pointed toward the tower. "Not that this parking lot tour isn't fascinating. The fumes, the public restrooms, the trash cans, the arguments over handicapped spaces . . ."

Rising up in front of them, almost in the middle of the lot, was a deep-green hill, so perfectly smooth and conical that it looked fake. It *was* fake, Peggy told them, insisting on risking bodily harm by reading while walking.

"It's not a hill, it's a motte," she said, squinting at the book. "An artificial earth mound. William the Conquerer again. The city's too flat, and he needed a hill for his castle."

"Little-known fact," called Jeff, who was leading them toward the hill. "It's named Clifford's Tower in honor of Clifford the Big Red Dog."

" 'Henry Clifford, fifth earl of Cumberland,' actually," Peggy read. " 'The Cliffords were hereditary constables of the' . . . oh, whatever."

She closed the book and stuffed it into her bag.

"Are we there yet?" asked Rob.

The only part of the castle that remained was a fat, rounded, roofless tower. It was perched like a stone crown on the top of the hill. The only way up was via a long, concrete staircase, slippery with icy damp. Apart from a pair of preoccupied geese pecking away at the grass at the top of the hill, and the ticket seller in the booth, the Tennants seemed to be the only ones there.

Inside the tower was an empty shell, a stone-flagged open space flecked with patches of moss. Miranda was pleased, in a way. She liked the idea of ruins. It was so much easier to imagine how things used to look hundreds of years ago if there weren't parts changed or added on, or — even worse — turned into rooms of worthy but dull exhibits. Here the tower had been left carved out and skeletal. A snaking stone staircase led to what used to be the upper level, where the king would have had his apartments.

Now, in the absence of floors and walls and a roof, there was just the "wall walk," where visitors could pace their way around the tower's perimeter and look out across the city. Miranda's parents, of course, went nuts at the prospect of a 360-degree view because — she'd often observed — anyone middle-aged thought that gazing at views and gardens and distant horizons was the most interesting thing in the world. But even Rob was eager to bound up the twisting staircase, despite its close confines, to reach the top of the tower.

Miranda lingered downstairs for a while, reading the information signs and trying to imagine what this level of the castle looked like hundreds of years ago. William the Conqueror had built the hill but not this stone tower, she read. The original tower was wooden, and known as York Castle. It was replaced by William's descendants two hundred years after it had burned down twice.

The flagstones beneath Miranda's feet weren't exactly flat, and the uneven slope seemed to be giving her sea legs. She felt wobbly, and for a moment she worried she was actually sliding backward toward the entry gate. This was strange. She'd been walking around York all day, along cobbled streets and uneven pavements: She should be used to this by now.

"What is wrong with you?" she muttered to herself. They were in York, not California; the ground couldn't possibly be moving. It couldn't possibly be . . . rumbling. The distant sound she heard couldn't be coming from deep within the earth. It was probably a train, or a truck crossing the river.

"Come up, honey!" Her mother was leaning over the railings two stories above. "You get an amazing view of the Minster from here."

Miranda stumbled rather than walked to the spiral staircase, annoyed with herself for being so clumsy. She also wished that the soles of her boots were thicker. Icy darts were prickling her feet.

At the top of the stairs, Miranda took a few tentative steps, all too aware that the wall walk sloped as well. It felt as though it was drooping toward the empty space in the center. There were railings, of course, but they seemed very insubstantial — flimsy, even — now that Miranda was up so high. The ground beneath her feet still felt weirdly fluid, not firm and stonelike at all. Rob and her parents were wandering around with no problem, leaning over the low outer wall, taking pictures. They weren't sliding around or desperately gripping the railings, as Miranda was now. What was happening? Was this what people called vertigo?

With each step, Miranda felt as though she was about to be tipped into the abyss. The stones beneath her feet were alive, writhing and twisting out of place. Tendrils of frigid cold laced up her legs. Just a few steps away, the members of her family were pointing things out to each other; Rob was crouching to balance his camera on the outer wall. Miranda didn't have the strength to cry out. All her energy was focused on staying upright, of not being jerked over the railings and down, down, down to the mossy stones below. Some force was tipping and dragging her, and she couldn't stop it. With both her hands trembling on the slippery railings, she faced the pit of the tower, willing herself to stay upright.

"Don't look down," Miranda told herself in a cracked whisper, trying to ignore her rising panic. Her skin was pulsing, prickling with cold, even though she was wearing a woolen jacket, jeans, and thick socks under knee-high boots. She had to step away from the brink. She had to throw herself on the ground if necessary, and claw her way to safety, fingernails digging into the crevices between the stones. The one thing she should *not* do was look down.

But she was so dizzy now, so disoriented, Miranda couldn't help it: She looked down. At first her head flopped and her eyes couldn't focus. Rather than seeing anything at all, she heard the rumbling again, except now it didn't sound at all like a train or anything mechanical. It was the sound of mumbling voices — lots of voices, rising up from the stones below. And there was whispering, too, like the rustle of trees in a summer breeze. A whole forest of trees, swishing and shaking in the wind.

But there were no trees on this man-made hill. And below her, there weren't treetops — or even stones. Where earlier there'd been a courtyard with a few signs and small gift shop, there were only faces. Dozens of faces. Hundreds of faces, all staring up at her. Gray faces attached to ashy bodies, crumbling, dissolving, and re-forming in front of her eyes. Up they rose, a charcoal cloud of . . . what? Were these ghosts? If only Nick were here, to explain what on earth was going on.

They didn't look like the ghosts she'd seen before, like the farmer, or the woman in white on the Shambles, or the little girl ghost from yesterday — no clothes, no wounds. They looked like creatures of ash and smoke, not real people.

Their hands stretched toward her, shooting cold beams into her body. All the faces looked stricken, as though *they* were the ones looking at a ghost. Maybe she *was* the ghost, Miranda thought, her mind racing. Maybe she'd died this summer in the cornfield, and everything after that had just been some grand delusion. But how could that be possible? How was any of this possible?

Miranda closed her eyes. She couldn't look at them anymore. She was leaning, she knew it, stretching over the top of the railings, unable to keep her balance. Any second now she would topple over and fall into the whooshing gray mass, that ashy pit of open mouths and reaching hands.

"Did you bring your camera?" Her mother took her arm, gently pulling her back from the brink. Wildly, Miranda grabbed at her, eyes still clenched shut. "What is it, honey — are you okay? Don't you feel well? Jeff! Come here! Miranda, you look so pale."

With her parents on either side of her, leading her away from the railings, Miranda opened her eyes. Walking was so easy when they were holding her. The mumbling and whispering faded away. One, two, three steps, and she was sitting on the ground, her back against the low outer wall. When her mother let go of her arm, Miranda grabbed her again, pulling her down.

"Don't let go," she whispered. Her legs were still tingling with cold, and she was shaking. Her father leaned over, pressing the back of his hand against her forehead and then her cheeks.

"You feel all clammy," he said. "Maybe you're coming down with something."

Miranda nodded. That was the easiest thing to do. No point in trying to explain what she'd heard, and seen, and felt, because instinctively she knew that nobody else here would experience any of it. Rob was leaning over the railings at this very minute, taking a photo, not looking startled or appalled in any way.

"One of those geese has managed to infiltrate," he called over. "Looks like it's settling in for the winter. Hey, Dormouse — what's up with you?"

"Nothing," squeaked Miranda. Her parents had had enough to worry about the past six months without adding "daughter's supernatural hallucinations" to the list.

"Maybe a touch of vertigo," suggested her father. "The height might be bothering you. This wall is pretty low."

"I wouldn't have brought you two up here when you were small." Peggy, crouching beside her, planted a soft kiss on Miranda's hair. "Rob would have been headfirst over the wall by now. Or dangling from those railings."

"Tired?" Rob sauntered up. He stood next to Miranda and nudged her with his knee.

"I'm okay," Miranda said, reaching up for his arm so she could pull herself to her feet. All she wanted to do was get out of there before the ash people came swirling up for her again, with their terrible agonized faces and crumbling bodies of smoky cloud. "Walk me down the stairs?"

"Only a touch of vertigo," her father said again, as though he were reassuring himself.

"Great," Rob muttered, so only Miranda could hear. "Just what we need in this family — another basket case."

Miranda's father walked her back to the flat while Peggy and Rob set out for Little Bettys to wait in line for a table. She needed to sleep, she told her parents; she'd feel better after getting some rest.

Waiting for them at the flat was a very small brown-paper package. It had been pushed through the brass slot in the front door.

"It's for you," her father said, scooping it up and examining the faint spidery handwriting. "Miss Miranda Tennant."

There was no address on the package and no stamps; it must have been delivered by hand. Miranda leaned against the wall to rip it open. Her legs still felt like Jell-O, though the cold darts shooting up from the soles of her feet had disappeared as soon as she got out of Clifford's Tower.

By the size and shape of the package, Miranda could tell it contained a book. She slipped it out of the brown paper. It was as small as a notebook. Its faded cover was green, and some of the stitches in its spine had worked themselves loose. The words *Tales of Old York* were spelled out in Gothic gilt letters on the cover.

"No note?" asked her father, taking the book from her and running a finger over the indented lettering. Miranda shook her head. But they both knew, without having to say it, that this was the book Lord Poole had mentioned. It looked about as old as *he* was, Miranda thought, and when her father flicked through the opening chapter, Miranda could smell the pleasant mustiness of the pages.

"How nice off him to drop it off." Jeff gave an appreciative sniff. "Look at these illustrations."

The pictures in the book were drawings done in intricate detail with black ink. The caption of one read THE TIMELESS SHAMBLES, which was true: The street looked pretty much the same as it did now, minus the tourists and holiday decorations. Jeff flicked forward to a double-page spread of small, almost fussy drawings of columns, a large stone basin, and some kind of stone plaque carved with demons pushing screaming people into a giant cauldron licked by flames.

" 'The Doomstone, from the crypt of York Minster,' " Jeff read aloud. Miranda shuddered, thinking of the desperate ashen faces at the tower, and her father snapped the book shut. "Sorry, Verandah. You're supposed to be taking a nap. Sure you'll be okay here by yourself?"

Miranda told him she would. Sleep would help, she thought. The ghoulish faces of the ash people would disappear when she fell asleep. With any luck, she'd be asleep for a long, long time.

When Miranda awoke, the flat was quiet. According to her cell phone, almost two hours had passed since she'd climbed into bed. The curtains were closed, something her father must have done before he went off to meet the others at Little Bettys. On the table next to her bed, he'd left *Tales of Old York*.

Miranda picked up the book and flipped through, pausing at a full-page illustration of York Minster engulfed in flames. Her mother had said something about a fire there, after the Minster was struck by lightning and badly damaged — but that had been relatively recent, some time in the 1980s. This book was over a hundred years old, according to the date on its copyright page. Even older than Lord Poole, she thought, smiling. THE MADMAN'S FIRE, 1829, the picture's caption read.

She noticed that another page was hanging loose from the binding, and she opened the book to tuck it back in. The heading at the top of that page read MASS SUICIDE IN CLIFFORD'S TOWER. Miranda wriggled up into a seated position, jamming her pillows behind her and twisting to get as much light as possible.

On the third day of September, 1189, Richard I, later acclaimed as Coeur de Lion after his crusades to the Holy Land, was crowned at Westminster Abbey, having banned all Jews from attending the service or playing any part in the subsequent feasts and celebrations. On the day of the coronation itself, a destructive anti-Jewish riot erupted in the streets of the capital, during which Jewish homes were plundered and burned, the mob believing itself to be acting on the wishes of the new monarch. Similar violent attacks followed in King's Lynn and Norwich, but the most bloody of all took place in York in March of 1190. After the murders of the family of Benedict of York, several hundred Jews sought refuge from the mob in York Castle. As fury outside the castle gates mounted, with instruments of the siege about to burst through the locked gates, the families seeking sanctuary within chose to die by their own hands rather than face the violent rage of the mob. On the night of

Friday the sixteenth of March, 1190, at the urging of their rabbi, the men killed their own women and children, and then set the wooden castle keep alight, so they might die, too, their bodies to be cremated by the great fire. Nothing but ash remained by the end of the night, the few survivors of the conflagration slaughtered without mercy by the enraged mob.

Nothing but ash remained. Miranda sank back into her pillows. The stone tower — that was why it was built. She remembered the sign she'd read before the dizziness came on. The old wooden tower, the castle keep, had burned down. And now she knew the awful reason why. The Jewish people of medieval York had set it on fire, choosing to die there together rather than be murdered.

Those were the ghosts she'd seen at Clifford's Tower today, the spirits of ash rising up from beneath the flagstones. But why? Why rise up from the earth, like some kind of whirling dervish of despair, to try to drag her down into the underworld?

Miranda thought about the things Nick had said about ghosts. Sometimes they reached out to certain people because they had unfinished business, because they wanted you to see them, because they thought you could help them. But she couldn't help the ghosts of Clifford's Tower any more than she could help Mary and the other workhouse orphans haunting Bedern, or smiling St. Margaret Clitherow serenely floating in the Shambles.

Any more than she'd been able to help Jenna after the other car smashed into theirs.

Miranda lay still, the book upside down in her lap. She was almost afraid to pick it up again. The thought of those desperate people dying there, of their ghosts haunting the place, was too awful. She absolutely didn't *want* to see these ghosts. But apparently, whether she was in Iowa or York, Miranda didn't have much choice. Maybe she could ask Nick some more questions about it when — if — she met up with him on Monday afternoon.

And somehow she knew she couldn't say a word about that to anyone. Like seeing ghosts, seeing Nick had to be Miranda's secret.

CHAPTER FIVE

That night, Rob insisted they go to the White Boar Inn for dinner, even though there were other restaurants that were much closer.

"It's the oldest inn in York," he said over his shoulder to Miranda, striding ahead of her through the courtyard. The building looked pretty old, she had to admit, its whitewashed walls crisscrossed with beams of black timber. Weathered picnic tables were pushed to one side of the cobbled courtyard, out of use until the summer.

"The white boar was Richard III's personal emblem," Jeff told them, pausing to fiddle with the flash on his camera. "Many inns changed their name from the White Boar to the Blue Boar after he was killed in battle. Didn't want to be associated with the losing side."

"I knew you'd like it here, Dad." Rob was holding the door open for them. "It's a grade eleven listed building or something. There's a sign over there."

"Grade two, idiot!" Miranda stepped past him into the warmth and noise of the inn. "I can't believe you don't know how to read Roman numerals yet."

"Now, now," said Peggy, unraveling her scarf and surveying the warren of crowded rooms. All the small, round tables were crammed with people — eating, drinking, laughing — and some customers had drawn their stools up in front of the crackling fire. "This was a very good idea, Rob. Should we find a table first? Do we order food at the bar?"

"I'll go get us menus," Rob offered, and promptly disappeared. What was *his* deal? He was like some one-man pep rally tonight.

"It wasn't this crowded at the place on Swinegate," Miranda lamented, following her parents until they wound their way back to a just-vacated table near the door.

"Yes, but . . ." Her mother flashed Miranda a significant look as they sat down. Jeff reached for Miranda's coat, bundling it next to him on the long banquette seat. "The other pub lacked a certain something. Or should I say . . . someone."

"That Richard III thing?" Miranda asked, bracing as someone opened the door behind her and let in a gust of cold air. "I thought Rob didn't care about that."

Jeff smiled. "I suspect a certain young lady made more of an impact on your brother than any number of my history lessons."

Miranda had no idea what they were talking about.

"The pretty blond girl at Little Bettys," Peggy explained. "Remember — she served us yesterday? Well, this afternoon when we went back while you were napping, she was working upstairs in the tearooms. Her name is Sally."

"We had to pass on four tables before we got one in her room," Jeff said drily. "I thought we'd be waiting there all afternoon."

"She mentioned that her parents own this place," continued Peggy, gesturing around the inn. "She just finished her first semester at the University of Manchester, and she's home for the holidays."

"She told you all this when she was taking your tea order?" Miranda thought this Sally sounded weird.

"Your brother was interrogating her." Jeff raised one eyebrow, a trick that Miranda used to think was awesome. She'd never been able to master it herself. "He's suddenly grown very interested in local culture."

Miranda stifled a laugh.

"And she said she helps out here in the evenings, when it's busy," said Peggy, rearranging the salt and pepper shakers on the damp table. "Oh — she's coming now! With Rob. Pretend we were talking about something else."

"Be cool," Jeff instructed Miranda in a mock stern voice, which made Miranda smirk: Her father was the most uncool person she knew.

"Sally!" her mother said in an ostentatiously casual way. "How nice to see you again!"

"Hello there — so glad you found me!" Sally stood at their table, Rob lurking doofus-like in the background. Miranda wouldn't have recognized her. At the Little Bettys shop yesterday, she'd worn a prim black-and-white uniform, like some kind of maid from another era, and her curly blond hair had been tied back in a ponytail. Here, her hair was loose, bouncing on her shoulders, and she wore jeans and a long-sleeved T-shirt. Her bright blue eyes sparkled. Miranda liked the soft burr of her accent and the open way she smiled, as though she was genuinely pleased to see them.

"This is Miranda," Peggy said, gesturing so wildly that Miranda had to duck to avoid getting smacked in the face.

"I've heard all about you," said Sally, beaming. "I hope you're feeling better now."

"What?" said Miranda stupidly, and it sounded ruder than she'd intended.

"You were feeling poorly this afternoon, over at Clifford's Tower?"

"Oh yeah." Miranda repressed a shudder at the very mention of that place. The whole experience seemed so surreal now. Almost everything in York she'd experienced so far was surreal, like a strange and unsettling dream. "Thanks. I'm . . . fine."

"Good." Sally smiled again. "Look, I've got to get back to work, but I just wanted to say hello. Rob's got the menus. . . ."

Rob held some laminated sheets in the air, and gave a goofy smile. He was the polar opposite of suave. Miranda had never seen him like this before.

". . . but I should warn you that we've already run out of the beef hot pot *and* the seafood pasta. I'm really sorry."

"Busy night." Jeff nodded, looking around.

"Yes. Two of the staff left today," Sally explained breathlessly. "They got jobs at a ski resort in France and didn't give any notice. It's a madhouse here during the festival, so it couldn't be worse timing. My parents are at their wit's end."

"I can help, you know," Rob spoke up. "Clear glasses and plates and stuff."

Miranda couldn't believe her ears. Her brother could barely clear his own dishes off the table at home, let alone help out at a busy inn.

"Oh, I don't want to spoil your —"

"It's fine, no problem, really." Rob sounded desperate. Miranda's parents looked at each other, obviously as bemused as she was. Her mother's mouth was twitching with a smile. "I like to have something to do. Keep busy, you know."

This was such a blatant lie that Miranda had to choke back laughter. At home, Rob's idea of "keeping busy" was lying across the sofa, scattering pistachio shells across the coffee table, and watching the director's cut of *Blade Runner* for the ninety-ninth time.

"Well," said Sally, and when she looked at Rob his face turned red. "When you've had your meals, if you can spare some time, I'd be very grateful."

After Sally had dashed away, and Jeff and Rob had ambled off to the bar to place the Tennants' orders, Miranda asked her mother why Rob was acting so weird.

"You think it's weird?" Peggy rested her hand on one of Miranda's. "I think it's quite sweet. And it's very nice to see your brother happy and enthusiastic for a change. It's good for him to meet someone his own age who . . . you know. Has nothing to do with everything back home."

"I guess," said Miranda, flinching as the door opened again and cold air swirled in. It wasn't like Rob at all to fixate on a girl and chase after her so blatantly. He'd had girlfriends at school before, but they always seemed to do all the chasing. A girl asked *him* to junior prom, not vice versa. And since the accident, he hadn't seemed interested in going out with anyone at all. He'd barely been out at night this summer and fall. He and Miranda had gone to precisely one party, at Halloween, and only then because it was close enough to walk there and back.

But now, all of a sudden, he meets a girl in a foreign country and gets a dazed look in his eyes and starts hanging around her like a lovesick adolescent? Lame, in Miranda's opinion. Even though she had to admit that Sally seemed nice without being gushy or sickly sweet, confident without being brash. She wasn't fawning over

Rob in a sappy way, like too many of his ex-girlfriends. Still, Miranda was annoyed.

"There's no need to worry." Peggy said, apparently reading her mind. Miranda had no idea how her mother could do that. "Or be jealous."

"Jealous?" Miranda repeated, startled. Peggy patted her hand.

"You know what I mean. You and Rob have been hunkered down for a while now, just the two of you. It's time, maybe. Time to venture out into the world again. Do things with other people."

Miranda couldn't trust herself to speak. She wanted to protest that her mother was being unfair, that she couldn't care less if Rob fell in love with every waitress in York, that she'd ventured out into the world *loads* of times without Rob since the accident. She'd been out with Bea and Cami on that trip to the river, the one she'd like to forget; they'd dragged her along to the movies twice as well, and . . . what else? The class trip to the ice rink at the mall. That was it, pretty much. It didn't mean Miranda was clinging to Rob. She wanted to be on her own this week, after all. Didn't she?

Anyway, Miranda was meeting people here in York herself; she just didn't make a big show of it. There was Nick, who she was meeting up with tomorrow at dusk — actually meeting him, to go somewhere, not just stalking him the way Rob kept turning up everywhere Sally worked. And then there was the mystery guy in the attic window, who she'd seen the night they arrived. If they opened their windows, they'd be close enough to talk. Close enough, Miranda thought with an uneasy shiver, to touch.

"Here they come," said Peggy, rearranging the salt and pepper shakers again to make room for drinks and cutlery. "Not looking where they're going, as usual."

Jeff and Rob were squeezing through the crowd, so intent on their conversation that they seemed oblivious to the way their drinks were slopping onto the floor. Her father practically stepped on a black cat that was sidling, tail curled, around the wall from one room to the next.

"Dad almost tripped over that cat," Miranda said. She was making an effort to sound normal, not strained and upset and sulky — even though that was pretty much how she was feeling.

"There's a cat?" Peggy raised herself out of her seat to look. If it were up to her mother, Miranda knew, they'd have a dozen cats at home, but Rob was ferociously allergic. "Where?"

"There," Miranda pointed. The cat had stepped onto the hearth, arching its back against the stone fireplace.

"I don't see it," said Peggy, sounding disappointed.

"It's right there, Mom," Miranda said. She jabbed her finger toward the fireplace. "See it? It's licking its paw now. Cute."

"I can't see anything. Maybe I need to get new glasses. Jeff, can you see a cat in here? Miranda says you almost stepped on it."

"No cat." Jeff lowered two drinks onto the table, spilling both of them. "But I did see a very interesting old Blue Boar sign in the next room. I'll point it out to you later, after we eat."

"You guys are all totally blind," Miranda said, almost snapping at them. "It is RIGHT THERE by the fire."

"They don't have cats in pubs," Rob said, dragging his stool closer to the table. He looked very pleased with himself. "People are allowed to bring their dogs in, so there'd be fights all the time."

"You're quite the expert now," Peggy teased. Miranda kicked him under the table, but Rob pretended not to notice. When she looked again, the black cat by the fireplace was gone.

That night, Miranda couldn't sleep. She was too hot, then she was too cold. When she tried to read *Northanger Abbey*, she felt sleepy and had to put the book down, but as soon as she turned off her light, she was wide awake again. At first, there was a little noise outside — people calling to each other and laughing, the tap of heels along the cobbles — but soon everything was eerily quiet. When she was too restless to lie still any longer, Miranda rolled out of bed and pulled one curtain back. Snow was falling again, soft and wet. The street was empty.

She knelt by the window, arms resting on the sills. Through streaks of snow she could see the attic window opposite, dark as the night sky. Miranda yawned, tugging at the curtain to draw it back into place, but a glimpse of sudden light stilled her hand. Across the street, blurred by snow, a candle flickered.

Then he was there, too, his face as pale as the moon, staring straight at her. Miranda felt breathless, something between excited and apprehensive. Slowly, she raised a hand to wave, but waving felt too silly, too girlish. She pressed her palm against the cold glass, not sure of what to do, wondering how long it would take for her to feel embarrassed and look away.

A ridge of mashed snowflakes fell from the window, and now Miranda could see the guy in the attic more clearly. He wore a white collarless shirt, open at the neck. There was something across the base of his throat — a dark line, like a ribbon or a leather string. Miranda squinted, trying to make it out. The candle flickered again, its flame dancing and quivering. And she realized that it wasn't a ribbon around his neck, or any kind of jewelry. It was a wound, dark with blood or bruising.

The guy in the window smiled at her — just the glimmer of a smile — and raised his right hand to the window, resting his palm on the pane in an exact mirror image of her gesture. A chill rippled through Miranda's hand. The glass was cold, of course; it was snowing outside. But this was a sudden, intense cold, turning her fingertips numb and shooting some kind of electric currents down her arm. Miranda knew this cold. She knew exactly what it meant.

Miranda wanted to pull away from the window, but she couldn't. This was different from seeing the face in the river, or the farmer, or the little girl in Bedern, or the ash people. She wasn't scared. She didn't want to cry out or run away. All she could do was keep looking into that beautiful face with its sad, dark eyes, feeling the cold of his hand burn its way into hers.

The candle's flame dwindled and then, as abruptly as last time, was extinguished. Miranda could see nothing but inky darkness through the haze of snow, and her hand, still pressed against the class, stopped tingling. It just felt limp and heavy, not zinging with electricity. Her legs started to feel stiff, cramped from kneeling in one position.

Her heart was still hammering. She'd thought he was real, but the guy in the attic was a ghost. A ghost with a terrible wound.

Crawling back into bed, Miranda flicked on her bedside lamp. The book, she thought, reaching for it — not *Northanger Abbey*, but the book she'd been reading earlier that afternoon. The Shambles was a famous old street; maybe there was something about the gorgeous ghost in *Tales of Old York*. She turned its musty pages, looking for a chapter on the Shambles. Maybe there would be something here to give her a clue.

Many local folk claim to have seen ghostly apparitions along the Shambles, although for a street so ancient and alive with history, it has surprisingly few consistent legends of hauntings and supernatural occurrences. But during the nineteenth century, numerous witnesses reported a sighting in an upper window of one of the oldest houses in the street. The spirit in question was a young man, purported to be the ghost of an apprentice garroted by his cruel master.

Garroted — that meant strangled, Miranda remembered, though where she'd learned that word, she wasn't sure. Probably one of her father's gory stories about some medieval king's evil hobbies. The dark stain at the young man's throat: It had to be a bruise, the kind caused by a rope drawn tight around his neck. This was the ghost she'd seen tonight, the ghost who'd appeared to her in the attic window. He could be two hundred years old by now. Still sad, still haunting the street where he died. Still insanely beautiful — dark, handsome, angular.

Miranda lay the book down and wriggled low under the covers. If only *this* guy were living and breathing, and Nick were the ghost, she thought, feeling instantly guilty for thinking something that mean. Nick was just so odd — spiky and caustic. There was something beyond edgy about him. She was sure he was going to get her into trouble, somehow. Even though she wanted to meet up with him tomorrow at dusk, it was out of curiosity, not infatuation. This was nothing like the thing Rob clearly had for Sally, where he was all puppy-dog smitten with someone he barely knew. Nick could see ghosts, just like Miranda could; he seemed to know how to navigate that world. She wanted to hear what he had to say, to see what he had to show her.

The guy in the attic window, on the other hand: He didn't need to say anything.

When he looked at her, everything else seemed to disappear — all her self-consciousness, sadness, confusion. Nick had said that ghosts couldn't hurt her, and Miranda was beginning to believe him. This ghost wouldn't hurt anyone. Miranda could gaze into his eyes and let the chill sear through her body without feeling afraid. She didn't want to look away. She wanted more.

CHAPTER SIX

"Miranda, listen to me. I never ask you for anything." Rob was pouting, squeezing the cushion on his lap as though he were trying to subdue it.

"Whatever. You ask me for things all the time," Miranda retorted.

It was Monday afternoon. Their father and Lord Poole had gone out somewhere. Their mother was meeting up with the orchestra at a rehearsal room. Miranda and Rob were sitting around in the flat: The TV was on with the sound turned down, and newspapers lay strewn across every flat surface. Outside, there was a strange greenish tinge to the dense gray sky, something Miranda always associated with snow moving in.

"The other day you ordered me to make you another English muffin."

"I did not!"

"You gestured at me and, like, pointed to the toaster."

"Did I say anything with my mouth?"

"What?"

"Answer the question. DID I SAY ANYTHING WITH MY MOUTH?"

Miranda sighed.

"Are you just going to sit around here bugging me *all* day?" she asked him.

"No." Rob sprang to his feet, the cushion tumbling to the floor. He clapped his hands together like a camp counselor. So obnoxious. "We should do something. How about I take you to afternoon tea at Little Bettys?"

"You're so original," she drawled. Really, he couldn't stay away from Sally for two minutes.

"You can have hot chocolate with real cream and chocolate flakes. Hmmm?"

"I'm not six years old, you know."

"And there are these little pancake things called peeklets. . . ."

"*Pike*lets," Miranda corrected him. "I haven't even eaten at Bettys and I know that. Maybe if you read books, you wouldn't be so ignorant about the foodstuffs of other cultures. Why don't you just go by yourself?"

"Guys just don't go to tea shops by themselves. It's not manly."

"You're not manly," muttered Miranda, heaving herself out of the armchair. She was starting to get nervous about meeting up with Nick later on. Maybe he'd forgotten all about it. Maybe it wasn't a great idea. She didn't know anything about Nick. He could be a lunatic. Her English teacher that fall had said that Lord Byron was once described as "mad, bad, and dangerous to know." Was that a description of Nick as well?

"Come on." Rob zipped up his hoodie, ready for action.

"But, you know, I can't stay long," she said quickly.

"What — you got somewhere else to go?" he scoffed. Miranda looked away, pretending to search for her woolen hat. Part of her really wanted to tell Rob about Nick. There were times, especially lately, when she did feel close to her brother; the accident was an unspoken bond between them, something that nobody else could understand. But talking about Nick would mean talking about ghosts. Maybe at Little Bettys — somewhere neutral, where he couldn't shout at her or walk away — Miranda would find the courage.

Upstairs at Little Bettys, they skirted a cart laden with cakes and tarts, and were led through a rabbit warren of little rooms to the very back of the building. Miranda wriggled into a woven chair jammed in the corner. This was more a nook than a room. It was very cozy, she thought, with its exposed brick and dark beams, a shelf of teapots mounted above the black fireplace. She and Rob could barely squeeze around their table. He sat sideways, his legs sticking out like a scarecrow's.

"You can't have anything that costs over five pounds," he muttered.

"But I really wanted to try the Yorkshire cream tea. . . ."

"God, Miranda — everything's not always about you! Can you see Sally?"

"She's walking toward us," said Miranda sulkily. Sally was far too pretty for Rob, she decided. Even in the old-fashioned waitress uniform, Sally looked attractive. She had lovely skin — creamy white, with pale pink cheeks. This must be what people meant when they talked about an English rose.

"Good afternoon," she said, with a beaming smile. "What a nice surprise, seeing you here!"

"Miranda really wanted to come," Rob lied, all nonchalant. "So I said I'd bring her along."

"That's so kind of you," said Sally, lifting her order pad. "I was hoping you'd stop by. This is my very last shift here. I've had to resign. I'm needed at the White Boar in the afternoons as well, not just in the evenings."

"That sucks." Rob looked crestfallen. He was never going to have a chance to see Sally now, Miranda realized. She was going to be working at the inn day and night.

"Maybe," Sally said, "if you're not too busy later on, you could come by and give my dad a hand with the barrels? Only if you don't mind, of course."

"No problem at all." Rob grinned.

"Thanks so much." Sally grinned back. These two were starting to make Miranda feel sick. "So, sir and madam, may I bring you something to drink while you read the menu? Or maybe you'd like to look at the cake trolley?"

"No need." Rob slapped his menu onto the table. "We'd like two hot chocolates and a plate of those peek — I mean, pikelets. To share. Thanks."

"Hey!" complained Miranda after Sally bounced away. "I hadn't decided yet. Did you just order the cheapest thing on the menu?"

"Maybe," said Rob, looking over his shoulder, "we should swap seats so I can see her when she walks by."

"Whatever," Miranda grumbled, getting up anyway and stepping over Rob's long legs.

"Thanks, Dormouse." He slithered around into her chair, still grinning like a fool. Miranda hadn't seen him smile like that for a long time. "I owe you one."

"You owe me at least ten," she told him. She pulled *Tales of Old York* out of her coat pocket, and the book fell open to the page she'd been reading last night, the chapter on the Shambles and the ghost of the apprentice garroted by his cruel master.

"Rob . . ." she started.

"What?" He was distracted, peering around her — at Sally, probably.

"Nothing."

"I hate it when people say 'nothing' when they obviously were about to say something. It's really annoying."

"I was just wondering if . . . if you've ever thought about things like ghosts." Miranda's throat was dry, and her stomach was twisting itself into knots. She just wanted Rob to hear her out.

"Things *like* ghosts?" he asked, still not looking at her. "Like werewolves and vampires? I don't mind zombies, but you know I can't get into all that other girly stuff about a love that never dies and who's on Team English-Wussy-Guy versus Team American-Big-Jaw —"

"I'm not talking about that," interrupted Miranda. She toyed with the table's small vase of flowers. Maybe trying to discuss her secret with Rob was a mistake. The problem was, she had nobody to talk to anymore. The other girls at school were no replacement for Jenna, and her parents didn't count, because they were busy and worried too much and would probably send her off to see yet another doctor type who wanted to talk about stuff like coping mechanisms and "working through your grief."

Finally, Miranda made herself say it. "I mean — what would you say if I told you that I — I think I can see ghosts?"

"What?" Rob wasn't really interested, she could tell. He was just filling in time until Sally came back. "Like that movie, you mean? You know — 'I see dead people.' That kid was dead, you know. Or was it Bruce Willis who was dead? It was confusing."

"Forget I said anything," said Miranda, irritated now. This was a waste of time. She might have known that Rob wouldn't listen, wouldn't even try to understand. She picked up her book and held it up in front of her face.

"Hey," he said, flicking her book and leaning closer. "Tell me."

Miranda put the book down. It was now or never, she thought.

"The night Jenna — the night of the . . . accident," she began, stumbling over her words.

Rob stared at her, his eyes muddy with pain, and Miranda wished she'd kept quiet. They never talked about the accident. Rob had been driving that night, and he blamed himself — that's what Peggy had told her. He thought he should have reacted more quickly, sped up or braked — something, anything. He thought he should have saved Jenna.

"What about it," he said softly. Miranda swallowed, trying to summon the courage to continue.

"I saw her . . . her ghost," she said at last. "I think it was her ghost. Yeah, it was. I saw her . . . I don't know how to explain it. I saw her leave her body behind and walk away."

Rob stared down at the table, tracing one finger along a pale swirl of marble.

"You're saying you saw Jenna get out of the car and walk away?"

"Not exactly." Miranda felt confused. What *had* she seen? Jenna walking into the field, even though her crushed body was still trapped in the car. "I mean, I saw her and *felt* her walk by me."

"You were in shock."

"I know, and I thought that maybe I imagined it.

That's why I never said anything to anyone. But then —
the thing is, I keep seeing them. In Iowa. Here. On the
street. At Clifford's Tower. In the . . ."

Miranda was about to say "in the attic across the
street" but changed her mind. She didn't want Rob staked
out at her window — or, even worse, insisting on swap-
ping rooms.

Rob raised his eyes to meet hers. He looked so sad,
she thought, so wounded. She shouldn't have brought the
accident up again.

"It's just your overactive imagination," he said. His
eyes were hardening; his voice was cold. "It's just one of
the ways some people react to all this . . . stuff. That's
what one of those doctors told me. Some people are in
denial about losing someone close to them, and they start
imagining they can see them, or talk to them, or contact
them in the spirit world or something."

"That's not what I'm saying!" Miranda raised her voice
without meaning to. "I don't think I can talk to Jenna. I
only saw her that one time. But I can see other ghosts.
On Saturday afternoon, one of them spoke to me — this
little girl."

"What the —" Rob shook his head.

"Here we go!" Sally appeared, sliding big white cups
of hot chocolate onto the table. "I'll bring a selection of
jams for your pikelets. They'll be out in just a moment."

"Thanks," said Rob, flashing her a weak smile. He
looked grateful for the interruption. When Sally had
gone, he picked up a teaspoon and started slowly stirring

the chocolate flakes into the frothy cream, not looking at Miranda.

"You have to believe me," she pleaded. "I'm not making this up. I don't know why I can see ghosts right now, but I just can. Someone said to me that maybe Jenna wanted to say good-bye."

"Who've you been talking to about this?" Rob hissed, banging the teaspoon on the side of the cup.

"Nobody you know." Miranda felt miserable. She couldn't say a word to Rob about Nick, that was obvious. If he didn't want to hear about ghosts, he wouldn't want to hear about someone who possibly planned to take her on some kind of private ghost tour.

"Just don't say any of this crazy stuff to Mom and Dad, okay?" Rob looked annoyed now. Accusing. "They're trying to have a nice time this week, and the last thing they need is you whining about seeing dead people. They'll get all worried and it'll ruin everything. This family trip thing is a big deal for them. They're trying to forget about . . . what happened. Just for a week, they're trying to forget, okay? *I'm* trying to forget. You should, too."

Miranda's eyes prickled with tears.

"This isn't about what happened," she hissed. "Maybe I've been able to see ghosts for years but I never realized it."

"*Everything* is about what happened," Rob said. He sucked his spoon clean and clanged it onto the table. "But this week I'm pretending that I'm not a psycho who can't get into cars without freaking out, and you're pretending you're not a psycho who can't climb a stair-case without freaking out, and we're all pretending that we're a normal family. Okay?"

Miranda said nothing. She didn't want to make a fool of herself by crying in public, especially now that Sally was leaning over them again, arranging white china jam pots in the center of the table.

"*Tales of Old York?*" Sally said, glancing at Miranda's book. She set out plates, lining up shining cutlery and small triangles of pristine white napkin. "That sounds interesting. You should have a proper tour of the White Boar, you know. Part of the building dates back to the thirteenth century, and an archaeologist told us once that some of the stones in the cellar may have been part of the old Roman road. You can come over with Rob later on, if you like."

"I have to be somewhere," Miranda blurted. Did Rob look suspicious, or was that just her imagination?

"Another time, then," Sally said, smiling, and Miranda did her best to smile back.

"Where are you going, anyway?" Rob gave her a sour look. Miranda didn't reply. She wasn't going to tell him about meeting Nick by the green door on Petergate. She wasn't going to tell him anything ever again if he was going to act in such a belligerent way. She thought he'd be the one person who wouldn't dismiss all this as fantasy, but she was wrong.

Both Rob and Sally were looking at her expectantly, so she had to say something.

"City walls," she mumbled. "Just for a walk."

Sally glanced at her thin silver wristwatch.

"You better hurry," she said. "They start closing the walls at dusk, and in the wintertime that's . . . well, it's now."

"I should go, then," Miranda said, cramming *Tales of Old York* back into her bag. She was out of her chair before Rob could say a word. He looked startled and grumpy, but Miranda didn't care. Nick may have seemed a little weird, but he didn't mock and berate her. He believed her.

Sally was right. Dusk sounded like a mysterious and romantic time of day, but the sign on the city walls told Miranda otherwise. As far as the City of York was concerned, dusk in December began at half past three in the afternoon.

Miranda found Bootham Bar, one of the city's old fortified entrances, without a problem; they'd passed it on the taxi ride from the train station — just days ago, though it already felt like weeks. But she couldn't see a green door anywhere. Miranda paced back and forth, confused. Maybe there was no green door. Maybe Nick never intended to meet her this afternoon, and the meeting place he'd told her didn't exist. Maybe he *was* going to meet her, and then take her somewhere quiet and murder her. She really didn't know what was making her heart beat so fast — anticipation at seeing Nick, anxiety that he wouldn't show up, or fear.

She couldn't just stand there like an idiot, so Miranda walked through Bootham Bar toward the steps up onto the wall. The roads were much busier outside the medieval walls; York suddenly felt like a modern city again, with trucks lumbering through intersections and people impatiently leaning on their car horns. Nick was nowhere in sight. It was only when Miranda turned around to retrace her footsteps that she saw it. The green door was right there, practically set into the city walls, impossible to see from Petergate itself. The door was the darkest of greens, almost black. It had a brass knocker but no bell of any kind. On the doorstep, Miranda hesitated, wondering if she was too early. Wondering if it was too late to change her mind.

"Hey," said a voice behind her.

She swung around, not really surprised to see Nick standing there. He seemed to have a habit of popping up out of nowhere. At least he was almost smiling at her now, his face softer, less hostile, than it had appeared Saturday morning. Still pale, of course. His face looked as though it were chiseled from chalk.

"Is this . . . where you live?" she asked shyly, gesturing at the green door.

"Where I'm staying." His voice was gruff. "Come on. We should get onto the walls."

"Aren't they about to close?"

"Don't worry. It'll be twenty minutes before they're sweeping this stretch, and by then we'll have jumped off."

Miranda didn't like the sound of "jumped off" at all. The walls looked way too high for any jumping — and why, exactly, did they have to jump anywhere? But even a semi-smiling Nick made her feel nervous, and before she could get another word out, he was hustling her through a squeaky barred gate and onto the stairs.

Within moments they were up on the city walls. On one side, there were the rooftops of the houses along Gillygate. On the other, across lush lawns streaked with the shadows of trees, sat York Minster, the last of the afternoon light catching its intricate ivory carvings and stained-glass windows.

"This was a Roman road," Nick told her, pointing back to Bootham Bar. "The Romans had their own gate-house here. Roman legions marched north out of the city this way, up to Hadrian's Wall."

"You know a lot about York," she said, running her hand along the golden stone of the battlements. It was a lame thing to say, but it was all Miranda could think of right now. It was a whole lot better than "are you planning to kill me?"

"Like I said, I grew up here. I moved away. But you don't forget things."

"When you moved away, where did you go?"

"Here and there. London, mostly. I've only been back for a week or two."

"Oh." Miranda wished her heart would stop beating so fast. Her voice sounded squeaky. "Does your family still live here?"

"No." He was walking more quickly now, his black boots clomping along the stone walkway. "I'm leaving on Monday."

"So are we," Miranda called after him, hurrying to catch up. "Where are you going?"

"Anywhere but here," Nick said, his voice dark, and he stalked away, his black coat flapping in the wind.

CHAPTER SEVEN

Nick finally slowed his pace and walked down a set of steps that led into a stark garden. Miranda followed him. All the flower beds were dug over, and the trees were spindly and bare. The lawns here backed onto a jumble of old buildings that crowded around the towering Minster. Miranda still had no idea where they were going. She opened her mouth to ask and then closed it again. She had to trust him. But part of her wondered what she was doing, if this was remotely safe.

Nick jumped over the low, locked gate in one easy movement: He was very agile for someone so tall. He reached out a hand for Miranda, but she hesitated before taking it. His grip was firm; the skin felt cold and a little rough. Miranda felt herself blushing, though she knew there was nothing romantic about this. Nick was just hauling Miranda over the gate, steadying her when her boots slipped on the damp ironwork. There was no reason to feel this flustered. Even so, Miranda was relieved when he dropped her hand, and at the second gate, she scrambled over without his help.

Hand holding was something surreptitious that happened when (before the accident) she had gone with some boy from school to the movies — clammy, tentative, under cover of darkness. Nick was nothing like those boys, and not just because he was older, and English. Miranda knew what to expect from the boys at school. Nick was still an enigma.

In a few confident strides he crossed the grass and ducked into the shadow of a high brick wall. Miranda scampered along behind him.

"Keep low," he said to her over his shoulder. He stopped next to the wall of what might be a shed, and crouched down.

"Where are we going?" Miranda asked, crouching alongside him, trying not to sound as nervous as she felt. She hoped they weren't going to break in somewhere. Getting arrested would definitely fall into the "ruining the family vacation" category.

"The Treasurer's House." Nick peered around the corner of the shed. "The courtyard. The place is closed for the winter right now; otherwise we'd be able to walk right up. They're doing renovations, too, building work. We should wait here a little while, until it gets darker. All right?"

"Okay," said Miranda. It wasn't okay, really. They weren't supposed to be here. It was cold and the ground was damp. The sky looked heavy, ready to burst with sleet or snow. The city walls were about to close for the night. The only people passing by up there were an old lady walking a yappy terrier and a jogger thudding past toward Bootham Bar.

"Here," Nick said, maneuvering until his back was against the wall, and then spreading the tails of his long coat out around him before he slid down. "Sit on a bit of this."

Miranda hesitated. She didn't want to get damp grass all over her butt, but if she complied with Nick's request, they'd be sitting very close together. Uncomfortably close. Nick was looking away, gazing up at the stretch of city wall, and Miranda slowly, awkwardly sat down next to him. Their shoulders and arms were brushing now. There wasn't anything she could do about it.

"What are we going to see at the Treasurer's House?" she asked him, desperate to fill the silence.

"Not see. Hear," he said. She waited for him to explain, but he was still staring up at the walls.

Miranda tried to take the conversation in a more normal direction. "Did you grow up near here or, you know, in the suburbs?" Her knee touched Nick's and she jerked it away, embarrassed.

"Here in town. Various houses. My mother liked to move."

"But she doesn't live here now, right?"

"She buggered off." Nick's voice betrayed no emotion. "Not long after I ran away. Moved to Spain. Didn't surprise me. I didn't really care."

"You ran away?"

"When I was fifteen. Wasn't the first time. The first was after . . . someone died."

"Your father?" asked Miranda. Nick had only talked about his mother moving away.

He gave a contemptuous snort.

"No, he's still alive. Getting fat, probably, on his estate up in Scotland. Ripping off investment bankers who'll pay through the nose for a chance to shoot a deer. They got divorced, him and my mother, when I was small. Haven't seen him for years."

His parents sounded as though they had money, Miranda thought. So why did Nick dress in such ragged clothes? Maybe it was all just a big Goth pose. But she couldn't ask him any more questions. The sun was setting, any warmth seeping out of the day. The darkness made her feel more self-conscious rather than less, painfully aware of the slight pressure of Nick's arm against hers.

"My brother," Nick said suddenly, his voice soft. "He was the one who died. When I was thirteen. He was a lot older than me — he was twenty-one. But I hadn't seen him for several years at that point. He'd been . . . away."

"At college?" Miranda asked, glancing at him. Nick's face was obscured by the shadows.

"In a mental hospital. Just outside the city. That's where he died. He committed suicide."

"How awful," Miranda said, because she had to say something, even though there was nothing to say. Losing someone you loved was unbearable, unspeakable. She knew that firsthand. Losing your brother in such a terrible way just had to derail you completely. If Rob had been killed in the accident . . . Miranda couldn't bear to think about it. No wonder Nick had run away to London. No wonder his mother had moved to another country.

"My mother wanted to have the funeral in the Minster." Nick sounded far away. "My parents got married in there. Big society do. They said no, of course. Mental case, killed himself. Not entitled to anything, as far as the Church was concerned. He's buried in the village where my grandparents live, way out there, where nobody has to know about him, or think about him, ever again."

"*You* think about him." This was such a sad story, Miranda thought. She looked up at Nick. The shadows softened the angles of his face.

"I saw him," he said. "Day of the funeral. We were walking away from the gravesite, and something made me turn around. He was standing by the grave, looking at the pile of dirt. I only saw him from the back, but I knew it was him. Then he walked through the churchyard and disappeared into a field. I told my mother — pointed to him, when he was walking past all the graves. She couldn't see anything. Nobody could. That was the first time I realized . . ."

". . . you could see ghosts," said Miranda, waves of relief washing through her. She wasn't a freak. She wasn't crazy. This happened to other people as well.

"Same for you?" Nick turned his head, leaning into

her. "The friend you mentioned, the one who died? Six months ago, right?"

"This summer," she told him, almost whispering. "Jenna and me and my brother — we were in a car accident. Rob and I were okay, more or less, but Jenna . . . They told me she was dead, but I swear to you, she walked past me and into the field. Her body was still there in the car . . ."

". . . but her spirit had other ideas." Nick scuffed at the wet grass with the toe of his boot.

"I'm still getting used to it, this seeing-ghosts thing. You've had longer to figure it all out, I guess." Miranda didn't feel quite so scared of Nick anymore. In one very crucial way, they were two of a kind.

"Seven years." He sounded weary. Sad. "Your friend's name was Jenna?"

"Yes. What was your brother's name?"

"Richard."

"Richard Gant," said Miranda. Nick wheezed out a laugh.

"That's not my real last name," he said, tapping his chest until Miranda leaned forward to look. The logo on his sweater, embroidered in a slightly darker gray, read GANT. "It was the first thing that came into my head the other day. Not used to talking about myself, I suppose. I usually don't tell people about any of this. But you . . . you're not like other people."

Miranda stared down at her knees, her cheeks burning.

"Look up there," he said, and he nudged her with his shoulder.

Miranda followed his gaze to the city walls. Some kind of night watchman in a long coat, holding a swinging lantern, was making his way along.

"He's closing the walkway," she said, but Nick shook his head.

"Watch," he said. Another jogger, visible mainly because of his fluorescent orange armband, pounded along the walkway toward Bootham Bar. Instead of running around the man with the swinging lantern, he ran straight through him, as though the night watchman were no more than a puff of mist. Miranda gasped.

"How did you know?" she asked. The night watchman had looked completely real and alive.

"I've seen him before," Nick admitted. "Tried talking to him once, but he didn't seem to hear me. Didn't answer, anyway."

"Jenna didn't speak to me," Miranda told him. It was so strange and liberating to be able to talk about that night to someone who understood. Miranda couldn't believe she was saying these things out loud. "Did your brother speak to you?"

"Not then." Nick frowned. He squirmed away from her, and Miranda regretted asking the question. "Come on, it's dark enough now. Keep low, and follow me."

Miranda struggled to her feet, freeing up Nick's coat so he could creep around the shed. He wended his way between two tall buildings, stooping as he passed windows.

Miranda followed him, wishing that the crunch of gravel wasn't so loud beneath her boots, only vaguely conscious of passing landmarks — a wooden garden gate, a moss-covered basin surrounded by terra-cotta pots, stone lions perched on their hind legs on the tops of columns.

Soon they were stealing across cobbles through a parking lot at the side of a grand stone house. The lot was empty except for a line of orange bollards and some yellow DO NOT CROSS tape strung across a stubby makeshift fence. Behind them, the cobbles had been lifted and the ground was being excavated. Pipes were exposed and, beyond them, the pit was even deeper. The ground along the lowest floor of the building itself — the basement, judging by its low windows — had been dug away by several feet. A paint-streaked tarp, held down by bricks, covered only some of the area.

Nick dragged the temporary fence post out of place, so there was enough room for them to squeeze through. Miranda, stumbling on a dug-up cobble, couldn't understand where they were going. There were no doors anywhere in sight. She hoped that Nick wasn't going to break a window.

But he stopped at the tarp, moving a brick to check underneath it.

"Here," he said, and folded the tarp back into place. "This is about as low as we'll get. We can sit on this. I don't think it'll get in the way."

He sat down with his back against the wall, legs outstretched, and looked up at Miranda expectantly.

She scuttled into place next to him, her back against the wall, too. She was going to have to get changed as soon as she got home: Every part of her felt damp and cold.

"Put your hands on the ground, like this," Nick instructed, pressing his palms flat against the tarp. "Take your gloves off."

"Why?" asked Miranda, but doing as he said.

"York was an important Roman city," he told her, as though that was the logical answer to her question. "The emperor Constantine was crowned here. Remember at Bootham Bar, when I said that's the way Roman soldiers marched north? Petergate was a Roman road, the Via Principalis."

"And Stonegate," Miranda said, remembering something her father had said. "That was a Roman road, too."

"Via Praetoria," said Nick. "And right underneath us, cutting through this building and running down the street beneath the Minster, is the old Via Decumana. The two roads used to meet in the middle, at what would have been the big HQ, the center of the Roman fort. The Minster was built on top of it."

"So we can see Roman ghosts here?" Miranda asked, suddenly excited. All this scrambling and hiding — all this breaking and entering — would be worth it if she could see Romans. But Nick was shaking his head, his smile dismissive.

"Too high up," he said. "The Roman road was much

lower — almost twenty feet down. We'd have to be in the cellar to see anything."

"Oh," said Miranda, disappointed.

"They've been spotted a few times over the years down there," Nick said. "Always around this time of day, in the wintertime. Tours go in there sometimes, to wait for them. But what they don't get is that only a few people can see ghosts."

He raised his eyebrows at Miranda, and she smiled back at him.

"There's all sorts of rubbish talked as well, about them being the famous lost Ninth Legion," he continued. "Marching off into the northern wilderness, never to be seen again. This was the last place they were stationed in Britain."

"How do you know so much history when —" Miranda stopped herself. She was about to say "you didn't even finish school?" but it sounded too rude a question. Nick glanced at her, amused.

"This isn't stuff you learn at school," he said. "I read books — I always did. You can't trust the stories people tell, especially around here, where there's profit in it. Saying the ghosts down here are the lost Ninth Legion, thousands of Roman soldiers about to be wiped out forever, makes a good story for the tourists even if it's not true. Here — can you feel them?"

Miranda didn't understand until Nick waved his hands at her and then pressed them firmly against the tarp. She pushed down with her own hands, feeling the tarp give way a little as it was tamped into the soft earth. From deep within the ground she felt a vibration, something shuddering. The motion made her hands tremble.

"What is it?" she whispered.

"Men. Horses. Dozens of them. They're getting closer — can you tell?"

She nodded. It felt like thunder rumbling underground. The soil beneath her was pulsing, the way a car seemed to pulse with the bass when the driver had the stereo turned up way high. It was rhythmic like the bass, too. Footsteps and hooves clopping along the road. When Miranda closed her eyes, she could hear them as well as feel them. Heavy, trudging steps. A shout — guttural, echoing — and then a shrill blast of sound that made her jump.

"Trumpet," said Nick. He must have heard it, too. "Announcing their arrival."

The footsteps kept thudding, but they were growing more distant now. Miranda realized she was clawing her fingers into the tarp, eager to feel the last of the procession.

When the ground stopped pulsing, she and Nick sat in silence. Miranda didn't want to open her eyes. Roman soldiers, ghosts for almost two thousand years, had walked the road beneath her, and she'd heard them. This wasn't frightening, like the ash ghosts in Clifford's Tower. This was exhilarating. She'd been so silly, wondering if Nick was going to harm her or drag her into some criminal activity. She wished she could come here every night.

"There might be something about them in here," she said, fumbling for *Tales of Old York* in her coat pocket. "It has tons of stuff about ghosts."

"Where did you get —" Nick began. He frowned at her, stretching a pale hand toward the book.

"This? Someone gave it to me. Have you read it?"

"No." He dropped his hand. "It's just — my mother had a copy of it. I never read it, though. You don't, when you grow up in a place. You find things out by seeing them for yourself. Especially when you can . . . see more than other people can. You know."

"I . . . I guess," stammered Miranda. She had never realized that she could see more than other people could. She'd had no idea that she was some kind of ghost whisperer. But when Nick talked about it, he made it seem almost normal.

"Just don't believe everything you read or hear about ghosts." He sounded stern. Miranda wanted to ask him about the ghosts she'd seen on the Shambles — Margaret Clitherow and the apprentice in the attic window — but there was something about Nick's dismissive tone that made her keep quiet. Rain was falling now — cold rain, splotching onto her face.

"Come on — we should go." He pushed himself up off the ground.

"How do we get out of here?" Miranda got up, stiff and unsteady, dusting off her jeans. The walls were closed by now, she knew. The gates in Bootham Bar were much bigger and sturdier than the ones they'd vaulted to jump down into the garden. She didn't want to be stuck in this creepy courtyard all night.

"Now that it's dark, we can climb over the fence," he said, gesturing to the spiked wrought-iron railings on the other side of the courtyard. They looked too high and too menacing to Miranda, but Nick showed her how to use the stone basin and a piece of brick jutting out of the adjoining wall to hoist herself up. She swung down onto the street on the other side, feeling pleased with herself, like an accomplished cat burglar. Nick came soaring down after her, a black-feathered bird of prey.

"Well, thanks. Good-bye." Miranda awkwardly held up a hand, more like swearing an oath than waving.

"Tomorrow night at Monk Bar, okay?" Nick demanded rather than asked. "We can make it later — six o'clock. One of the Vikings' victims. Nailed to a door, I should warn you."

"Oh," said Miranda, startled. He'd seemed almost anxious to be rid of her, but now he wanted to meet up again. The thought of seeing him again made her nervous, but in a good way. At least, she thought it was in a good way. "Sure. Okay. Monk Bar at six. I'll see you there."

Nick looked down at her. A half smile flitted across his face.

"I'll see you first," he said, and headed off into the night.

CHAPTER EIGHT

Everyone seemed on edge at breakfast. Rob crunched his way through two bowls of cereal, staring glumly into space.

"Thanks for leaving, like, a drop of milk for everyone else," Miranda complained, sitting down next to him. He ignored her.

"Rob, you look tired," their mother said. She stood over the table, sorting through a sheaf of music, pursing her lips and frowning at the score. Today was the first rehearsal with the singers, Miranda knew, which was why her mother was so agitated. "I hope you're not going to be working at the White Boar again tonight."

"It's not *working*," Rob spluttered. "I'm just helping Sally's parents out. All their staff took off. They're really shorthanded."

"Surely Sally's father can find . . ." their father began, shaking the cereal box. "This is empty already?"

"They can't find anyone," snapped Rob. "It's a really busy time, in case you hadn't noticed."

Peggy gave him a look. "Don't speak to your father like that, please."

"Rob's just, you know . . . carrying barrels for them and stuff," Miranda said. "And clearing glasses and cups . . ."

"Stay out of this," said her father and Rob simultaneously. Miranda couldn't believe it: She was actually trying to back Rob up, and he was turning on her. She banged her spoon in the bowl.

"And there's no need for that," said her mother sharply.

"Could everyone just CHILLAX!" Jeff brought the cereal box down onto the table, but it didn't make much of a noise. He looked disappointed with the lack of dramatic effect.

"Dad, nobody says 'chillax' anymore," Miranda told him, picking up her spoon again.

"Nobody ever said it," added Rob.

"Please, could you all stop talking." Peggy shuffled all her pages together. "You two, if you're going to drop in to the rehearsal today, come by around eleven and don't make any noise. I'll be home tonight by six at the latest. I thought we could have an early dinner at that Indian restaurant around the corner."

"I'll still be out then," their father said, folding the newspaper so only the crossword was visible. "Drinks thing with the Richard III Museum people, remember?"

"I'll be out then, too," said Rob.

"So will I," said Miranda quickly.

"Where are *you* going?" Rob muttered, pointing at her with his spoon. Milk dribbled from the side of his mouth. Miranda hoped he acted more civilized in front of Sally.

"None of your business," she whispered.

"Could everyone please be home no later than six thirty," said Peggy, sliding papers into her portfolio. It was a statement rather than a question.

"Seven," said Miranda. It meant she wouldn't have much time with Nick, but anything was better than nothing. She wanted to see the Viking ghost. She wanted to see Nick.

"Ten," said Rob. He was pushing it, Miranda thought.

"I could possibly make it." Jeff sounded uncertain, but then he seemed to notice Peggy's look of exasperation and disbelief. "Of course, darling — six thirty. No problem. You two! Home by six thirty. You can run wild other nights. Your mother and I have the medievalists' banquet tomorrow night, which, by the way, you're very welcome to attend."

"No, thanks," said Miranda. She'd been tricked into one of these medievalist shindigs before, in some conference-center ballroom in Chicago. Dry chicken, boring conversation, old people dancing. It was hideous.

"Count me out," said Rob. "Not that it doesn't sound, you know — fun."

He and Miranda started laughing, snickering into their cereal bowls.

"You are horrible, horrible children," their mother declared, swinging her bag onto her shoulder. "I'm going."

"See you at the rehearsal!" Miranda called as her mother pattered down the stairs.

Luckily, her parents were so preoccupied with their own activities, they'd forgotten to grill Miranda about what she was planning to do tonight until six thirty. The less they knew, the better. How could she begin to explain Nick — who he was, how they met, what they were doing together?

Their mother often told them that they needed to be better listeners. Miranda just thought it was something all mothers said, with the same pained expression and tortured tone. It was probably in some parenting book, one of a list of things you should say to annoy your teenaged children, along with "take that look off your face" and "what's that long sigh for?" and "I don't know what happened; when you were little you were so sweet."

But, apparently, Peggy was right. Rob and Miranda had assumed that today's rehearsal was at the Minster, but when they got there — dead on eleven, as agreed, racing up the side steps and through the revolving doors — they found out they were wrong.

"No rehearsals here today," said the cheery woman at the ticket counter, after trying to get them to cough up some outrageous amount to come in and look around. "There's a concert tonight — the Tallis Scholars. Is that what you're here for?"

"Our mother is conducting *Dido and Aeneas*," explained Miranda. Rob was useless, staring up at the huge stained-glass window behind their heads. Probably dreaming about his wedding to Sally, she thought.

"*Dido and Aeneas*," said the ticket seller, tracing a finger down a printout on the counter. "A staged performance of Purcell's opera by the Spenserian Consort — yes? Conducted by Peggy Tennant."

"That's our mother," said Miranda. She didn't want to have to buy a ticket just to get inside the Minster for a rehearsal.

"Performance at eight P.M. on Saturday evening. Let me check my other sheet — yes, I see. There *will* be a rehearsal here in the Minster on Wednesday. Today's rehearsal is in Victory Hall. Do you know where that is?"

Back out on the wet, chilly street, Miranda clutched the map the ticket seller had given her. The route to Victory Hall — on the other side of town — was marked in squiggly blue pen. She and Rob set off at a good pace, loping through the crowded streets and squabbling, not very seriously, about the best route. Even though Miranda was the one with the map, Rob thought he had a better idea of how to get there.

"I've walked around much more than you have," Miranda argued. "You've spent most of your time at the White Boar. I'm surprised you're not there now, hanging around Sally like a lovesick moron."

"Whatever," said Rob, and something about the way he sounded — sheepish rather than brash — and the way he hung his head made Miranda suspicious.

"What's up?" she asked. "Has Sally dumped you already?"

"No," he said. "Nothing like that."

"Like what, then?"

Rob came to a stop outside a store, his gaze fixed on something in the window. Miranda took the opportunity to check on her own reflection. The hat she was wearing was cute, she decided, even if it did make her hair go all flat. She wondered what Nick would think of it — or if he would even notice whether she looked pretty or not, let alone care.

"Do you think Sally would like that?" Rob pointed at a mannequin dressed in a patched suede jacket. It was a charity shop, Miranda realized, its window display crammed with everything from ugly china animals to scuffed winter boots, paperback thrillers lined up against the glass. As well as the suede jacket, the mannequin was wearing a long taffeta skirt and a canary yellow wool beret. "She was saying yesterday that she's saving all the money she earns for college, and not spending it on clothes and stuff."

"It's not bad," said Miranda. Rob had surprisingly good taste. Then again, he might just be drawn to charity-shop gear because of the price. He was nothing if not cheap.

"Last night," said Rob, looking at the coat in the window, not at Miranda. "Last night, Joe — that's Sally's dad — he took me down to the cellar to show me how to change a barrel. We weren't down there long, but . . ."

"What?" Miranda's mind started leaping to the worst possible conclusions. "Did he threaten you or something?"

"No!" Rob looked at her as though she were crazy. "Really, you need to just — chillax, as Dad would say."

"Well, what happened then?"

"I got all — you know." Rob stared at the window again. "It's this really small old cellar. Ancient Roman or whatever. It's a really tiny space. Low ceiling, steep stairs to get down there. Like some kind of cave."

"So you freaked out."

"I just couldn't breathe. I thought my head was going to explode. I hid it pretty well, I think. Joe didn't seem to notice anything. I just don't want Sally to find out."

"Find out about . . ."

"Everything. The claustrophobia. The . . . you know."

"You haven't told her about . . . you know."

"I don't want her to feel *sorry* for me. I'm tired of everyone feeling sorry for me. For us. I don't want her to look at me the way everyone looks at me at school, like I'm some kind of special-needs case."

"I'm sure she wouldn't."

"Really?" Rob said, his voice accusing. "You know how they all talk about us."

Miranda knew what he meant. Rob was the guy who was driving the car, the night that girl was killed. And what did they say about her? Was she the girl who did nothing, the girl who just sat on the side of the road without trying to help her dying friend? She'd heard the whispers. No wonder neither of them wanted to go out anymore.

"Sally just thinks I'm a normal guy," Rob said.

"Well, she's wrong about that," Miranda joked, hoping to cheer him up. But it didn't work. Rob just looked pensive. Miserable, even.

"I really like her," he said quietly. "It's true I've only known her for —"

"Five minutes."

"Okay. Not very long. But she's a cool girl, even if she does have a weird accent. And she likes me, you know? For me. Not because I'm some tragic figure. The guy who killed somebody."

"You didn't kill anyone," Miranda told him, biting her lip. Her throat felt tight. "The other driver smashed into us. He killed Jenna."

She would not cry in the street, she told herself. She would not embarrass herself by crying in the street.

"Yeah, well," said Rob. He tapped the window with one finger, his breath steaming up the glass. "I think I'm going to buy Sally that jacket."

Miranda sniffed back an insistent tear. She didn't want Rob to see it.

"You do know it's twenty pounds," she said. "That's like a million dollars or something in American money."

"Yeah," said Rob. "I know. You're going to have to lend me some cash."

The door of the shop swung open, its bell jingling. Someone was stepping out onto the pavement, clutching a big bundle of what looked like sheets and blankets. The bundle was so big, in fact, that the person could barely see where they were going.

Where *he* was going, realized Miranda, with a shivery jolt of recognition. The person leaving the charity shop, lowering his cargo of blankets so he could negotiate the step down, was Nick. And he did not look happy to see her. Not happy at all.

"Hey," said Miranda, lifting her hand in a half-hearted wave. Nick glowered at her, clutching his lumpy bundle of secondhand bedding as though it were a child.

"Hey," he muttered. He shot Rob a ferocious glance, and then hurried away down Walmgate, his black coat flapping.

"Why are you talking to random guys?" Rob wanted to know. "Just because we're in a foreign country doesn't mean you have to curtsy to strangers. Who do you think he is, the Earl of Emo?"

"He's this . . . this guy I know," Miranda mumbled. She glanced down the street, watching Nick stride away. His back was poker straight, his hair spiky. He didn't look around. "I've met him already, I mean."

"What — *him*?" Rob was incredulous. He stood with his arms folded, facing her. "What are you talking about, you've 'met' him?"

"It's a long story," said Miranda, looking down. "Don't make a big deal out of it. You meet people, I meet people. Whatever."

"This isn't the . . . oh no, please tell me this isn't the reason you wanted to go out tonight. You're not going out with *him* somewhere, are you?"

"No," lied Miranda, but she could see Rob didn't believe her.

"Miranda, trust me. That guy is a creep. Stay away from him."

"What do you know?" she demanded. "You've never even talked to him. You're just judging him because —"

"Because he was rude, and he looks totally weird, and he's probably planning to sacrifice you at dawn or something. Not to mention he was carrying around his bedding like a homeless person."

"He's not homeless," said Miranda, though she wasn't sure if this was true or not. "Look, I'm not *eloping* with him. He's just showing me around."

"Yeah, well," snorted Rob. "He's not showing you anywhere, okay? I don't like the looks of him."

"Please!" Miranda couldn't stand it when Rob decided to play the role of overprotective, all-knowing older brother. "I can take care of myself."

"No, you can't. You're only sixteen."

"Going on seventeen."

"Miranda, this isn't *The Sound of Music*. You don't know anything about anything. Have you told Mom and Dad about this guy?"

"If you even think about telling them, I'll tell Sally about your claustrophobia. I mean it."

"Don't threaten me."

"Don't threaten *me*. You mind your business and I'll mind mine. Okay?" Miranda glared at Rob. They stood in silence for a long moment, staring each other down.

"I just don't like it," he said at last.

"You don't have to," Miranda retorted. "Everything's not always about *you*, Rob."

She stood outside the store while he went in to buy the jacket for Sally. Her heart was beating fast. Miranda hated arguing like this with Rob, especially when he was a little bit — just a tiny little bit — right. Nick had acted very strangely just now, abrupt and surly. The whole blankets-and-sheets thing was weird. But maybe they were for some of his Goth friends, or for the flat with the green door — lots of people might be staying there, and maybe they didn't have enough heating or bedding. Nick would probably explain everything when she saw him tonight.

*　　*　　*

At the rehearsal in Victory Hall, Miranda couldn't focus on the music. It was all too stop-and-start anyway, because Peggy wanted the musicians and singers to keep going over certain things, and the high-pitched laugh of the woman playing the First Witch grated on Miranda's nerves. The hall itself was dusty and cold. Rob sat three seats away, looking grumpy. Miranda wasn't sure if he was still mad at her or if he was just annoyed to be away from Sally for five minutes. She knew he was planning to spend the rest of the afternoon "helping" at the White Boar, so at least she'd be free to meet Nick later on without any interference.

She had some time between the rehearsal and her appointment — going to see a guy nailed to a door a thousand years ago was hardly a *date* — with Nick. Miranda didn't feel like doing anything, not reading, not sleeping, not sightseeing, not shopping. She marched down Goodramgate to Monk Bar at a quarter to six, hoping that Nick might arrive early as well. Six thirty was her curfew: That didn't give them much time.

Tonight, Miranda was determined to ask questions. Nick might look "totally weird," as Rob insisted, and he might be kind of spiky and intense sometimes, but unlike everybody else, he told the truth. Miranda wasn't sure how she felt about him, exactly. She wished he was as handsome as the guy in the attic window, and as . . . what was the word? *Charismatic*, maybe. But she and Nick had some kind of bond, a shared experience of death and sadness and ghosts. He'd never met anyone he could talk to about this; that's what he'd told her. What they had wasn't quite friendship and it wasn't quite romance. It was something more unique. Like a conspiracy.

At Monk Bar, Miranda paced around, uncertain of where to wait. Nick made a big thing about seeing her first, and he was right: She never managed to spot him, even though he had such a distinctive look. But just before six, when someone on the other side of the street called her name, Miranda wasn't relieved or excited. Her heart sank.

It wasn't Nick. It was her father.

CHAPTER NINE

"Such excellent timing," Jeff said, helping himself to more rice. "I left the museum, walked down the stairs, and there was Miranda waiting for me."

"That was very nice of you." Peggy smiled at Miranda across the table. They'd been seated in the window because they were the first diners of the evening. The restaurant, the Rajah, was small, its walls swathed with vibrant red and pink saris and hung with gilt-flecked paintings of bejeweled women riding elephants. It looked, Jeff had whispered, like the inside of the bottle in *I Dream of Jeannie*. "You know how your father tends to get lost."

Miranda couldn't think of anything to say that wasn't a lie, so she tore off a chunk of naan bread, dunked it into the lurid orange sauce of her chicken tikka, and stuffed it in her mouth. Of course, she'd forgotten completely that the Richard III Museum was in Monk Bar. She hadn't thought for a moment that her father would be leaving his "drinks thing," as he called it, just as she was about to meet Nick.

Nick. Miranda hoped he wasn't angry with her for standing him up. What else could she have done once her father had spotted her? The whole thing was so, so annoying. Maybe she'd never see Nick again now. Wondering if that awkward encounter outside the secondhand store would be their last meeting made Miranda feel miserable.

Luckily, nobody expected her to say much at dinner. Her mother was talking about how well rehearsals had gone today, and her father had various bad impersonations of museum workers to inflict on them. Between enormous greedy mouthfuls of lamb vindaloo, Rob was droning on about everything he was learning at the White Boar Inn, and how Sally's father had even entrusted him with a key to the cellar. That morning, Peggy had been telling Rob not to spend all his time there, but now she and Jeff seemed delighted to hear all of Rob's dull stories. Miranda noticed the significant looks her parents exchanged now and then, and she realized what was going on in the collective mind of the Parental Unit. After months of moping — depression, probably — Rob was suddenly a grinning chatterbox. *Look how happy Rob is*, they were thinking. *This is such a positive experience for him. He's getting over the accident at long last.*

That didn't mean her parents would be thrilled about *her* choice of activity in York. That conversation would be a different story. "Mom, Dad, I've met this guy. His brother committed suicide. He was a teenage runaway and he's as pale as a vampire. And guess what: He can see ghosts, just like me! Yesterday we jumped off the city walls and climbed fences so we could break into a building site and listen to the ghosts of Roman soldiers. And today I was planning to meet him again on the down-low so I could see the ghost of someone nailed to a door by the Vikings."

Yup. That conversation was a total non-starter.

The thing was, Nick's story was way too complex to even begin to discuss. He wasn't just a high-school-dropout Goth. The little pieces that Miranda had learned so far were sad and odd, like his brother dying young in that terrible way, and being refused a funeral in the Minster, or Nick running away from home and losing all contact with his parents. There were so many things she *didn't* know, of course. Why had he come back to York now? Why was he staying for such a short time? What had drawn Nick back to the place he'd grown up, and what was driving him away, Miranda didn't know. He made her feel nervous, even a little afraid, though he hadn't done anything to put her in danger. Not yet, anyway. He seemed to be in control of all these ghost encounters, not scared and confused the way she was. Why he was offering to show her things . . . well, that was another mystery. Maybe he was lonely, she thought. Maybe he couldn't talk to his Goth friends about his "gift," just as she couldn't fathom discussing it with Bea or Cami or any of the kids at school. Perhaps he'd tried to tell someone about what he could see, the way she'd tried to tell Rob yesterday, and they just didn't want to know.

"So, what else did you do today?" Peggy was asking, and Miranda struggled to find something plausible to say. Rob looking at her in a mean and suspicious way didn't help.

"Mainly . . . um, wandering around," she said, trying to be as vague as possible.

"Any shopping?"

"We did some shopping this morning," Rob said. He looked straight at Miranda. "In a secondhand store, near that hall place where you were rehearsing."

Miranda glared at him. He better not say anything about bumping into Nick. She would never forgive him. Nick was *her* secret. The second her parents found out she'd made friends with the Earl of Emo, as Rob called him, she'd probably be forced to spend every day page-turning for one of the singers or doing archival research for her father. She fixed her most steely gaze on Rob, willing him to shut up.

"It was pretty lame," he said at last, reaching for what was left of Miranda's naan bread. "Hey, does anyone want the rest of that chicken thing? I'm starving."

According to Miranda's cell phone, it was just after three in the morning. She'd woken up feeling a little sick — too much rich Indian food, she thought ruefully. In Iowa right now, it would be only nine in the evening.

If she could send texts, she could see what the girls were doing, maybe. But her phone couldn't send anything to the U.S. or receive anything, either, as she and Rob had discovered in Manchester airport. And anyway, what would the girls back home have to say? What happened on *Glee* that night, maybe. Who was and wasn't going to Matt Angeli's holiday party. Nothing that meant anything. Everything back home seemed more than thousands of miles away: It felt totally irrelevant.

The attic bedroom was stuffy and too hot. Miranda kicked off her quilt, swung her legs out of bed and padded over to the window. She pulled back a curtain and peered out. Nothing but silence and darkness. The Christmas streetlights were out, and no stars were visible. In the attic across the street, Miranda couldn't make out anything in the room beyond the window. It was just too dark.

She moved to twitch the curtain back into place, but something stopped her. A light flickering — the tiniest light. A candle.

The ghost was there.

Miranda froze, still clutching one of the curtains. He looked even more breathtaking this time, his face like chiseled marble. She was staring at him, she knew, but it was like staring at someone up on the screen of a movie theater. He was an idol, someone to gawk at, to admire. What he was thinking when he looked at *her*, Miranda wasn't sure. She was just a teenage girl wearing pajamas from the Garnet Hill catalog, her auburn hair messy and her eyes crusted with sleep. But there was something about his intense gaze that made her feel special. Picked out in some way. Only a few people could see ghosts: That was what Nick had said. The way this ghost looked at her — it was as though there was something between them. As though he *knew* her.

The ghost held up his right hand, just as he had last time, and a burst of cold, an injection of it, seemed to pierce her through the glass. Miranda pressed her own hand against the window. She knew what to expect now, the surge of cold playing through her veins, from her fingertips to her toes. And this time she wasn't overwhelmed by shock; she had enough sense to notice details about the ghost. The sleeves of his shirt drooped, like a pirate's shirt. She'd thought his fingers were dirty, but it was really just his fingertips, as though he'd been dipping them in something like ink — or blood. The wound across his neck, clearly visible, was a purple line.

Tonight he wasn't smiling at all, but his eyes were warm, velvety dark. Miranda wished there weren't two closed windows — and a stretch of very cold open air — separating them. She wanted to talk to him, like she'd talked to that little girl ghost, Mary, in the street. Maybe, like Mary, he had something to tell her. She'd seen him three times now: That had to mean something. When she saw Nick again — if she saw Nick — she'd ask him.

The ghost opened his mouth. Was he trying to say something? Then the flame of the candle leapt, just for an instant, and died. Everything was dark again — inside, outside. He was gone.

Miranda peeled her hand off the glass and staggered back to bed. The sharp jolt of cold had stopped as soon as the candle went out, but she still felt shivery. She pulled the quilt back up onto the bed and snuggled down, her heart racing. What was he going to say to her? What did he want her to know?

When she finally fell asleep, Miranda dreamed of walking along the city walls at dusk. Jenna was there, pleading with her to go on a double date with that cute Spanish exchange student, Alejandro. In the distance, the ghost watchman she and Nick had seen was pacing the battlements, holding a shining lantern. Miranda walked past Jenna, ignoring her pleas. All she wanted to do was get close to the ghost. As she grew closer, she could see that he was talking, but she couldn't hear what she was saying. "Press your hands down," Nick's voice told her, and the dream-Miranda dropped to her hands and knees. She was crawling along the stone walkway, the stones vibrating beneath the palms of her hands. The ghost wore a black coat, just like Nick's. It flapped open in the wind, the long tails wafting with every step. When she got closer, she realized that the man walking toward her along the walls wasn't the ghost at all. It was Nick, and he wasn't smiling. He was angry.

Someone was banging on the door downstairs — banging, banging, banging. Then there were thudding footsteps, and agitated voices. Miranda opened her eyes, still feeling groggy. She didn't know if it was nighttime or morning, or if she was dreaming or awake. Her father was bellowing Rob's name.

Miranda squinted at her cell phone: It read 7:53. Rob's door squeaked open.

"What?" he called, sounding sleepy.

"Sally's here," Jeff shouted up the stairs.

Miranda groped around the floor for a sweater to pull over her pajamas. Why was Sally coming by so early in the morning? The White Boar Inn didn't open for hours and hours, so they could hardly need Rob's amateur services at this very minute.

In the hallway, she bumped into Rob, still in his usual sleep gear of boxer shorts and an Iowa Hawkeyes T-shirt. Miranda followed him down the stairs. Sally was sitting at the kitchen table, her head in her hands. Jeff and Peggy were both standing, looking very serious. When Rob approached Sally, she started crying.

"What is it?" he said, hurling himself at her feet, one protective arm thrown around the chair. Miranda stood on the landing, swallowing back panic. Something terrible must have happened. *No more accidents*, she prayed silently. *Please, no more accidents.*

"There was a break-in at the pub," Jeff explained. "The pub cellar. It was vandalized — that's right, isn't it, Sally?"

Sally nodded, brushing tears away.

"What do you mean, vandalized?" asked Rob.

"Everything thrown around," Sally said, sniffing. "Barrels disconnected, beer poured everywhere. It's just a mess."

"But everyone's okay?" Rob asked in a low voice, and Sally nodded again. Miranda exhaled, relieved that nobody seemed to have been hurt. "Just a break-in, right?"

"It wasn't a break-in, though." Sally looked up at Peggy and Jeff, her face pale and streaked with tears. "That's the mystery. No sign of a forced entry at all, the police say."

"The police?" Rob echoed.

"They're over at the pub now. The door leading down there was locked, and the access in the alley — you know, the trapdoors. They were locked, too. Locked and bolted."

"It doesn't make any sense," Peggy said, her voice anxious, glancing over at Jeff.

"I know," Sally said. "That's why they want to see Rob."

"Me? Who wants to see me?"

"My parents. The police." Sally looked as though she was about to cry again. "You're the only other person with a key."

"They didn't think *I* did it?" Rob frowned. He stood up slowly.

"They don't know what to think," said Sally, her eyes welling up. "That's why I got so angry, and then all upset. I'm so stupid — I know this crying doesn't help. But it's so unfair to blame you."

"They're *blaming* me?" Rob ran his hands through his hair. He looked like a cornered animal.

"Not blaming — that was the wrong word."

"I'm sure they're not blaming anyone." Jeff sounded gruff. "But of course they want to talk to you, to see if you can help shed any light on all this. Sally, what about the employees who left last weekend? Maybe one of them still has a key."

Sally shook her head.

"They handed them in. And anyway, Dad had the locks changed on Monday, just to be safe. That's why nobody understands how this could have happened."

"I'll go talk to them now, if that's what you want." Rob looked at Sally, and she started to get up, pushing her chair back. "I just have to get dressed."

"I'll come with you," said Jeff.

"Okay," said Rob, and he bounded off up the stairs.

"I think I'll go with you, too." Peggy put down the coffee mug she'd been cradling throughout the conversation. "Rather than just stand around here worrying."

"I'll go get dressed, then," said Miranda, turning on her heels.

"No need for you to come," said her father.

"You're staying here," said her mother, practically at the same time.

"Why?" Miranda was indignant. Sally flashed her a sympathetic look.

"There's no need to make a family excursion out of this," said Peggy. "You can just stay here and have your breakfast. We'll be back soon."

"Very soon." Jeff nodded. "Once we explain to Sally's parents about Rob's condition . . ."

"No!" Miranda was amazed at how quickly she'd reacted, and how loudly she'd shouted. Everyone looked at her. "I don't think Rob would want you to . . . explain things. Or say . . . anything about . . . anything. You know."

Sally looked completely befuddled. Miranda wondered if she should ask Sally to go wait outside in the street while she ordered her parents to keep their mouths shut about Rob's claustrophobia. He would go nuts if he knew they'd breathed a word about it.

Her father seemed to be catching on.

"I hear what you're saying," he said. "But it might be important for them to know that Rob would never go into that cellar by choice."

"Why not?" asked Sally, genuinely puzzled. "He goes down there all the time. When he's helping my father, I mean."

"Really?" Peggy paused in buttoning up her trench coat. "I'm . . . surprised to hear that. That's . . . that's good."

"It's great," agreed Jeff, a little too enthusiastically. Sally looked from one to the other, as though they were crazy Americans she couldn't begin to understand. Miranda wished they would just stop talking.

Rob came thudding down the stairs again, asking if anyone had seen his shoes.

"By the door," said Peggy. "You have the cellar key with you?"

"It's in my wallet," Rob said, tapping his pocket. "Exactly where I put it last night. I checked."

"Everything's going to be all right," Sally said. Miranda thought she was trying to persuade herself, by the sound of it. Her cheeks had turned all flushed when Rob came downstairs again.

"Everything's going to be fine," echoed Jeff, and a few minutes later they were all gone, leaving Miranda nothing to do but sit at the table by herself, hoping that Rob wasn't in any trouble, and wondering why bad things just kept on happening to them.

fruit bowl. Rob ate it in silence, sprawled on the sofa. When he said he was going out for a walk, she didn't ask where he was going, and she didn't remind him about the Minster rehearsal later on. Miranda knew that when things went wrong, sometimes the only company you could stand was your own.

At the ticket desk inside the Minster's south transept, Miranda flashed the EVENT PERSONNEL laminated pass her mother had left for her. Although the concert itself was going to take place in the main part of the cathedral — the nave, according to the brochure she was handed at the desk — the rehearsal was closeted away in the Quire, behind the impressive carved Screen of Kings. Musicians from a different orchestra, their rehearsal over, were on their way out, with her mother's orchestra only just arriving. Musicians were easy to spot because of their instrument cases and — Miranda couldn't help noticing — dubious fashion choices. One man struggled to wheel his giant double bass out through the safety doors. Miranda remembered a random piece of advice her mother once gave her, something about never dating a double bassist: They could never go out for a coffee after a concert, or drive a car smaller than a station wagon, because the instrument was just too big and unwieldy. The double bass was the least of this guy's problems, thought Miranda. Peggy should have warned her about dating men who wore Crocs in the wintertime.

While her mother's musicians set up, Miranda wandered around the Minster, the biggest and oldest church she'd ever seen. On an overcast day like this, there was a chilly calm to the place. Though it was early in the afternoon, the church already seemed to be sinking into darkness, subdued purple-gray light filtering through the stained-glass windows.

People sat in the rows of red-cushioned chairs set up for a service. Some were praying, more were talking, several were asleep, and one was actually eating his lunch. Miranda's footsteps echoed across the marble floor. The stone of the columns and soaring ceilings looked scrubbed clean, like bones. Conservation work was going on all over the place. Miranda couldn't even see into the crypt, which the guide told her lay directly beneath the Quire, because it was all boarded up, and a sign informed visitors that there would be no entry at all to the crypt until March. The pictures she'd seen in *Tales of Old York* would have to suffice, Miranda thought, drifting toward the Great East Window.

This was another building site, she discovered. In the far corner, a stonemason sat on a low wooden stool, chipping at a stone embellishment set low in a column. In place of the tennis court–size window hung a giant printed banner, a reproduction. The real thing was being taken to pieces elsewhere.

"It's said that the Minster can never be completely finished," came a voice from behind her — so close behind her that Miranda could feel his breath on her neck. Nick!

Miranda swung around. Nick stood with his hands in his pockets, gazing up at the giant window poster.

"There's always scaffolding up somewhere," he continued, not looking at Miranda. "And the story is, a promise was made to return the Minster to the Roman Catholics, but only when it was finished. So the Church of England makes sure it's *never* finished."

"Is that true?" Miranda was so relieved to see him. Or rather — that he'd seen her first, as usual, and still wanted to speak to her.

"No." Nick grinned. "Nothing is true. Everything's just lies and stories and broken promises. Isn't it?"

Miranda felt a pang of guilt.

"I'm so sorry about last night," she said in a breathless rush. "I got there early, but my father was at the museum, the one in Monk Bar, and he saw me and . . . I just had to go. I hope you weren't waiting forever."

"I saw you go," he said casually, as though it was no big deal.

"You . . . you saw me?"

"I keep my eyes open." Nick looked at her. She could tell that he wasn't angry. He had the slightest smile on his face — sardonic, of course.

"So, are you following me?" Miranda teased. Something about being here in the Minster, standing in an actual building, made her feel more secure, more brave. Until now, she'd only ever seen Nick out in the streets.

"I could ask the same of you," he said. "I come in here every day. And now, all of a sudden, here you are."

"I thought you didn't like the Minster."

"Well, you know what they say. Keep your friends close and your enemies closer."

"Which am I?"

"Hmmm. Not sure yet." He was still looking at her straight in the eyes, and Miranda felt very shy all of a sudden.

"I'm . . . I'm here for the rehearsal," she said. The stonemason working on the column dropped something — some sort of tool, like a chisel, Miranda guessed, watching it shoot across the shiny floor. She leaned over to pick it up so he wouldn't have to get up from his low stool. But as her fingers reached for it, she grasped nothing but air. She could see the chisel, which looked homemade, but she couldn't feel it at all.

The man, his smile grateful, turned his head to look at Miranda. He was wearing the oddest floppy hat, and something that looked more like a tunic than an apron. He stretched out a dusty hand. Instantly, splinters of cold pinged through her, prickling the length of her body. Behind her she could hear Nick's soft laugh. Right in front of her eyes, the stonemason faded from sight. Moments later, there was nothing — not him, not his stool, not his wayward chisel.

"He's always here," Nick told her. "Somewhere in the

Minster. Always messing with some piece of stonework. Probably his mates murdered him because he was a perfectionist. Doesn't like me much, but he seemed to take to you. At least his dog wasn't around today. That animal's a menace."

"His *dog* is a ghost?" Miranda didn't even know that was possible. And then she thought of the black cat slinking around the White Boar Inn — the cat that her parents couldn't see. Maybe she'd already spotted an animal ghost without realizing it.

Nick was nodding.

"Loads of people have heard him bark. Even people who can't see him can hear him. You'll see people looking all around for him — they think someone's brought a dog in. He hates me, for some reason. Barks like mad whenever he sees me."

"I didn't think about ghosts in the Minster," Miranda confessed. She should have realized the stonemason was a ghost. She wondered how many other ghosts she was passing every day, stupidly unaware that they'd been alive in another century.

Nick opened his mouth to say something, but the next voice Miranda heard was her mother's, distant and muffled, but recognizable nonetheless. She was calling the orchestra to order. A violin squeaked; there was some laughter.

"The rehearsal's beginning," she told Nick. "My mother's conducting the orchestra. Do you want to sit in for a little while? It's in the Quire."

Nick's face clouded over, as though Miranda had just said a terrible thing. As though he'd just decided *she* was a ghost.

"Go ahead. I'll catch you up." He stood with his hands in his pockets. Miranda hesitated — was he just planning on leaving abruptly, the way he usually did? She walked away slowly, willing him to follow, looking for the entrance to the Quire. It wasn't far. On the stairs, she looked back; Nick was still standing there watching her.

"Sit in the back," he called, and she nodded.

Sitting in one of the choir stalls — in the back, as instructed — Miranda felt overawed by her surroundings. The Quire was a sanctuary at the heart of the cathedral. It looked like a beautiful jewelry box, exquisitely carved and upholstered. The orchestra and singers sat on ordinary folding chairs, but Miranda, tucked into a corner so she could see *everything*, felt as though she were sitting on a throne. Above her head loomed the shining pipes of the organ. Colorful shields and heraldic emblems were set into the wood all around the stalls. A hymnbook sat in front of her, and there was a cushioned rest at her feet, to kneel on during prayers. In the very center of the Quire, separating the choir stalls from the orchestra's area, stood an imposing golden lectern shaped like an eagle.

The orchestra was playing the overture now, mournful at first, but then faster, more frantic, the urgent song of the violins sailing up into the Minster's cavernous spaces. After a few minutes, Peggy stopped them, tapping with her baton on the music stand. It was always strange watching her mother in this mode as opposed to wife-and-mother mode. Even though Miranda could see her only from the back, her mother seemed so relaxed and happy. She held her arms in the air in an expansive gesture, her wavy hair bouncing as she moved her arms down. The stop-start went on for a while, her mother singling out various sections of the orchestra and asking them to play a few phrases.

Nick padded up the tiny wooden staircase leading to Miranda's corner and slid onto the pew next to her. He must have come in a different entrance — through the gates in the Screen of Kings, maybe. Everything he did had to be secretive, thought Miranda.

"So that's your mother?" he asked in a low voice. Miranda nodded. "If she sees me with you and asks who I am, tell her I'm one of the beadles here."

"What's a beadle?"

"No idea," said Nick. Miranda smiled.

"What makes you think I haven't told her all about you already?" she whispered.

Nick gave her a long, disbelieving look.

"I'm not the kind of boy you take home to Mummy and Daddy," he said. "You took off as soon as your father turned up yesterday, didn't you? I bet you've never told them that you can see ghosts."

"No," Miranda admitted, hanging her head.

"So how are you going to tell them about us meeting, and what we've been up to since?"

The music soared again and stopped. The musicians riffled through the pages of their scores. One of the singers — tubby, balding, wearing a too-tight red sweater — stood up and sat down again. There was laughter. Nick sat in silence, brooding, one foot up against the woodwork.

"It's so beautiful in here," said Miranda. The brass-mounted candles — which were electric but looked real — cast a golden glow against the honeyed wood of the choir stalls. "I've never been in so many medieval buildings before. All this carving must have taken them years."

"Originally," said Nick. "But everything you can see in here, in the Quire, is a replica."

"What do you mean?"

"There was a fire in here, in 1829. Brought down the roof of the Minster, destroyed the organ. Most of the woodwork in here burned as well. They did their best to copy the medieval work, but it's all nineteenth century."

"That's a shame," she said, disappointed.

Nick shrugged.

"Doesn't matter much one way or the other," he said. "People build temples, or churches, or forts, and other people come and sweep them away. The Vikings had a palace where King's Square sits today — that's *why* it's called King's Square. No trace of it now. One day there'll be no trace of this place. It doesn't mean anything anymore."

"It must, to some people."

"This isn't a very religious country, in case you hadn't noticed. This place," Nick said, with a dismissive wave, "is all about tradition and prestige and empty rituals. Dressing up and incantations. People come here to take pictures, and they don't even do that so much anymore, now it costs eight pounds to get in."

"*You* pay eight pounds every time you come here?" Miranda whispered. "Every day?"

"Not me," said Nick, pushing his coat open and slumping back in the seat. The hem of his gray sweater was frayed. "I'm a beadle, remember?"

One of the female singers, a very pretty young woman, stood up, and Peggy was telling the orchestra they were going to run through Dido's Lament.

"You'll like this," Miranda told Nick, though she really had no idea whether he would or not. *She* liked it when her mother played the CD at home. "It's a very sad and beautiful aria. Dido's asking everyone to remember her, but to forget her fate."

"What does that mean?" Nick leaned his head close to hers. They were so close, Miranda thought their foreheads were about to brush.

"I guess it means to remember her as she was when she was alive," Miranda whispered, "and not the way she died. She's about to . . ."

Dido was about to commit suicide, but Miranda felt uneasy about bringing up the subject around Nick.

"That's not possible, though, is it? Forgetting the way people died."

Miranda said nothing. She was thinking of Jenna, crushed and lifeless in the car. Like Nick said, it was hard to forget. But she couldn't keep going over that night again and again in her head — thinking if only they'd left five minutes earlier or later, if only they hadn't gone at all. If only she'd done something, anything, to save Jenna. Eventually, Miranda's mother had told her, she'd think more about her friendship with Jenna and less about the way it ended. One day, Miranda thought, that might be possible.

The strings started playing, until Peggy rapped her music stand.

"So — what's the opera about, then?" Nick asked.

"Um . . . it's about a queen named Dido," said Miranda, trying to shake all the awful thoughts out of her head. "She's the queen of ancient Carthage. She's in love with a handsome Trojan prince named Aeneas."

"Fatty over there?" Nick smirked.

"I think so. And he's tricked into dumping Dido by the Sorceress and various Witches who want to destroy Carthage. Someone dresses up as a god and persuades Aeneas that the will of the gods is for him to leave Carthage forever. He's completely duped by this guy. But just as he's about to go, Aeneas sees Dido again and changes his mind. It's too late, though."

"Why?"

"She can't forgive him. You know, for listening to the fake god and betraying her. So she sends him away. And then she kills herself."

It just slipped out. Miranda could have kicked herself. She snuck a look at Nick, wondering if she'd upset him, furious at herself for being so insensitive. But it was almost as though he hadn't heard her. He was staring at one of the singers, the one dressed in a gray hoodie, her auburn hair piled on her head in a messy bun. When she started singing without any accompaniment, Nick nudged Miranda.

"She's got the same color hair as you," he said.

Miranda felt herself blushing again. Luckily, she didn't have to reply because the strings started playing, soft and melancholy. It might sound too restrained to Nick, Miranda thought. Too pretty or old-fashioned.

"*When I am laid, am laid in earth,*" the soprano sang, her voice pure and clear. "*May my wrongs create no trouble.*"

Miranda closed her eyes. Something about the Minster's acoustics made the aria's simplicity and sadness even more intense, much more moving than on the stereo at home — even though they had a good stereo, according to her father, who could be a boring techie about these things. But hearing the soprano's yearning voice soar in this cavernous, resonant space was something else. No wonder people wanted to give concerts in the Minster. This place had magical powers.

"*Remember me, remember me,*" sang Dido, and the Quire seemed to fill with the aching strings. "*But ah! Forget my fate.*"

The last notes faded, and Miranda opened her eyes. The redheaded soprano was sitting down. Peggy was talking to one section of the orchestra, humming to show them how she wanted them to draw out a particular phrase.

Miranda snuck a look at Nick, trying to figure out if he'd liked it.

"Sad," he said, resting his head against the back wall. "Like you said. Dido was probably better off without Aeneas. You know, if he couldn't be trusted."

"It wasn't his fault, though. Aeneas gets tricked by the Sorceress and the Witches. By evil spirits."

"Evil spirits." Nick wriggled lower in his seat. "People are always talking about evil spirits, aren't they? Why are spirits always evil, and people always good?"

Miranda shrugged. She didn't know what to say.

"All spirits really want," said Nick, leaning toward her again, "is to rest in peace. And the reasons they can't can all be traced to their lives. The real world. The one full of 'good' people."

"Listen," Miranda said. The singer was standing up again, holding her score.

"Should I close my eyes, the way you did?" Nick asked, and Miranda thought he was teasing her. But when she looked at him, the usual sardonic smile wasn't there. The gaunt angles of his face looked less severe in this light. And there was something in his eyes she'd never seen before — an uncertainty, perhaps.

"If you like," she said. She closed her eyes, but this time she wasn't facing the orchestra. Her head was turned toward Nick, her hands resting on the soft cushion of the pew.

"Remember me, remember me — but ah! Forget my fate."

Nick's hand brushed hers. His touch was gentle, tracing soft lines down her fingers. Miranda kept her eyes closed. She held her breath. His hands didn't feel as cold as they had on Monday, when he helped her down from the city walls. Nick's skin was rough, but there was a tenderness to the touch, the movement. Goose bumps prickled her arm — not the brain-freeze cold of the ghosts, just the hint of a thrill.

The music stopped abruptly. The singer asked Peggy a question; the musicians were rustling pages again. Nick withdrew his hand. Miranda opened her eyes.

"You know, you could come to the performance on Sunday night," she said quickly, trying to fill up the awkward silence. Nick stared straight ahead. "I could get you a ticket."

"No," he said. There was no softness in his voice or expression now. "I can't."

"Oh," said Miranda, regretting that she'd even made the suggestion. He was always the one who made the plans, the one who told her when they'd meet again. She'd said the wrong thing.

"I shouldn't even be here now, mucking around," he said, restlessly shifting in his seat. "Got things to do."

"Oh," she said again. She tried not to feel offended by the "mucking around" comment. Was that how Nick saw the time they spent together? Miranda felt like a stupid little girl who'd been fawning over an older guy, deluding herself that he liked her. All he was interested in was ghosts, she reminded herself. That was the thing they had in common. When he'd stroked her hand just now, it didn't mean anything. Or whatever it *did* mean, she didn't understand. Miranda really didn't understand guys at all.

Nick stood up as though he'd just remembered something, and then, without looking at her or saying another word, he swooped down the stairs and around the corner. Gone, just like that — no good-byes, no talk about meeting again. That's it, Miranda thought. She'd pushed things too far by asking him to go to the concert with her. Going to hear an opera in a cathedral wasn't the kind of thing other kids did, especially not guys like Nick. Miranda would never dream of asking a boy back home to go to one of her mother's concerts. She was a fool to think that Nick would be different.

When she left the rehearsal, Miranda wandered around the Minster for twenty minutes, hoping to find him. But all she saw were tourists, and tour guides, and ushers arriving for that evening's concert. The ghost stonemason was hard at work at a different column, his wiry little dog visible now, too, lying half asleep at his master's feet.

If Nick was still in here somewhere, she couldn't see him. Maybe he didn't want to be found by anyone — especially not Miranda.

CHAPTER ELEVEN

S orry, buddy," said Jeff, zipping and unzipping his fleece as he always did when he was preoccupied. "There's just no way to get there on the train. The house is way up in the Yorkshire Dales."

"That's okay," said Rob. He was seated precariously on a window ledge in the living room, looking down onto the Shambles. "I was just planning to hang out today anyway."

Miranda was just planning to hang out today as well. She'd thought that she'd wander around for a bit by herself, sticking to busy streets where ghosts were less likely to bother her. Maybe Nick would find her, the way he always did. He might have gotten over his little freak-out by now. They could just pretend the hand-holding thing and her embarrassing request for a date — because that must have been how it sounded — had never happened.

But no, her father had other plans. Lord Poole was taking time out of his busy schedule of foxhunting or boar baiting or however else elderly nobles spent their twilight years. He was driving into York in his ancient Land Rover to collect Jeff and take him out to Poole Castle, or wherever it was that he lived. Peggy was busy all day today — "Singers!" she exclaimed with irritation on her way out of the flat that morning — but Miranda and Rob were invited. The difference was: Rob had an excuse. They could get to the Land of Poole only in a car, and Rob didn't do cars. Miranda had no excuse.

"You'll come — won't you, honey?" Jeff asked. "He's been so nice to us. And he gave you that book, which is obviously a first edition and probably worth a fortune."

"I think he just lent it to me," said Miranda, wishing that everyone would leave her alone. Rob was allowed to do anything he wanted, but she was always at the beck and call of everyone else in the family.

"He has an amazing library out there, which you'll love. And a maze, I think. Really, an actual maze. It's a genuine English stately home, and you'll get the insider's tour."

"Can't I just stay here?" Miranda moaned.

"To do what?"

"Stuff. You know. Look after Rob."

"I don't need anyone looking after me, thank you." Rob sounded affronted. Couldn't he tell she was just saying anything to get out of going? If it weren't for Miranda, Sally and her parents and the entire police force of York

148

would know about his claustrophobia by now. As usual, he wasn't remotely grateful.

"Verandah, this is going to be great. You can sit around reading at home anytime. Now, I'm going to go get organized, because we have to wait for Lord Poole at the corner. Grab your coat and whatever else you need." Jeff headed up the stairs. End of discussion.

"I'll probably go along to Mom's rehearsal this afternoon," Rob called after him.

"Liar," muttered Miranda.

"Whatever," he said, breathing on the window and drawing a smiley face with his fingertip. "Sally's parents gave her a couple of hours off this afternoon to show me around. We're going to take a walk along the river."

"It's freezing outside today," Miranda pointed out. "But then, I suppose you two will be all snuggled up together. Don't fall in and get swept out to sea."

Rob bared his teeth in the fakest of smiles.

"Your ignorance of British geography astounds me," he said smugly. "Have fun in the maze. Make sure you ask Dad and Lord Poole lots of questions about the rise and fall of the Plantagenet dynasty. That conversation is sure to be *fascinating*."

Yorkshire was a much bigger county than Miranda had realized — if she'd ever given the subject more than five minutes of thought — because it took Lord Poole over an hour to drive them back to his house. At first, there was nothing to see but gas stations and supermarkets, glimpsed through the mist that had settled like a sodden blanket. But eventually they left the highway, driving up into hillier country where snow still lay in patches. On high fields hemmed in by rugged stone walls, black-faced sheep grazed. The roads were narrow, crossing streams via small arch-shaped bridges. They passed cottages with low windows, their walls rammed right up against the lane, and farms with vast stone barns and big muddy yards. There was a bleak beauty to all this, Miranda thought, just as she'd imagined when she first read *Wuthering Heights*.

Lord Poole's place wasn't called Poole Castle at all: It was Lambert House. The driveway was very long, lined with sturdy trees. On one side, there were more trees, like some kind of rambling dark forest, and on the other stretched miles of rolling countryside, flecked with snow and sheep, divided into a rough grid by stone walls.

"I warn you — this isn't one of those elegant Georgian estates with a gatehouse and a folly and a mansion built by Vanbrugh," Lord Poole said over his shoulder to Miranda, who had no idea what he was talking about. She was concentrating on staying upright in the backseat as the Land Rover made a sharp turn from the rutted drive onto a lower road spread with gravel. "It's largely a Jacobean house with various poorly executed additions. Stairs all over the place, and it's rather cold, I'm afraid. The maze is that way."

Lord Poole jabbed a finger to his right, and Jeff and Miranda looked out their windows. All she could see in the distance was a thicket of scruffy bushes and someone driving a beaten-up tractor.

"On sunny days," continued Lord Poole, "the walk to the local village and the churchyard is very pleasant, but I don't like the look of that sky."

"Snow," agreed Jeff, who, Miranda had to admit, was a weather expert. Back home, watching the Weather Channel was one of his major hobbies, along with making turkey chili and piling towering stacks of books and papers on the Ping-Pong table in the basement.

"I hope you won't be bored, stuck in the house," Lord Poole said apologetically, peering at Miranda in the rearview mirror.

"Oh no," she reassured him, trying to sound more positive than she felt, leaning as the car rounded a corner. "I'll just — wow!"

Whatever Lord Poole said about the house being cold and ordinary was British understatement. The house was nowhere near ordinary. It soared three stories high, reddish-brown, with what looked like a massive oak front door, and windows made up of dozens of tiny diamond-shaped panes of glass. Miranda half expected someone in a long velvet gown to come sweeping out to greet them, and maybe the Brothers Grimm to drop by later for tea.

Lord Poole screeched up outside, the Land Rover skidding on the gravel. He clambered out of the car, calling to a man — checked cap, cocked gun, three dogs — walking up from another part of the garden.

"This looks amazing." Jeff sounded as impressed as Miranda felt. He opened his door, almost hitting one of the dogs running in wild figure eights around the car. Miranda slid out, her boots crunching when they hit the gravel. The air smelled sweet and clean, though it was even colder up here than it was in York. One of the dogs (a yellow Labrador: She could have bet money that Lord Poole would have an entire litter of Labradors) hurled itself at her legs, lapping at her hands. Miranda braced herself, waiting for a jet of cold, but no: This appeared to be an actual dog, not a ghost.

Lord Poole finished his chat and shouted at the dogs in some impenetrable British shorthand, sending them reeling away.

"Just had to check something with the gamekeeper," he said. Miranda and her father exchanged glances: a gamekeeper! Who would they meet next — a butler? A lady's maid? Although she'd resisted today's visit, and although she'd never concede this particular point, Miranda was kind of glad her father had made her come along. There was only one thing that made her hesitate before crossing the threshold.

"Lord Poole," she said quickly, watching him swing the great door open. "You don't have any . . . any ghosts here, do you? That you know of, I mean. That someone's seen."

"Well . . . ah, I don't think so." He looked at her — almost suspiciously, Miranda thought. "Of course, this house has only been in the family — my wife's family, I should say — for the past two hundred years."

"Only!" said Jeff, who was — to Miranda's embarrassment — pulling his camera out of his jacket pocket. If they stayed out here much longer, he'd be lying on his stomach in the gravel, trying to get a good angle, or making her pose with a hunting rifle and/or dog.

"There are ghosts over in Richmond Castle, I hear. And the house where I grew up, just outside Northallerton — well, that's a different story. But I've never heard any accounts of hauntings here at Lambert. All the deaths here have been peaceful, or so it would seem. I hope that doesn't . . . disappoint you too much."

"Not at all," said Miranda, smiling, and she walked through the open door with a much lighter heart. It would be a relief to get away from ghosts, even if it was just for a few hours. For the first time in a few days, she could pretend to be normal.

Inside, the house was as drafty and eccentric as Lord Poole had threatened, but Miranda and her father agreed that this was essential to its charm. It was all dark wood, looming furniture, and, up the creaking stairs, tiny angled landings leading off to dark hallways and closed doors. The kitchen had last been renovated somewhere around World War II, Miranda suspected, with dish towels hanging on a rack suspended from the ceiling, and a big range — an Aga, Lord Poole called it — throwing off a very welcome heat. A red-faced woman named June bustled in from the vegetable garden, smiling and nodding at them. She wasn't Lady Poole, Miranda knew: Her father had whispered that Mabel, Lord Poole's wife, had died a year ago. June was a sort of part-time housekeeper. She offered them tea and had a lengthy conversation with Lord Poole, during which the only words Miranda could decipher were "potatoes" and "rot." She also said something, translated by Lord Poole, about a meat pie ready to go in the Aga whenever they wanted lunch.

"Probably one of the old Labradors," Jeff whispered to Miranda, on their way out to resume the tour. Miranda couldn't help laughing, though she and Rob had agreed years ago not to do anything to encourage their father's lame jokes. "No, really! They don't waste anything out here in the country."

The best part of all was the library. This was on the ground floor of the house, and Miranda wondered if Lord Poole spent more time in here than in the dark, dusty living room — or drawing room, as he called it — where they'd poked their heads in for just a moment. In the library, tall shelves lined almost every part of every wall; there were even shelves above the doors, crammed with books. Many were first editions, Lord Poole told them, including three of the novels of Sir Walter Scott.

The relative warmth of the room was the product of three antique-looking electric heaters, strategically placed to radiate feeble heat across the threadbare Turkish rug. An impressively large desk, longer than their dining table at home, was stacked with folios, books, and what looked like the printout of a very hefty typed manuscript. A map was spread out across the center of the desk, littered with pens, a magnifying glass — which Miranda couldn't resist playing with — and at least six empty coffee cups.

"June will tell me off if she spots those," said Lord Poole, looking guilty. "Maybe we should smuggle them back into the kitchen later."

Before long, her father and Lord Poole were deep in a discussion of some article in the *Ricardian* — something about new evidence on Edward IV's alleged premarriage contract to Lady Eleanor Butler blah blah blah — and Miranda was free to roam. Lord Poole had said she could take anything down from the shelves; he'd pointed out the sliding ladder she could use for higher shelves, warning her of its tendency to roll at a quick speed along the uneven floor. He'd also gestured to a cozy window seat, a nook built into the walls, with squashy tapestry cushions.

"That's where my children liked to read, and my grandchildren," he said with a forlorn smile. "A long time ago."

He stared into space for a moment, lost in some personal reverie, and then recovered himself, urging Miranda to take her boots off, put her feet up, and generally make herself at home.

Miranda didn't know where to start. So many of the books looked very old and fragile, and a number of them seemed to be in Latin. She sat for a while reading *The Mysteries of Udolpho*, which she recognized only because one of the characters in *Northanger Abbey* had mentioned it. After lunch — the pie was steak, Lord Poole reassured them, not Labrador — she decided to go looking for a really old copy of Mary Shelley's *Frankenstein*.

The men were sitting across from each other at the giant desk, spilling coffee on the map and jawing about something — the second wife of John of Gaunt — which was of interest to practically nobody but themselves. Miranda paced along a section of shelves she hadn't examined yet, at the far end of the room. Shelves towered on either side of a fireplace that was clearly never lit: Paperback books were stacked on the hearth. Above the mantel hung an enormous black-and-white print of some apocalyptic scene. In the foreground, people were huddling, wailing, and lamenting. In the background, their city was on fire. A great swirl of flame was devouring walls and columns and some kind of tower.

"Ah!" said Lord Poole, slowly getting up from his torn leather chair. "I see you're taken with the John Martin."

"The what?" Miranda stood with her hands clasped behind her back, a habit from childhood when her parents used to take them to the Art Institute of Chicago, with strict instructions not to even *think* about touching anything. Jeff came and stood next to her, giving Miranda an affectionate pat on the shoulder.

"The engraving — it's a mezzotint," Lord Poole said. "Early nineteenth century. Round 1819, I believe. Very impressive, don't you think? The artist is John Martin. Wildly popular in his day. The Brontës had one of his engravings in their parlor at Haworth Parsonage, you know."

"What's it . . . about?" Miranda knew this was a stupid-sounding question, but the city in the picture looked like something out of a sci-fi epic.

"It's called *The Fall of Babylon*," Lord Poole told them. "The way it was predicted in the Bible — God's wrath, and all that — rather than what actually happened. I believe the Persian invasion was a fairly bloodless coup, and Babylon was never burned to the ground in the way it's depicted here."

"Just faded away," mused her father. Miranda shook her head. Did he know something on *every* historical topic? "The greatest city of antiquity, lost."

"The interesting thing about this engraving," Lord Poole said, giving the elaborate frame an unceremonious tap, "is the artist's connection with York."

"Really?" Jeff and Miranda said at the same time.

"He was from the north, but most of his career was spent in London. His older brother, Jonathan, moved to York sometime in the 1820s, though I've never been able to find out exactly where he lived."

"Oh," said Miranda. The story wasn't turning out to be quite as interesting as she'd hoped. But Lord Poole was still talking.

"There was a lot of instability in that family. Emotional instability. Mental illness, I'd suppose we'd call it today.

John Martin was a volatile character, but Jonathan — well, he was mad as a hatter. He started hearing voices in his head, or some such thing, and decided to burn York Minster down."

"I remember this!" Miranda thought about *Tales of Old York* and the caption THE MADMAN'S FIRE. "In the book you lent me. I haven't read it all yet. But someone was telling me —" She glanced at her father. "I mean, I heard about the fire. When I was in the Minster yesterday. It destroyed the Quire completely, didn't it?"

Lord Poole nodded. "If the roof hadn't collapsed, the entire Minster would have burned to the ground. People watching the fire said it looked just like one of John Martin's pictures — the huge flames engulfing the building at night. Not realizing, of course, that the arsonist was his brother."

"Did they hang him?" Jeff asked matter-of-factly. Away from Miranda's mother, he'd obviously forgotten the don't-mention-death rule. "Jonathan Martin?"

"The people of York wanted him to hang," Lord Poole said. "But at his trial he was judged to be insane. So they locked him in Bedlam for the rest of his life."

"Bedlam — that was an asylum, right?" Miranda asked. Another thing she didn't realize she knew.

"That's right. A lunatic asylum, as they called them in those days. The fire was in 1829 and Jonathan Martin died — let me think — about nine or ten years later."

Jeff gave a low whistle.

"I don't know," he said. "Hanging doesn't sound so bad compared with ten years in Bedlam."

"Those places," said Lord Poole. "They were terrible then. Not much better now, I have to say."

The grandfather clock by the door chimed, and Jeff checked his watch.

"He that hides a dark soul and foul thoughts, benighted walks under the midday sun," said Lord Poole in a quavery voice, and it took a second for Miranda to realize he was quoting from something, rather than just waxing lyrical. "Himself is his own dungeon."

Even Jeff looked puzzled at this.

"Milton," said Lord Poole. "It's a passage from Milton, from his poem *Comus*. Jonathan Martin quoted it at his trial, though no one was quite sure why. I think he felt that the fire had cleansed him in some way. So even though he would be imprisoned in Bedlam, he'd be free."

"As you said, crazy," said Jeff. He tapped his watch. "I'm wondering if we should be getting back soon. I feel terrible asking you to make another two-hour round trip, especially in weather like this. And it'll be getting dark by the time you're driving back."

Lord Poole protested, but although she could have happily stayed in this library — despite the fading light and lack of heat — for hours and hours, Miranda knew her father was right. These weren't great roads to be driving along after dark. She picked up her discarded boots and followed the others into the high-ceilinged hall, where Lord Poole had lain their jackets and bags on an enormous coffinlike chest. There were more pictures on the wall here, ones she hadn't noticed on the way in, small family photographs in black frames, hanging askew.

One old picture was of a man in military uniform who looked exactly like Lord Poole, including the beard: He *had* to be Lord Poole Senior, Miranda decided, wrapping her scarf around her neck. The next photo was much more recent — a snapshot of a skinny teenaged boy leading a horse, a grinning younger kid perched on it. Both boys were dark-haired and barefoot, and the older boy was holding his hand up to the camera, as though he was protesting having his photo taken. Next were several photos of floppy-eared spaniels, presumably the pet predecessors of the Labradors racing around outside.

And then there was a photo that made Miranda gasp out loud and press a hand against the wall to steady herself. A photo of a lanky teenage boy: an older version of the little boy who'd sat on the horse. His dark hair was tousled and he was dressed in a school uniform. He was smiling at the camera in an uncertain, almost sardonic way.

Nick.

CHAPTER TWELVE

On the car ride back to York, Miranda thought she was going to explode with curiosity. She *had* to ask Lord Poole about the picture in his hallway. But how could she, without revealing that she knew Nick? Finally, her father made some remark about the holidays, and Miranda grabbed her chance.

"Does your family come home to Lambert House for Christmas?" she asked, her voice trembling with excitement. "I mean, your children and grandchildren?"

"My daughter lives abroad now," Lord Poole said, his tone neutral. "She rarely returns to England."

"That's too bad," said Jeff. "How about your grandsons?"

Thanks, Dad, Miranda thought, relieved that her father was inadvertently helping out.

"My grandsons?" Lord Poole sounded startled.

"The ones in the photos — sorry, I just assumed they were your grandsons." When Miranda was standing staring at the photo of Nick, Jeff had walked over to look as well. She'd managed to keep calm — on the outside at least — and not give anything away, even though she wanted to scream and point and jump up and down.

"Yes, you're quite right. My grandsons." Miranda felt a little sorry for Lord Poole. Part of her hoped he would say more, to confirm or refute the story Nick had told her. But she liked Lord Poole: He was kind, and generous, and probably a bit lonely as well, rattling around in that big cold house by himself. It would be hard for him to have to disclose his sad family history to people who were, basically, strangers.

"Unfortunately," he said, negotiating a particularly tight corner, "my grandsons . . . well, it's a long story."

"Say no more," Jeff said quickly. "I know how family relationships can change, especially as kids get older."

"Alan Bennett, the playwright — do you know his work?" Lord Poole asked, and Jeff mumbled a vague assent. "He has a very good line about this. Every family has a secret, he says, and that secret is that they're not quite like other families."

"Very true," said Jeff, with an overly hearty laugh. Miranda sat quietly in the back. It would be rude to ask any more questions. More than rude: It would be cruel. But Lord Poole wasn't changing the subject.

"I'm afraid our family, rather like that of John Martin, has had more than its share of unhappiness. We saw a lot of the boys when they were young. They spent large parts of every summer at our house. But my eldest grandson — he died seven years ago."

"I'm sorry to hear that," said Jeff. He glanced over his shoulder at Miranda, a wary look in his eyes. She wasn't sure if he was concerned that the forbidden subject had come up again or if he was trying to tell her not to ask any more nosy questions.

"Yes — it was terribly hard on the whole family, but especially on his younger brother. Richard — that was my eldest grandson's name — he'd had a very troubled adolescence. Let's just say . . . well, when I was talking about mental institutions earlier today, we were unfortunate to have a lot of experience of them."

"Ah," said Jeff. Miranda was rigid with tension. Richard — that was Nick's older brother, the one who had killed himself seven years earlier. Nick *was* telling the truth.

"Yes, well — he was away in one hospital or institution of one kind or another from the age of seventeen, when his brother was only nine or ten. They never saw each other again. Mabel and I believed that was a terrible mistake, but their parents thought it best at the time."

"Well, you never know whether you're doing the right thing," Jeff said evenly.

"He idolized his older brother, I suppose," said Lord Poole. He sounded tired now. Old and tired. Miranda felt bad knowing that after he dropped them off he'd have to turn around and make this drive again, in the dusk, with fog swirling in, maybe even snow. "He was very upset. Very upset with all of us. He has very little to do with any of us now. The last time I heard anything, he was living in London. I hope he's all right."

Miranda resisted the impulse to tell him that Nick was alive and well and staying in York. If Nick wanted his presence there to be a secret, that was his decision. But she did feel terribly sorry for Lord Poole.

"What about last year, when Mabel died?" Jeff asked.

"His mother got some kind of word to him, I believe. But he didn't attend the funeral. He was very close to his grandmother — to both of us, when he was a child."

"Very sad," Jeff said, and then there was silence in the car for quite a while, in a way that made Miranda incredibly tense. Women, she thought, would have changed the subject and talked about something — or someone — else. She wished her mother were there.

It was awful to think of Nick all alone and bitter and saying he had no family when Lord Poole was right here, desperate to see his grandson again. Lord Poole had nobody now: His wife and one of his grandsons were dead, his daughter lived overseas, and Nick was AWOL. It wasn't fair that Lord Poole had to spend Christmas alone; Nick *had* to forgive him for what happened all those years ago. It wasn't Lord Poole's fault that Nick hadn't been allowed to see Richard, or that Richard had committed suicide.

All the awkwardness and embarrassment at the

Minster yesterday — Miranda resolved to forget it. Tomorrow, she had to find Nick and try to talk to him. Whether he wanted it or not.

On Friday morning, Miranda left the flat immediately after breakfast. Luckily, everyone was distracted, talking about the latest bad news from Sally. There'd been another break-in overnight at the White Boar. Once again, the cellar had been trashed — barrels overturned, beer sloshed all over the floor, and a new development: graffiti daubed on the walls. Once again, there was no sign of a forced entry. Rob couldn't possibly be suspected this time because he didn't have a key to the cellar anymore. Not that Sally's parents ever thought he'd had anything to do with it: Sally's mother had told Jeff and Peggy that Rob was "a lovely lad."

Miranda slipped away from the table, murmuring something about shopping she needed to do. She tugged her coat off the peg by the door, and shoved *Tales of Old York* into one of the pockets. Before anyone could ask any questions, she was out the door and bolting down the street.

She'd woken up that morning feeling almost elated with anxiety, her mind spinning with what she'd discovered yesterday. It wasn't going to be easy, Miranda knew, but she *had* seen Nick in the street twice before. The first time was when she'd arrived in York, and he was lurking in that boarded-up doorway in the Shambles. The second time was when she was in King's Square, watching the juggler, and he'd waved to his Goth friends. True, since then he'd tended to surprise her by materializing — usually behind her — in a startling and often disconcerting way. But York wasn't a big city like Chicago, and if she wandered the streets for long enough, Miranda was sure she'd find Nick again.

This was the theory, anyway. Miranda spent all morning roaming central York, drifting down Coney Street, hanging around St. Helen's Square, pretending to watch the enthusiastic troupe of street dancers entertaining people shivering in the line for the Jorvik Viking Centre. She strolled past the Treasurer's House, staring through its locked gates for a while and thinking about the Roman soldiers marching every night through its bowels. She walked the city walls from Bootham to Monk Bar and back, even venturing briefly into the Richard III Museum, just in case. She strolled up and down Stonegate so many times, she could have recited the name of every shop.

In the Minster, where Miranda had to pay the entrance fee to get in, wiping out half her remaining cash, she saw the ghost stonemason working on the door of the chapter house. She gave him a nervous smile and was surprised when he smiled back. His little dog stood up, wagging his tail, and gave an explosive bark in greeting. Miranda nearly jumped out of her skin, as did two women walking past at that moment.

"Someone must have brought a dog in here," one

murmured to the other. "These British take their dogs everywhere!"

Then one of them walked right through the dog, seeing and feeling nothing.

Miranda wished that Nick was as easy to spot as the stonemason. After half an hour dawdling in the Minster, she was even considering walking back to Clifford's Tower, though nothing would persuade her to climb those stairs again. She hadn't even told Nick about that experience yet. Not about the ashy, scary ghosts in Clifford's Tower, or St. Margaret Clitherow, or the handsome guy in the attic window. And now she might never see Nick again.

Finally, in desperation, Miranda decided to seek out his friends, but the Goths weren't hanging out in King's Square today. Maybe they took Fridays off. Maybe it was the day they all sat at home polishing their piercings and re-dyeing their hair.

That was it: home. Miranda realized, with a mental smack to the head, the first place she should have gone today. The flat with the green door, at the end of High Petergate. Nick had said he spent "some nights" there, at least. If he wasn't home, maybe one of his friends would know how to find him.

Miranda was almost running down Petergate, dodging shoppers and delivery vans, her breath puffing out in steamy bursts. But on the doorstep of the green door, she hesitated. Maybe Nick wouldn't appreciate her just turning up like this. He was so intensely private and enigmatic. He might think she was still trying to persuade him to go to the concert with her on Sunday night, like some desperate stalker.

Too bad. She summoned up all her courage and rapped the brass door knocker — once in a sort of pathetic, muffled way, and the second time giving it more gusto. Miranda waited. Nobody seemed to be home, but she decided to try again. Three raps this time, as loud as she could manage. Still no answer. Just as she was about to turn away, Miranda heard footsteps thudding down the stairs. After some mumbled swearing, and the jingling of keys, the door squeaked open, just wide enough for someone to poke his head out.

"What?" said the guy in the doorway. He looked as though he'd just woken up — or been woken up by Miranda's knocking. He wasn't one of the Goths, she registered with surprise. He had wavy, sandy hair and his blue T-shirt read BATH RUGBY. He frowned at Miranda. "If you're looking for the door to the English Language School, it's the next one up Petergate. Just past the gallery, number One-A. I should put a bloody sign up."

"No," she said quickly, because he seemed to be closing the door. "I'm not looking for the language school. I speak English already."

"Not properly," he sniffed. He sounded like a member of the royal family, Miranda thought. "Look, I'm not interested in talking about becoming a Mormon, okay?"

"I'm not a Mormon," Miranda hastily assured him.

"I thought all Americans were Mormons."

"We're not. I'm just here looking for Nick."

"Who's Nick?"

"Nick . . . Gant." Miranda's heart sank. His real friends might know what his real last name was, but Miranda didn't.

"Never heard of him."

"He's been staying here," Miranda pleaded. "This week."

The sandy-haired guy rubbed his face, yawning so wide Miranda could see his fillings.

"No one's been staying here this week," he said. "Classes have finished for this term. Everyone's gone home for Christmas."

"Dark hair, really tall, really thin. Wears a long black leather coat. You don't remember him?"

"No. Oh — hang on."

"Yes?" Miranda was desperate.

"Do you mean Jim's friend — Nick Fullerton? The one he went to school with?"

"Maybe," said Miranda uncertainly.

"I remember that coat. He never took it off. Said it belonged to his dead brother or something creepy like that."

"That's him," Miranda blurted, her heart thumping. It had to be Nick. It just had to be.

"He hasn't been here in ages. More than a year, at least."

"Are you sure?"

"Of course I'm sure. This is my flat!"

"But . . . but . . ." Miranda didn't know what to ask next. This guy was her one lead to Nick, and he wasn't leading her anywhere useful.

"Look, I don't want to freak you out," he said, leaning against the doorjamb. "But I thought Jim said that Nick Fullerton was dead."

"Then we can't be talking about the same person," Miranda told him. She felt a horrible churning in her stomach — nerves and dread and fear.

"Maybe not," shrugged Sandy Hair, as though he didn't care one way or the other. "But he's not here, anyway. Sorry."

He didn't sound sorry, Miranda thought. She stepped back into the street, not sure of what to say or where to look, almost as dizzy as she'd felt in Clifford's Tower. If the guy they were talking about was the same Nick, and Nick was dead . . .

Then Nick was a ghost.

It had started to rain, but Miranda didn't care. She was wandering now without a purpose, without even trying to look for Nick. What was the point? If he was a ghost, he would show himself when he wanted to be seen. Wasn't that what he'd said to her, when she said she'd see him around? "I'll see you first." Of course he'd see her first. She was a real live person. He was a ghost. He could decide when, and when not to appear.

Lord Poole hadn't said anything about his younger grandson dying, but maybe he didn't know. He hadn't heard from Nick in years. And the Goths in King's Square had seemed to "see" him, but maybe they were all ghosts themselves. Miranda had no idea. Obviously, she couldn't tell a ghost from an orangutan.

Her face was wet — rain, tears, whatever. She'd been completely duped. She'd thought she'd figured out the code, that she knew when someone was a haunting rather than a human. Nick's hands were cold, but not *that* kind of cold. He'd touched her hand, and she'd felt him — not just his presence, but his actual hand, his actual skin. She'd leaned against his shoulder! He'd felt completely real.

The strange thing was this feeling that Nick had betrayed her. Miranda knew it wasn't rational or fair. He simply hadn't mentioned that he was a ghost, that was all. She didn't know why she was crying. Maybe the cold rain was stinging her face, making her miserable. Or maybe it was . . . no. That was ridiculous. Today was Friday. A week ago, she'd seen Nick for the first time. Just one week. Only today, courtesy of the sandy-haired rugby fan, had she discovered his real last name. Miranda had no right to be *sad* about Nick. But sad was exactly how she felt.

Back in the flat, her father was making coffee in the kitchen, whistling "Greensleeves." Miranda darted up the stairs — wet, cold, and utterly defeated, not in the mood for any questions.

On the landing, the bathroom door popped open and Rob loomed in front of her. He reached out one of his long arms and dragged her into the bathroom.

"What?" Miranda almost shouted. She was sick of people jumping out at her or materializing behind her: It was turning her into a bag of nerves.

"Ssshhhh." Rob closed the door and leaned against it so she couldn't get out. "I need you to do something for me. Ask for a spare key to this place."

"The bathroom?" Miranda asked sarcastically, peeling off her scarf.

"No, dummy. The flat. Either Mom's or Dad's key — it doesn't matter. They'll be suspicious if I ask. *You* have to ask for it."

"Why would they be suspicious about you asking to take a key to the flat?"

"They'll know I'm planning to stay out way late tonight with Sally. They already think we're getting 'too serious.' I heard them talking about it last night — in the kitchen, when they thought I'd already gone upstairs."

"They're really happy about you and Sally." Miranda sat down on the edge of the tub. She felt shaky after all the hours of walking around. "They think it means you're all normal again, whatever that means. And anyway, if I ask for a key, they'll want to know why. Where I'm going, who I'm going out with — you know what Dad's like. There's no reason for me to have a key. How late are you staying out, anyway?"

"All night," said Rob, as though it was no big deal. "After the pub closes tonight, Sally and I are going to lock ourselves in the cellar, so if and when someone tries to get in, we can nab them red-handed."

"That's absolutely ridiculous. You won't last ten minutes in that cellar, let alone all night."

"Whatever," Rob said sulkily. He walked over to the window and slid it open, sticking his head out. He couldn't even stand being shut in the bathroom, Miranda thought. He'd never cope with locking himself up belowground at the White Boar Inn. "Look, this is our plan and we're sticking to it. If someone breaks in, we'll catch them. If nobody tries, I need the key so I can sneak back here before Mom and Dad get up in the morning."

"You're overthinking this." Miranda sighed.

"I thought you always said I underthink things."

"You're either over or under. You're never thinking things through in a rational way. What if whoever is breaking in is some kind of violent thug? They could beat you up or kill you."

"We'll surprise them." Rob closed the window partway to stop the drizzle from coming in. "We have weapons."

"What kind of weapons?"

"A cricket bat and a really big flashlight."

"As I said, ridiculous."

"We'll be fine," said Rob, but even he didn't sound convinced.

"Rob, believe me," Miranda pleaded. "You're getting antsy in this bathroom. How are you going to cope with being locked in the dark in that tiny cellar?"

"I have to get over this," Rob said. "I have to. I can't go through my life cowering because of . . . what happened. For Sally's sake, I need to do this. If I don't, she's going to be alone in there tonight. I don't want anything to happen to her."

"Look," said Miranda, realizing she was never going to talk him out of this stupid scheme. "Just sneak out tonight, and whenever you need to come home, get Sally to send me a text. I'll let you in."

"I thought we couldn't get texts here."

"Not from the U.S. But didn't you say Sally sent you a text the other day?"

"Oh yeah."

"Problem solved."

"I'll be okay in the cellar," Rob said, now not sounding convinced at all. He closed the window all the way, shutting it with a bang. They both flinched. "I have to be. This is for Sally."

"You still haven't told her?"

"No need," Rob said firmly. He checked his watch. "What time do we have to meet Mom at that Italian place? I said I'd help Sally's dad for an hour before dinner."

"We're meeting at seven," Miranda told him, inwardly groaning. She'd forgotten about the dinner plans for tonight. All the singers would be there, talking in overloud voices. Miranda had way too much on her mind right now — tracking down Nick, worrying about Rob. *There better be good pizza at this restaurant*, she thought, dragging her feet out of the bathroom and up the stairs. And she'd better not get stuck next to the tubby guy or, even worse, the Second Witch.

CHAPTER THIRTEEN

ou're sure you know how to get to the restaurant yourself?" Jeff asked her for the hundredth time. Miranda nodded. Rob was already over at the White Boar, and one of her father's Richard III cronies had turned up to lure Jeff out for a quick drink. All his weird early modernist chums had arrived in town for this weekend's conference, and they had swarmed some pub nearby called the Lamb and Lion, probably driving out all the locals and other normal people.

"I'll be fine, Dad. I'll see you at L'Avventura at seven, okay?"

"I don't like you walking around in the dark by yourself." He frowned. "You can come to the Lamb and Lion with me, you know. Have some pop, read your book."

"No, thanks," Miranda said quickly. "It's not late, and there are tons of people out. Really, I'll be fine. You go and have a good time. Just don't be late for dinner. You know how Mom gets about that."

"If you're sure you don't mind . . ."

"Go already!" Miranda couldn't wait for Jeff to leave. She had exactly ninety minutes until dinner, and she planned to use every single one of them walking the streets of York again, looking for Nick. It was Friday night; on Monday morning, the Tennants were leaving York, and Nick would be gone as well. She had to talk to him, to find out — once and for all — if he was a real person, a ghost, or some figment of her imagination. And she wasn't going to achieve anything sitting around in this flat, or stuck in the corner at the Lion and Lamb, surrounded by history-obsessed academics.

She'd told her father the truth: The streets really were crowded at this time on a Friday night, some people still shopping, others going out after work, or heading to the evening concert in the Minster. It was Christmas party season, big groups parading around wearing tinsel headbands, hurrying into crowded pubs. Holiday lights sparkled overhead, and street musicians were out on King's Square, and St. Helen's Square, and along Stonegate, despite the bitter cold. Miranda marched along, hands in her pockets because she'd left her gloves at home, head lowered against the chilly wind rising off the river. It was busier, if anything, than this morning. Nick was going to be harder to find — if he was even out here, of course.

Time whizzed by, Miranda's agitation increasing with every step. She had to start making her way to the restaurant if she was going to be on time: One minute late and her parents would send out a search party of hysterical singers to find her. Miranda turned up St. Andrewgate, almost stomping her feet with annoyance. She was never going to find Nick.

Then someone grabbed Miranda's elbow and yanked her hard, pulling her into the dank confines of a snickelway. She opened her mouth to scream, but Nick — of course it was Nick — clamped his other hand over her mouth. He loomed over her, his eyes wild and intense.

"Calm down," he hissed. "It's only me."

She pushed his hand away, spluttering with indignation. Her heart was pounding so hard she thought she was about to hyperventilate.

"Why don't you just walk up to me in the street like a normal person?" Miranda rubbed her arm. Nick had practically wrenched it out of its socket.

"I just wanted to talk to you in private," he said, sounding bemused. "I didn't mean to hurt you."

"Well, you did." Miranda had been looking for Nick for hours, but now that they were standing close together in this dark, confined space — a narrow tunnel right here, stinking of urine and damp — all she felt was limp, useless.

"I'm sorry," he said softly. "There's something else, isn't there? Something's wrong."

"Everything's wrong." Miranda felt miserable. "I've been looking for you all day, because I wanted . . . I wanted . . . I just don't even know where to begin."

Nick stepped closer, his eyes boring into her, but he said nothing.

"I mean," Miranda continued, no longer sure of what she wanted to say, exactly, or how to begin saying it, "there's no point, is there? Because I found out you just lie to me about everything."

Nick frowned.

"What do you mean, you *found out*?"

"See — this is what I mean!" Miranda was annoyed with him now. "You don't care when I say you're lying. You only care about how I found you out. You always have to be in control, keeping everything secret. Well, how about this. I know your real name is Nick Fullerton."

"You never asked me my real name, did you? I would have told you."

"I don't believe you." Miranda pushed a hank of damp hair off her face. "You said you had no family here, but you do. Your grandfather, Lord Poole. I saw a picture of you at his house!"

This news seemed to have more of an effect on Nick. He swallowed hard, and the shadow of something — guilt, nerves, doubt — clouded his face.

"You didn't tell him . . . you didn't say anything about seeing me here?"

Miranda shook her head. "No. Then I would have to explain how I knew you. But I wanted to tell him, I really did. He's so sad, it's just awful. I mean —"

"Thanks," Nick said, interrupting her. He clearly

didn't want to hear any more about his grandfather. "Thanks for not saying anything."

"Don't thank me. Just stop lying to me. Stop pretending to be staying somewhere where they barely know you. And stop pretending to be real when I know you're . . . you're a ghost."

Nick's eyes widened.

"What?"

"You heard me. I know you're a ghost."

He gave an exasperated laugh and reached for one of Miranda's hands, squeezing it hard. It didn't feel cold at all. It felt just the way it did the other day — a little rough. Strong.

"Miranda, I'm not a ghost," Nick said firmly. "I thought that you, of all people, would be able to tell by now."

"That's not what that . . . that guy said!" Miranda could barely speak, distracted by the sensation of Nick's hand grasping hers.

"What guy?"

"The one who lives in the flat where you pretended you were staying! The flat with the green door."

"Him! He doesn't know anything," Nick scoffed. He squeezed her hand again.

"He said you went to school with someone named Jim, and Jim told him you were dead. Are dead. Whatever."

"Well, maybe that's what I wanted him to think. What I wanted them all to think." Nick was speaking softly now. The more flustered Miranda got, the more calm Nick seemed. "But it's not true. I'm alive, even though sometimes I wish I wasn't. I'm not a ghost."

"Prove it," Miranda said, and Nick pulled her toward him. She instinctively turned her head away, her heart skittering. But the two of them were pressed close now, the leather of his coat soft against her cheek. With one finger he tipped her chin up, turning her face toward his. She looked deep into his eyes — so dark against the pallor of his skin. And then he kissed her.

His lips were soft, but there was a strength, an urgency to the kiss that was almost intoxicating. Miranda felt light-headed and floaty, as though her feet might lift up off the ground. Her eyes were closed now, but she didn't need to see: She could *feel* the kiss. It was nothing like any kiss she'd experienced before. There was nothing tentative about it, nothing halfhearted. It was intense. It was real. *Nick* was real.

"'Scuse me," said a gruff voice, and Miranda opened her eyes. A man carrying plastic shopping bags was trying to squeeze past them.

"Sorry, mate," said Nick, wrapping his arms around Miranda and holding her close. When the man had passed, she slowly pulled away. Her cheeks felt flushed and her heart was still flip-flopping. She could barely bring herself to look at Nick.

"I have something to tell you," Nick said. He leaned back against the wall, still holding her hand. His cheeks were flushed, too. "I don't know whether to tell you or not. I don't know whether . . . whether I can trust you."

"Of course you can," Miranda whispered.

"You can't tell anyone," he said. "Especially not my grandfather. Not that he'd believe you. Nobody would believe you."

"Believe what?"

Nick gave her a long appraising look, staring at her in that intense way she'd found incredibly disconcerting when they first met.

"Richard," he said. "My brother. He's the reason I came back to York. I just had this overwhelming feeling about him. I knew I'd find him here."

"What do you mean, find him here?" Miranda was confused. Was the story of his brother's death another lie? Had Lord Poole been duped as well?

"His ghost," Nick explained, almost in a whisper. "Richard's ghost. He's back. Here in York — he's back."

"Are you sure?"

"I've seen him. I've talked to him. I was right to think that I was being called back here. It's seven years since he died — seven years on Saturday. He needs my help. There's something he needs me to do for him."

"I still don't understand," Miranda said. "How can we help ghosts? Whatever happened to them happened long ago. Centuries ago, maybe. We can't change the past."

She thought of the ghosts in Clifford's Tower reaching out to her with their hands of crumbling ash, and of little Mary tugging at her jacket. How could she possibly help them?

Nick stood gazing intently at her. She could still feel the imprint of his lips on hers.

"I can't explain," he said at last. "Sometimes they want our help and we can't do anything. But sometimes we can. Look, I shouldn't say any more. At this point, the less you know, the better."

"Don't do anything stupid, Nick." Miranda didn't know what he was planning, but she didn't like the sound of this.

"Wouldn't you do anything to help *your* brother?" he asked her.

"Not *anything*. Please, Nick. Don't do something crazy or dangerous. Please look after yourself."

"I'll look after me," he said with a wry smile. He let go of her hand. "And I'll look after *you*. See you round."

He headed off down the snickelway, holding his hand up in a good-bye salute. Miranda leaned back against the damp brick wall, breathing hard. Her head was spinning.

"Next time," she whispered at his retreating back, "I'll see you first."

At dinner with all the singers, Miranda didn't feel like talking much — not that she could have got a word in edgewise with the Second Witch, who insisted, despite general skepticism, that she was once practically engaged to Prince Albert of Monaco. ("Really! His mother —

that's Grace Kelly, darling — *begged* me to be his bride. But music was always my true passion.")

Later that night, full of pizza, Miranda again had vivid and unsettling dreams. She and Rob were in the bathroom, choosing from a cake trolley. Lord Poole's Land Rover was driving at top speed through a towering, bright green maze that started off looking like hedges and ended up looking like waving corn. Her father was telling her she needed to go look for the dog before it got baked in a pie. "We don't have a dog," she kept telling him, but he wouldn't listen.

And then she dreamed about Nick. The green door on Petergate swung open, revealing a big empty room. Candles lined the windowsills, their quivering flames the only light. Nick, standing behind her, put his hands over her eyes. Then they were sitting in the Minster Quire again, but this time they were kissing. Nick pulled away, asking Miranda to remember him. Of course she'd remember him, she told him, but he kept shaking his head. "May my wrongs create no trouble," Nick said, and then they both looked up. The Minster roof was open to the night sky, and Miranda tilted her head back, feeling the rain drum onto her face. Nick kissed her again, but now his lips felt cold and papery. She opened her eyes and saw that it wasn't Nick she was kissing at all. It was the ghost in the attic across the street. When she recoiled, he pursed his lips and started humming, but all that came out was a horrible buzzing, like an angry cloud of wasps drawing closer and closer.

This was what jolted her awake — the incessant buzzing. Miranda rubbed her eyes and tried to sit up. Either she was still dreaming or the wasps were in the room, because the buzzing hadn't gone away. She reached out wildly for her bedside lamp, bumping the shade before she clicked on the light. The buzzing, she realized, amazed at her own stupidity, was coming from her phone, vibrating in a jittery dance around the tabletop.

Miranda picked up the phone.

"Hello?" she croaked.

"I've sent you five texts already." It was Rob and he sounded furious. "What the hell are you doing?"

"Sleeping."

"I'm standing around outside, freezing my butt off. I've got Sally's phone. This is probably, like, an international call."

Miranda padded downstairs as quietly as possible, wincing when one of the steps creaked, holding her breath as she crept past her parents' closed bedroom door. The time on her phone had read 2:18. Rob hadn't even left the flat until after midnight: He was going to wait, he'd told her, until the lights were off and he could hear their father snoring. He hadn't lasted very long in the cellar. No wonder he was in a foul mood.

Miranda slithered down the last of the stairs and slowly unlatched the door. Rob was standing right outside the door, arms wrapped around himself, shivering. They didn't speak until they were upstairs in his room with the door firmly closed.

"What happened?" Miranda whispered. Rob flopped onto the bed, staring up at the ceiling.

"What do you think?" he murmured. "I freaked out. I just couldn't handle it. When we turned the light off, it felt as though the walls were closing in on me. The smell was getting to me as well. Stale beer and mold, maybe. I couldn't breathe. I thought I was going to black out. God, I'm such a loser."

"What did Sally say?"

"She thought I was joking at first. Then — you know, she was concerned, and sweet and all. Said the whole thing was a stupid idea anyway."

"I'm glad *she's* got some common sense."

"She was just trying to be nice. She'll probably never see me again."

"I doubt that," said Miranda.

"We tried turning on the flashlight, to see if that helped, but that was even worse. They haven't cleaned off the graffiti yet — I'll offer to do it tomorrow. During the day, when you can open the trapdoors, it's not so suffocating down there."

"I thought you said Sally won't want to see you again."

"Yeah, well." Rob sounded dejected. "I have to return her phone."

"What does the graffiti say, anyway?"

"It's not like tagging or words or anything," Rob said, sitting up so he could pull off his sweater.

"What, then?"

"Hard to explain." He peeled off his socks and dropped them one by one onto the floor. "It's just like someone's gone crazy with a paintbrush."

"Weird," said Miranda, the word turning into a yawn. Rob looked tired, too, his eyes red.

"Everything is weird about this," he muttered, flopping back onto his back. "And now Sally knows that I'm weird, too. So much for pretending to be someone else this week."

"You should try to get some sleep," Miranda told him. It was late and they were both exhausted. She whispered a quick good night, and then tiptoed back to her room and shut the door. She felt bad for Rob — she really did. But things would be better tomorrow. Sally didn't seem the kind of girl who'd mock him about his claustrophobia, or decide to dump him because of it.

A sliver of light shone into Miranda's room through the gap between the curtains. The moon hadn't been visible a single night since they arrived in York, and it was too late for the Shambles holiday lights. Miranda drew back one of the curtains, feeling that familiar twinge of excitement, curiosity, and dread.

The handsome ghost sat in the attic window, a candle burning in its usual position on the sill. He was staring directly at Miranda's window, as though he'd been waiting for her. Her heart was thumping. There was something so breathtaking about him, she thought, something sad, something magnetic. In her dream, she'd recoiled from his kiss. But was that what she'd really do? If somehow she could leap across the chasm between their two windows — their two worlds — would she hesitate? What would it feel like to kiss someone that perfect?

Perhaps ghosts couldn't kiss the living. Nick had kissed her to prove that he was real. Maybe if the ghost reached for her, pressed his face to hers, she'd feel nothing but a chill wind.

Or maybe it would feel like the most intense, exhilarating thrill she'd ever experienced.

The ghost started raising his hand to the window, as he did every time she saw him. Miranda pressed hers against the pane in anticipation of the jet of cold that would surge through glass and space and dimensions, the freezing shock that would tingle through her body. This time, she noticed, he was lifting his left hand. As he pressed it against the window, Miranda gasped, and not just because an icy tide was shuddering up her arm. The palm of his hand was dark with blood. Dried blood, a crude rainbow of it, as though someone had dragged their fingers through it when the blood was still flowing, swirling the blood in a wild, violent circle.

The ghost seemed pleased with her reaction. He gave her a slow smile, his top lip curling in a way that was almost cruel. The cold pulsing through Miranda rooted her to the spot. She couldn't take her eyes off the ghost — his haughty, irresistible face, his bloodied hand.

A police car's siren sounded in the distance, its wail breaking the silence of the night. Miranda tried to steady her breathing. The ghost had never appeared to her for this long before. He'd never been waiting for her, either, the way he'd seemed to be doing tonight. She wondered why he was showing her the blood on his left hand for the first time. Ghosts reach out to us sometimes; that's what Nick had told her. They think we can help them, he'd said, and sometimes we can. Was the ghost in the attic reaching out to her? How could she help him?

Another siren joined the chorus — this one higher and louder. The ghost smiled again. Then, carefully, with the thumb and finger of his right hand, he extinguished the candle.

"No," Miranda whispered, the sharp cold of his touch draining from her hand. But he was gone, the attic window dark and empty. The second siren was getting closer. It wasn't the only noise: Footsteps thumped along the hallway outside her room.

"Miranda." It was Rob, on the other side of her door. She peeled her hand off the window. "Miranda!"

"What?" she said, opening the door. "Keep your voice down."

"Sally just called," he said, brandishing her cell phone as evidence. He was struggling to pull his jeans on with the other hand. "We have to go."

"Where? Why?"

"Stonegate," he said, out of breath. "The White Boar is on fire."

CHAPTER FOURTEEN

Ten minutes later, all four members of the Tennant family — hastily dressed and wrapped up against the cold — were striding toward Stonegate. Miranda could tell the precise location of the White Boar from the plume of smoke drifting into the sky.

"Just one thing after another for those poor people," Peggy was saying to Jeff, still pulling on her gloves as they hurried along Swinegate. Rob ran ahead, beckoning at them to hurry up. He was frantic with worry.

Stonegate smelled like a bonfire. The fire engine had pulled up on St. Helen's Square, blocking off that end of the street. The firemen were shouting, running up to the White Boar, maneuvering the hoses into position. An ambulance reversed in jerks down Stonegate, its back doors already hanging open. The police, in their domed hats and dark uniforms, talked into their radios, waving people away to the Petergate end of the street. Miranda couldn't see flames — just smoke, billowing like smog from the chimney and the windows.

Rob stopped to make a call to Sally, who was using someone else's cell phone. Miranda kept walking.

"Help me," groaned a man's voice, and she turned her head to look. He was sitting on the ground outside a bookstore. His head was crudely bandaged and he was wearing breeches of some kind, and rumpled leather boots. As soon as she caught his eye, cold radiated through her body. Not a victim of the fire, she realized — just another ghost. He groaned again, and reached out to her. Miranda recoiled, almost stepping on Rob's foot. One of the man's hands was simply a bloody stump.

"Come on," said Rob impatiently, jabbing her in the back. "You can look at books tomorrow."

Miranda walked on, staring back at the wounded man — a Cavalier from the English Civil War, maybe? — until she blinked, and he vanished. More people were out in the street now, stepping out of doorways, wandering down from Petergate. Jeff and Peggy had stopped outside a shop some distance from the pub.

"This is as close as we should get," said Jeff, slinging a protective arm around Miranda.

"I have to find Sally," said Rob. Peggy grabbed his arm.

"She and her parents are safe, remember?" she said, sounding both calm and stern — her specialty, thought Miranda. "When she called you, they were already outside."

A wild lick of flame had darted through a window, flaring out into the street, and the watching crowd gave a collective cry. The firemen trained a steaming jet of water onto it, straining to keep the powerful hoses under control, and the orange flame disappeared as abruptly as the soldier ghost had, a thick cloud of smoke taking its place.

"If the White Boar goes, the whole street could go," someone nearby said cheerily.

Jeff bent to mutter in Miranda's ear. "I doubt that," he said. "It looks as though the worst of it's over. You can't see any flames in the windows."

Firemen were moving in through the inn's front door now, bellowing and signaling to each other. The whole sky was misted with smoke. Miranda's eyes were watering. Rob stood with Sally's purple phone clamped to one ear, his hand pressed over the other ear to block the noise.

"We're right outside the armor store," he shouted. "Sal — can you hear me? Do you want me to . . . come to you? Where are you?"

"This is just awful," Peg said, shaking her head. She pulled her coat tightly around her. "I feel so terrible for Sally's parents. First the break-ins, now this."

Sally was making her way toward them, pushing through the crowd. She was wearing some kind of foil blanket like a cape over her T-shirt and sweatpants.

"Rob!" she cried. She rushed up and hurled herself into his arms. Then Peggy hugged her, and Jeff stepped forward to hug her as well, and Miranda wanted to hug her, too, because Sally was shaking so much and because she looked so distraught.

"It's lucky that I was still awake," she told them, her teeth chattering. She and Rob exchanged quick looks. Lucky, thought Miranda, that they weren't still down in the cellar when the fire broke out. For once, Rob's panic attack was a godsend.

"Very lucky," Peggy said, rubbing Sally's arm.

"As soon as the smoke alarm went off, I ran downstairs, but the fire was already — it was already behind the bar. Some of the bottles were broken, and . . . and there was this line of fire on the floor, and I thought that the whole place was going to explode. My father sprayed it all with the extinguisher, but it was spreading and . . . and we just had to get out."

"And you're all okay?" Peggy wanted to know, not sounding as certain as she did five minutes ago. "We saw the ambulance . . ."

"My parents — they inhaled smoke, and my father burned his hand. Nothing too bad, though. He'll be okay. My mother, she's just in a nightgown. That's why they gave us these." Sally flapped the foil cape. "My father didn't even have his shoes on."

Her eyes filled with tears, and Miranda felt herself welling up, too.

"Take this," said Peggy, rapidly unwinding her scarf and draping it around Sally's neck.

"Will your father fit in my shoes?" Jeff asked. He crouched down and started unlacing one of his sneakers. "I can run home and get another pair."

"You're all right," Sally said, brushing away her tears. "Derek from the Punch Bowl gave him a pair of his. Everyone's being so kind. The police got here really quickly. And the fireman — the one in charge . . ."

She turned around to point, but there were too many people in the way.

"He said . . ." Jeff prompted.

"He said it didn't look too bad, all things considered. No danger of the roof coming down. It looked bad to us, though."

The crowd was oohing now, the way they would at a fireworks display, because snow had started to fall. Sally lifted her face to the sky, and Miranda did the same thing, looking up at the flakes dropping through the cloud of dark smoke. They splattered onto her face, soft and wet. They were implausibly clean.

Rob was back on Sally's phone, this time talking to her father.

"It's out," he reported. "Just downstairs that's damaged. Just the bar in the front."

"Just," said Sally, shaking her head. She looked at Peggy and Jeff, whose faces were as worried as hers. "It's our livelihood."

"They'll be closed for weeks," Jeff murmured to Peggy as Sally walked away, hand in hand with Rob, to rejoin her parents. Snow splotched the paving stones around them. "Come on, you two. There's nothing we can do to help tonight. Let's go back and try to get some sleep. This snow looks like it might be sticking."

"What about Rob?" asked Peggy, looking around for him.

"He'll be all right," Jeff said, gently steering her away. "He'll make his own way home when he's ready. I gave him a spare key. The lady in that pie shop downstairs made a set of spares for us this morning — she thought it might be useful with four of us coming and going." Jeff handed Miranda a key of her own.

So Rob had managed to get a key to the flat that night after all, Miranda thought, following her parents down Stonegate. This wasn't quite the situation he'd imagined, though. It all could have been much worse, she realized, shuddering at the thought of it. Sally and her parents could have been trapped upstairs. Or Sally and Rob could have been trapped in the cellar. If anything had happened to him, her parents wouldn't have been able to bear it. None of them would be able to bear it. It was silly, Miranda knew, to cry about something that hadn't even happened, but she couldn't help herself. She was glad her parents, walking arm in arm, couldn't see her.

Miranda turned to look back at the smoldering pub, watching the smoke rise like mist. A dark-haired girl walked toward her, looking around wildly, as though she was searching for someone. She must be freezing, Miranda thought: Her long dress was gauzy and flowing, more like a summer party dress than something you'd wear outside on a winter's night. Strangest of all, she wasn't wearing any shoes. As she overtook Miranda, weaving like some dark butterfly, Miranda felt a sudden blast of icy cold. The whoosh of it was so strong, Miranda felt herself falling, as though someone was pushing her out of the way. She staggered a few steps, reaching out a hand to stop herself from tumbling onto the cold cobbles. The girl in the floaty dress drifted on, still looking from side to side. This must be the ghost that Nick had talked about, the one he'd heard about but never spotted — the girl searching for her lover. "Women are the only ones who've ever seen her," he'd said.

"Miranda!" Her father was calling for her, waving her down Little Stonegate, and she hurried to catch up. High above them, people leaned out their windows, calling to each other across the street. One person was asking if they should all evacuate, and another was shouting at them to turn on the radio for the latest report.

On Back Swinegate, in the narrow entrance to a snickelway, one person stood gazing up at the sky. A young guy, with tousled dark hair. He might have been watching the gray cloud of smoke billow and disperse in the wind. He might have been watching the snow, heavier now, pelting down on his upturned face. Whatever it was he was looking at, he was absorbed in it. The one thing he couldn't see, Miranda realized, was her.

She squeezed between her parents, letting them each take hold of a gloved hand. They all quickened their pace, scuffing through the snow, arms swinging. This time, she thought, just this once, she'd seen Nick first.

Yellow police tape blocked the front door and windows of the inn, but Rob led Miranda down the side alley, past the trapdoors to the cellar, and through the yard door. It was twelve hours since the fire. The police had declared it arson: Both the internal cellar door and the back door had broken locks.

"I don't get it," said Rob. They were all crammed in the doorway leading to the flat upstairs, peering through to the front bar. All the tables, stacked with upturned stools, were charred. The inn's front windows had been boarded up. The ceiling was streaked with black, and the bar itself — doused with alcohol before being set alight — looked like a giant hunk of charcoal. "Someone broke in through the back door. Why did they need to get into the cellar, too? Nothing was taken or moved this time, right? And they set the fire behind the bar, not in the cellar at all."

"That's the million-dollar question," said Sally. "I thought maybe whoever was setting the fire only broke the lock to the back door to make us *think* that was the point of entry."

Sally wasn't exactly cheerful this afternoon, but she was trying to be much more upbeat about everything — kind of like Jenna would have been, Miranda thought.

The inn would need to be closed for only a week, maximum, she'd said. They could even start doing business again in the back before the renovations on the front room were finished. They wouldn't lose out on *all* the Christmas business.

"You mean, they had access to the cellar, like the vandals did?" Rob nodded slowly, as if he thought that made perfect sense. "Maybe through the trapdoors. And they used the cellar as a way in."

"Did you tell the police?" Miranda asked.

"Oh yes," Sally said. "And they asked me if I'd go and put the kettle on, to make them a cup of tea."

"Don't those guys watch, like, *Miss Marple*?" said Rob. "They should know that cops don't always know best. Especially ones who don't even carry guns, and wear helmets that look like upside-down sand pails with starfish stuck on them."

"Can we help clear up?" Miranda asked. "We're only here until Monday but . . ."

"I know," said Sally, pouting, and she and Rob gave each other long looks. It was like a high school production of *West Side Story*, Miranda thought, except without the memorable songs. "I hope seeing this place doesn't make you . . . doesn't bring back memories of your accident."

Miranda opened her mouth to put Sally straight, to tell her that on the night of the accident, the car hadn't caught on fire. But she didn't really want to talk about the accident. And neither — judging by the way he flinched a little at the mention of it — did Rob.

"It's okay," he said briskly. "Miranda, I'm going to be here helping today and probably tomorrow, too."

Miranda didn't think mooning around Sally would be very useful to her parents, but, hopefully, Rob would be better at cleaning up burnt furniture than he was at cleaning out the bathroom sink.

"I thought we had to go and hear Dad deliver his paper on Richard III," she said. "That's tomorrow afternoon, remember?"

"You can be the family representative." He patted her on the head.

"Gee, thanks." She glanced from Sally to Rob. The meaningful moment was continuing. They certainly didn't need her around, getting in the way of their significant looks. "Well, let me know if you need an extra pair of hands tomorrow morning. I'm going back to the flat now — okay? Rob?"

"Later," he said, punching her on the upper arm. He was trying to be affectionate, Miranda knew, so she tried not to rub her arm too ostentatiously as she made her way out through the pub kitchen and into the snowy yard.

Miranda decided to walk the long way home, past Bettys, down busy Davygate and along Parliament Street. Maybe she'd buy her mother some flowers in the market, to wish her luck for tomorrow night's concert. Her mother had rehearsals all day in Victory Hall, even though its heating had been malfunctioning all week, they could hear mice running around inside the walls, and the singers were threatening a revolt unless something called a Zip, used to make endless cups of tea, was fixed pronto.

At the flower stand, Miranda picked through buckets of cellophane bundles, finally choosing something aptly called, according to the flower seller, snowdrops. She wound her way past the stalls, careful not to slip on the snow-smeared cobbles.

It wasn't a surprise, really, when she saw Nick in the market, leaning against the brick wall that framed one of the cut-throughs to the Shambles. He was chewing on a match, one leg bent so his boot rested on the wall. The light fixed to a post on a nearby stall caught his snow-dusted hair, and the sole glass button still dangling from his coat. Maybe he was waiting for her, she thought, approaching him; maybe it was coincidence. But at least he wasn't leaping out from behind her, for a change.

"Hey," he said. It was strange seeing him in daylight. He looked very pale and tired, dark shadows under his eyes.

"Hey." Miranda felt shy with him. The kiss had complicated things. She wasn't sure what it meant, or if he regretted it. Did she regret it? Miranda didn't know. One thing she knew, though: They couldn't take it back.

"Tomorrow night," he said, throwing the match onto the ground. "Don't go to the concert. Come out with me."

"But it's my mother's concert," Miranda protested. "She would be really upset if I wasn't there."

"She won't know. She didn't even see you at the rehearsal."

"My father will know."

"Tell him you're going to sit somewhere else. Tell him you're going to sit with friends." Nick seemed agitated, rocking back against the wall.

"He doesn't know that I *have* any friends here," Miranda said archly.

"Please," said Nick. He was reasoning with her, not pleading. "It's our last chance to spend time together."

"We could spend time together this evening. Tomorrow. You could come with me tomorrow afternoon to hear my father's paper on Richard III, if you want."

Nick frowned at her, as though she were stupid.

"I can't see you at all until tomorrow night," he said. "And then that's it. You'll be gone on Monday, and so will I."

That's it. So this is what happened after a kiss, Miranda thought. Things ended.

"Um . . . what about after the concert?" she suggested, though she didn't really know how she was going to manage shaking off her family. There was going to be some sort of after-party in a restaurant on Swinegate.

Nick bowed his head. His dark hair was tipped with crystals of icy snow.

"After is too late," he said, still looking down.

Miranda wanted to see Nick again: That was the only thing she knew. She wanted to be alone with him. She wanted to feel him touch her hand again, his long fingers gently stroking her skin. Maybe she even wanted him to kiss her again. "I just . . . I don't know," she said.

Nick jerked his head up and looked her in the eyes. There was something in his gaze that was beyond intense. Something wild, like the look of a cornered feral animal.

"You have to," he said. "Please. I'll come for you around eight thirty tomorrow night, all right? I'll knock on your door. If I'm late, don't worry. I've just been . . . held up. Wait until I get there."

Miranda fingered the cellophane wrapping of the flowers. She didn't know what to do. Her heart was thumping. She wanted to see Nick again, but it was going to mean lying, and hiding, and skipping out of something. . . . It was all so complicated.

"Please," he said again. "It's important. To me. To you, I hope."

"Yes," she said, turning her head to avoid his gaze. It was too much. All of this was too much. "Tomorrow at eight thirty."

"Wait for me," Nick said. "Promise?"

"I promise," said Miranda, and he bent toward her, as though he was going to kiss her again. But he didn't kiss her. He just looked at Miranda, really looked at her, as if seeing her clearly for the first time.

When she got back to the flat, nobody else was home. Miranda was relieved. She didn't feel like talking to anyone. She was still thinking of Nick walking away through the market. The shape of his shoulders, the flare of his coat. She felt guilty, horribly guilty, at the thought of skipping out on her mother's concert. But not seeing Nick again would feel much worse. She'd never met anyone like him before. However strange he was, however abrupt and mysterious, he understood her. He understood ghosts. It was okay.

Miranda dumped the flowers in a tall drinking glass filled with lukewarm water, and arranged them on a place mat on the table. Upstairs in her room, she flopped on the bed, too agitated to nap. She reached out a hand for *Tales of Old York*, but it wasn't on the bedside table. It wasn't on the floor, either, though Miranda thought she might have knocked it there. It wasn't anywhere in the living room or — after she pounded down three flights of stairs to check — in her jacket pocket. She remembered slipping it in there on her way out . . . when was it? Yesterday morning? When she'd been walking around last night with her hands in her pockets, she'd felt it — or had she? Miranda couldn't remember. After that kiss, everything had been a blur. But even when she looked through everything all over again, Miranda still couldn't find the book. Yesterday she'd had it. Today it was gone.

CHAPTER FIFTEEN

Miranda had two conferences to attend on Sunday. The second, that afternoon, was taking place in the King's Manor, where the Richard III Society was gathering again to hear scholarly papers, drink coffee, and discuss exciting new theories about what might or not have happened at the Battle of Bosworth Field.

The first conference was that morning, in the bathroom, with Rob.

"I call this meeting to order," he said, attempting to sit on the closed toilet seat and, at the same time, rest his bare feet on the towel rail. "Ow!"

"What's wrong?"

"Someone's turned that thing on. My toes are scalded."

"Ssshhh! Stop making so much noise. Why are we in here, anyway? We could be having this conversation in your room. Or mine."

"But this is our meeting room," said Rob, looking at her as though she were stupid. "And I'm trying to get used to sitting around in small spaces. Okay. Present — Rob Tennant, chair, and his top advisor, the dormouse. On the agenda — one item only. How do I get out of going to the concert tonight?"

Miranda sighed. She wasn't in the mood for Rob's minor problems: She had other things on her mind. Last night she'd woken up sweating after the strangest dream, where *she* was the girl in the floaty dress, running along the street desperately looking for someone. There was a guy up ahead, but it was too misty to see clearly. At first he looked like Nick, then he looked like Rob. However fast she ran, she couldn't catch up with him.

"Well?" Rob demanded. "Could you put on your *thinking cap*?"

Miranda couldn't help laughing. This was something that Peggy used to say to them when they were little kids.

"Okay, okay," she said. "People can sit anywhere at this concert, right?"

"Except for the front row, which is reserved for VIPs. That's where Dad and Sally's parents will be sitting, and Lord Poole, and us. And the husbands of the Sorceress and all the Witches."

"So we go along with Dad, as planned. And then we tell him that a big group of Sally's friends are coming along, and they're sitting farther back. We want to sit with them, is that okay, blah blah blah. He'll say yes, because he's busy talking to Lord Poole, and Mr. and Mrs. . . . what's Sally's last name?"

"Framington." He said it lovingly. Miranda rolled her eyes.

"He'll be busy chatting up the Framingtons. We'll go to the back. Then you and Sally can slip out."

"Why do *you* have to say you want to sit with Sally's imaginary friends?" Rob asked. "And could you open that window? I can't breathe in here."

"I just . . . I just think it'll be more convincing if both of us go off to sit together." Miranda had decided not to tell Rob about her plans with Nick. He might disapprove. He *would* disapprove. He would start asking questions about Nick — how often she'd seen him, what they were planning to do that night. And what could she say? Miranda had no idea what they were going to do that night, but the most likely candidates — looking for ghosts, talking about dead loved ones, kissing — were not things Rob would want to hear.

"Okay. You're the brains of the operation, apparently." Rob stood up, clearly eager to open the door. "I gotta go — we're ripping out the bar today. You do know what they call Dumpsters in this country? Skips. Crazy name, crazy town."

Miranda waited while Rob loped up the stairs, two at a time, back to his own room. She picked up her toothbrush and put it down again: She'd already brushed her teeth. There was too much to think about today. Too much to worry about.

Her father stuck his head inside the door.

"What were you two conspiring about in here?" he asked, grinning at her. He was way overexcited about his conference.

"A present for Mom," Miranda told him, amazed at how easily the lie slipped out.

Down in the kitchen, her mother was scrubbing the counter with a little too much vigor. If Jeff was overexcited, Peggy was overanxious.

"I'll do that," Miranda told her, but Peggy shook her head. Her hair, still wet from the shower, was twisted up, held by a clip that looked ready to slide out. She was wearing a long sweater and leggings. Miranda had never seen her mother in leggings before. Probably that bossy Second Witch had talked her into buying them.

"Cleaning helps keep my mind off tonight," she said, moving on to polishing the faucet. "I'm trying to be rational. It's not a huge orchestra, or a complicated score. The venue is — well, amazing. The soloists, when they're singing and not talking, are really quite good. Everything should be fine."

"Everything's going to be *great*, Mom," Miranda said. *Oh, and by the way — your children are planning to skip the concert so they can get up to who-knows-what with who-knows-who.* Another secret to keep. Another sharp pang of guilt.

Peggy tossed the dishcloth into the sink and rinsed off her hands.

"It's just . . ." She was gazing out the window. Miranda couldn't see her expression. "I have this really bad feeling.

Not nerves, exactly. Just this feeling that something isn't quite right. Hard to explain. Silly."

"What do you mean?" Miranda asked, trying to keep her tone neutral.

Her mother shook her head, and swung around to look at Miranda.

"Nothing," she said, pretending to smile. Miranda knew that fake smile: She was an expert at it herself, saying there was nothing wrong, smiling. Peggy reached for Miranda's hand and squeezed it.

"Just nerves, probably," Miranda told her. Peggy smiled again.

"I'm sorry we haven't had any time this week. You and me, I mean. These rehearsals have just consumed my days, and in the evenings I'm so tired. . . ."

"It's okay," Miranda said quickly. "Really."

"I thought we'd have time to do some fun things, like more shopping," Peggy said, sounding forlorn. She squeezed Miranda's hand again. "But time's raced by, and I haven't even had a minute to look in a store window all week."

"Where did you get the leggings?"

"A gift. The Second Witch. Too young for me?"

"No. Cute."

"I swore I'd never wear anything I wore in the eighties," Peggy said. "If you catch me in leg warmers and an off-the-shoulder top, please stop me from leaving the house."

"No problem."

Rob was thundering down the stairs, shouting his good-byes.

"Bye, honey!" Peggy called. The front door slammed shut. "You'd think he had much more exciting plans for our last full day here than cleaning up after the fire. He's in such a good mood."

"Hmmm," agreed Miranda, thinking about their combined secret plans for later on.

"And you've been all right, haven't you?" Peggy looked anxious. Miranda hated making her mother worry — especially today, which was supposed to be her moment of triumph. "Your dad said you seemed to have a nice time at Lord Poole's house."

"Really nice." It was Miranda's turn for the fake smile. Thinking of Lord Poole's house made her think of the picture of Nick. It was too late to tell her mother about Nick now. There was too much to explain. Too much to withhold.

"Good." Peggy looked relieved. "You know, I have no idea why I'm so doom and gloom all of a sudden. I think this trip has been really great for us all. Rob seems so much happier. Despite everything that's gone on at the White Boar — the break-ins, the terrible fire — it's as though he's woken up again. Sally's been good for him, I think. I wish he would tell her about the claustrophobia — I'm sure she'd understand."

"But she . . . oh yeah," said Miranda, remembering that Sally's discovery of Rob's panic attacks — in the White Boar's cellar, in the middle of the night — was still in the top-secret file. "You're right. I'm sure she'd understand."

"The only thing is, with Rob so preoccupied, and Dad busy with his research, you've been left on your own, haven't you?"

"I've been fine," Miranda reassured her.

"You really should have come to the medieval banquet with us."

"Dad said that you two were the youngest people there by, like, twenty years."

"True. It's a shame you didn't have a chance to meet people your own age here in York. Make some friends."

"Sally's got some friends," Miranda blurted. "I mean, she's bringing them along tonight, to the concert. We're all going to sit together and hang out and everything. She says they're really nice, and that maybe we'll all go out afterward."

"Oh, honey!" Peggy looked delighted, and this made Miranda feel worse. She wasn't used to lying this much to her parents. She gripped the edge of the counter with her free hand, trying not to squirm. "That will be *so* nice for you. Don't worry about coming out with us afterward. You all go out and have a good time. Get Dad to give you some money."

"What's this?" Jeff appeared in the kitchen door. He was wearing a dark suit and his White Rose of York tie. "Do I have to pay you to come and listen to my paper?"

"Yes," Peggy told him, winking at Miranda. "A pound a minute."

"I'll have to read quickly, then," he said, pretending to look aggrieved. Everyone was a fake today, thought Miranda. Everyone was pretending. And, hopefully, they'd all make it through the day without anybody getting caught.

Her second conference of the day took longer than the meeting in the bathroom, and Miranda found it much harder to concentrate. Not that her father's paper wasn't interesting — in parts, anyway — and not that he expected her to stay for the rest of the afternoon session. But two things had proven really distracting and disconcerting.

The first was the walk up the stone staircase to the expansive paneled room lined with portraits, where an optimistic fifteen rows of chairs were set up for conference attendees. Miranda was following her father, listening to him chat with someone Scottish — who was wearing an identical White Rose of York tie — when a man came racing down the stairs so fast he was almost a blur. Her father and his new friend didn't flinch, but Miranda had to practically leap out of the runner's way. As he passed, a whoosh of intense cold whipped through her, as though she were wearing cotton in a snowstorm.

Great, she thought, hurrying to catch up with her father. King's Manor was haunted. Of course it was: It was built in the fifteenth century. Henry VIII had stayed here with Catherine Howard, his fifth wife, not long before he had her imprisoned and executed. No surprise at all that a ghost would be charging down the stairs past Miranda, giving her the big chill. But really — it was broad daylight. Couldn't they just leave her alone for five minutes?

The second thing unsettling her today was the sight of Lord Poole sitting in the front row of uncomfortable folding chairs. He clapped loudly at the end of each paper, even if the person giving it had read in a monotone or impenetrable accent.

He'd smiled broadly when he'd seen her, shaking her hand in his hearty way as though she were an adult. He was so genial, so kind. He'd been nothing but generous to her this whole week. And what had Miranda done in return? Lost the book he'd lent her, when he'd driven into York — a two-hour round trip — just to leave it for her. Miranda wanted to kick herself for being so careless. She must have dropped it somewhere in the street, not noticing when it fell out of her jacket pocket.

But something else she'd done — or rather, not done — was much worse than losing an expensive book. She hadn't said a word to him about Nick. Nick was Lord Poole's grandson, the only one he had left. He hadn't seen or heard from him in years, and it was pretty obvious that he was miserable about that. Miranda could have told him that Nick was alive, and right here in York. But she'd said nothing. At the house, she'd been too surprised, too confused. And then she'd made the promise to Nick.

Tomorrow, Nick was leaving town; it would be too late. Maybe tonight she could try and reason with him. Maybe Nick could be persuaded to write to his grandfather, even if he refused to meet with him in person. Lord Poole was all alone in that big, cold house in the country. And Nick was all alone in the world, too.

That was it, she decided, clapping when a bony woman from the University of Leicester ended a long-winded presentation by dropping her papers all over the floor. Her father, sitting at the table of panelists, was getting ready to read now, shuffling the pages of his talk together. He looked pale and a bit queasy. His tie was askew, and Miranda wished she could send him some kind of psychic message, telling him to straighten it, reassuring him that his talk was going to be awesome.

When his name was announced, and he stood up to move to the lectern, Miranda clapped so loudly that the man sitting in front of her turned around. Tonight, she promised herself, whatever else happened, she would talk to Nick about his grandfather. Your family was your family. You couldn't turn your back on them, or pretend they didn't exist. Families loved each other, and stuck together, no matter what. She hoped that Nick wouldn't get angry with her for interfering. She hoped he would listen. She hoped he would kiss her again.

"You must be Miranda," said Linda, who was obviously Sally's mother: They had the same curly hair and

213

bright blue eyes, though Sally's hair was a vivid yellow, and Linda's was skeined with gray. "I'm sorry we haven't had a chance to meet properly yet, with everything that's been . . . going on. It's been a terrible week."

"I'm glad you could come to the concert tonight," Miranda said, resisting the urge to hop from foot to foot with cold, or excitement, or a combination of the two. They were standing on the steps of York Minster, bundled up against the winter's night. Around them, people hurried up from the street and through the big doors. It would be a large audience, according to Lord Poole, who'd been in and out several times, to the detriment of the traffic flow through the revolving doors. Hundreds of people, he'd said.

"Your brother's been a great help to us today," said Linda, smiling at Rob, who was brazenly holding Sally's hand. "He's such a hard worker."

"Doesn't sound like anyone *we* know," Jeff whispered to Miranda, handing her a ticket.

"Aye, we'll have it all cleaned up soon enough," said Sally's father, Joe. One of his hands was bandaged, and the tips of his fingers looked blue with cold. "No thanks to the police. They want everything left, just to sit there for days on end while they poke around. I've got a business to run."

"We're due to leave in the morning, but I could come over first thing to help," said Jeff, in a great mood after the success of his talk, and still wearing his White Rose of York tie. "We all could."

"Very kind of you," said Joe gruffly. A gust of wind blew the flap of his heavy coat open, and a cold drizzle began to fall.

"You should all go in," Miranda said. "We'll wait for . . . everyone else."

"Sally, you know I would have got your friends tickets if —"

"It's no problem at all, Mr. Tennant," Sally said, blushing. At least she felt some shame. "We'll see you at the party afterward, right?"

"If you'd like to drop by, that would be very nice, but it's not necessary," said Jeff. He beckoned Miranda away from the others and slipped her two twenty-pound notes. "One's for sitting through my talk," he murmured. "And the other is for the talk on conflicting accounts of the color of Richard III's horse. Don't worry about the party. There'll be too many Witches there, and I think they're a bad influence. You kids should go to a disco."

"Nobody says disco anymore, Dad. But thanks."

As soon as everyone over eighteen was inside and — as reported by Miranda, after a brief espionage mission — settled in their seats on the far side of the Minster, Rob and Sally left.

"Bye, Miranda," Sally said, giving her an enthusiastic hug. "And thanks. We'll meet you outside the Two Keys at eleven, okay?"

"Enjoy the concert," said Rob. "We'll need a full report later."

"Sure," said Miranda. "See you."

Miranda waited for them to disappear down Stonegate, and then she counted to thirty. An usher who was even younger than Miranda appeared and hurried everyone in: The concert was about to begin.

"Are you coming in, miss?" he asked her, and she shook her head. She walked down the steps and across the street, following the path Rob and Sally had taken down Stonegate. It wasn't quite eight o'clock yet; she had more than half an hour to wait. Half an hour until Nick knocked at the door and she took a giant leap into the unknown.

It was strange being alone in the flat at this time of night. Usually they were all getting back from dinner somewhere, or clearing away the debris — take-out packages, newspapers, empty cans and bottles — from an evening in. The flat felt too hot and too empty. Miranda sat for a while in the living room, then she lay on her bed. She finished off the orange juice in the fridge and threw the carton away in the recycling bin. She made another fruitless search for *Tales of Old York*, in the hope it had fallen behind the sofa or found its way onto her father's bedside table. She searched through the TV channels, which didn't take long. Still no Nick. Eight thirty came and went; eight forty-five. Miranda wondered if she should go and stand in the street, because he might have got their flat confused with another. But when she went outside, there was no sign of Nick anywhere, and it was too cold and wet to be hanging around.

Nine o'clock. He'd said he might be late, she remembered. He'd told her to wait — made her promise, in fact. Miranda climbed the stairs to her bedroom and opened the window, her radiator clanking in complaint. If he called her name, she'd hear him, and she could stick her head out of the window every few minutes to try and spot him walking along the street.

Nine fifteen. Miranda put down her cell phone and walked to the window. The rain had stopped, at least. It was Sunday night, but still there were groups of young people out, dressed up — not warmly, despite the weather — and making their way, shouting and laughing, from one pub to the next. Miranda didn't know what to do. The waiting was gnawing at her stomach, making her feel ill with anticipation. He wasn't coming, something inside of her was saying. Nick wasn't coming.

But he said he would. He made her miss the concert so they could be together. She would wait downstairs, Miranda decided, out in the street, even if it was freezing. Then there'd be no chance of Nick going to the wrong door. She pulled her head back in and closed the window.

Just as she was about to draw the curtains, a light flickered in the attic window across the street. Miranda could see its beam darting around the room like a skittish insect. That was odd. Usually, the ghost's candle was lit in the window. But although no candle materialized on the sill, and the handsome ghost didn't appear, Miranda was sure that someone was up there. The light

kept moving, searching something out. And then someone stepped out of the darkness, walking right up to the
window, looking straight at Miranda.

Sally stood in the attic across the street, her mouth an
O of surprise. Miranda couldn't believe her eyes. She'd
been expecting the ghost, not Sally, of all people. What
was she doing in there? How did she get into the boarded-
up house?

Sally was jiggling the window, trying to open it, but it
must have been stuck fast. She mouthed something at
Miranda: It took several tries before Miranda could decipher *Go to the pub.*

"Okay!" she shouted, not sure if Sally could hear her.
But just as she stepped away from the window, she heard
a frantic banging on the glass across the street. Sally was
waving to her, trying to get her attention again. She'd
pressed something up to the glass, holding it high so
Miranda could see it. It was a small green book and, even
in the half-light, Miranda recognized it instantly. She'd
been looking for it today, after all. It was *Tales of Old York.*

CHAPTER SIXTEEN

Miranda was running — darting around people, breathing hard. It wasn't that far from the flat on the Shambles to the pub on Stonegate, despite the zigzag of the route, but there was no time to lose. She'd left a scrawled note for Nick — *At the White Boar*, it read — hanging out of the mail slot in the front door in case he turned up. If he'd ever planned to turn up, which she was beginning to doubt.

She didn't know what game Nick was playing tonight, but right now, there were more immediate questions dancing around in her head. How — and why — had Sally managed to get into the boarded-up house on the other side of the Shambles? Where was Rob? Was he okay? How did Sally come across the missing copy of Miranda's book? Why did they have to meet back at the White Boar? This evening's plan had been so straightforward, but now it seemed as though everyone was off on their own, doing things they shouldn't be doing. Miranda's stomach churned, and not just because the ghost with the bloody stump at the end of one arm was lying on Stonegate again, groaning in her direction.

The front of the White Boar was still boarded up. At the back door, Rob stood waiting.

"Get in," he said, practically dragging her by her arm.

"Sally," Miranda panted. "I saw Sally."

"I know. Come on — she just got back. She's downstairs."

"Downstairs," Miranda repeated stupidly. Sally must have run like the wind to get back so quickly. Odd that they hadn't seen each other.

"The cellar!" Rob exclaimed. He led the way through the pub's kitchen and into the charred, now-empty front bar. Sally was clattering up the cellar steps.

"Miranda!" said Sally, out of breath and flushed. She looked completely disheveled, her clothes and hair smeared with mud. "Has Rob told you?"

"He's told me nothing." Miranda was practically leaping out of her skin. What was going on?

"Jeez, give me a chance," said Rob. "So, we were upstairs in the flat, and we decided to come down and get something to eat from the big kitchen, the one where they make the food for the customers —"

"Get to the point!" Miranda shrieked. This was no time for Rob to be long-winded.

"That's when we heard it," Sally said. "The noise in the cellar."

"Like something being dragged or pushed or whatever," said Rob. "But the door down there was locked. I went outside, into the alley, to see if the trapdoors were open."

"We thought we could close them and bolt them, and whoever was in there would be trapped."

"And then we'd call the police," added Rob. "So don't start again about us putting ourselves in danger, okay?"

"Were they open?" Miranda asked, and Sally shook her head.

"Shut and locked," she said. "The security bolt my father added after the fire — it wasn't cut through or anything. When we went back inside, the cellar door was still locked and the noise had stopped. We couldn't hear a thing."

"So we went down to look," said Rob. "With the flashlight and the cricket bat."

Miranda rolled her eyes.

"And?" she demanded.

"There were footprints," said Sally, her eyes widening. "Only a couple. Big wet footprints, and they seemed to just . . . to just . . ."

"Come straight out of the wall," Rob said, smacking the wall next to him for emphasis. "And it took us a while, but we figured it out. Where the footsteps started, one of the stones seemed to jut out in a weird way."

"We were pulling on it," Sally explained, "and it moved. The stone moved! A whole panel, really — three big stones. It was some kind of secret passage: an entrance to a tunnel. *An entrance to a tunnel!*"

"A tunnel?" Miranda repeated. Wow. A tunnel leading to the White Boar cellar. No wonder vandals could get in without a key. This was amazing.

"So," said Rob, taking over the story again, "we decided to follow it, to see where it went."

"Are you crazy?" This was even more stupid than the plan to stay in the cellar overnight, Miranda thought.

"It was my idea," Sally admitted. She looked sheepish. "Rob said we should call the police — really, he did. But I was so sick of all this. I just wanted to find out for myself."

"She was pretty determined," Rob explained. "I couldn't stop her. And I couldn't . . . I just couldn't make it very far along. It's not really a tunnel. It's more like a low passageway. Really low and really narrow. I couldn't stand up in it."

"It's low and it's wet," Sally said. "And dark. Horrible." She shuddered, rubbing at one of the muddy streaks down her arm.

"And you followed the tunnel all the way to that house on the Shambles?" Miranda asked. She couldn't believe how brave — and foolish — Sally was. She thought of the handsome ghost of the apprentice, wondering if he'd been there in the attic. Sally had said nothing about him. But, of course, Sally couldn't see ghosts.

"I was going nuts, worrying about her," Rob said. "I got quite a way along, but I just couldn't . . . you know."

He looked embarrassed.

"And the tunnel led to that house on the Shambles?" Miranda pressed.

"To the cellar," Sally told her. "At that end, the stones were pushed out of the way, so I could crawl in with no problem. I had no idea where I was. The cellar wasn't locked, so I could get into the house, also no problem, but it was in total darkness. Nobody there. No furniture. No sign of life at all, except for the top floor."

"What?" Miranda's heart started thudding again. Sally *had* seen the ghost — is that what she was about to say? "What did you see?"

"A mattress and a few odds and ends. Your book." Sally lifted her sweater and pulled the book out; it was tucked into her jeans. "I saw it there, lying on the floor, and I remembered it from when you were in Little Bettys that day. But I still didn't know where I was. All the windows were boarded up. There was just that one window, up in the attic. I walked up to it to look out, try to get my bearings. And that's when I saw you."

"How weird is all this?" said Rob. Much weirder than he realized, Miranda thought. He didn't even know about the ghost in the attic — if the ghost was even a ghost. Why would a ghost need a mattress? Or a book, for that matter. Maybe the mark on his neck was just that, a mark. Miranda's head was spinning. Was he a ghost or not?

"I tried the doors downstairs, but they're boarded up. The only ways out of that house are along this tunnel and through a small trapdoor in the roof of the cellar. That probably leads into a yard, or an alleyway or something. But it was locked."

"Let me see," said Miranda, grabbing Sally's arm. "Let me see the tunnel."

"You're not going to that house," Rob said, frowning at her. "I forbid it."

Miranda rolled her eyes. "Sally, show me."

Sally looked hesitant.

"I don't know — maybe Rob is right. We should call the police now. Whoever's vandalizing the cellar and setting fire to the pub — either they're living in that house or using that cellar as an escape route. They might be dangerous."

The guy in the attic wouldn't hurt her, Miranda thought. He *knew* her. He'd seen her at least, in the window across the way, and smiled at her. She'd wanted to be in the same room with him and now, at last, she might have the chance.

"Let me look at the entrance to the tunnel, at least," Miranda pleaded. She was so excited it was hard to keep her voice steady. No way was Rob going to call the police before she had a chance to see for herself.

Sally gave Rob a long look.

"It's only fair," she said to him, and he shrugged. Sally started down the cellar steps, and Miranda followed her.

Miranda had never seen the cellar of the White Boar before. Rob had described it to her in his usual vague way — low ceiling, stone walls — and that was right. But the first time he'd been down there, he said, it was all very neat and organized. Now the metal barrels and their rubber tubes were in a jumble, some tipped onto their sides, so there was hardly any room to walk.

To the left of the stairs gaped a jagged hole in the wall, the block of three big stones pulled out of place, just as Sally had described. The right wall was still daubed with the graffiti Rob had mentioned earlier in the week. It was the strangest tag Miranda had ever seen, just a wild smearing of paint — orange, red, gold — in some sort of big, crude rainbow.

"See, the footsteps were leading out of here," Sally was saying, pointing to the opening in the wall. Miranda stood in the center of the cellar, gazing back and forth between the two walls. "They're a bit hard to see now, because Rob and I have tramped in and out as well. And if you look in here . . ."

She gestured to the tunnel, and Miranda stepped forward, squeezing between two upturned barrels. But there was something about the painted wall, something about the abstract shape of it, the color. Miranda looked over, staring directly at it. Where could she have seen it before?

"There weren't any paint pots in the house," Sally told her, answering a different unspoken question. "I looked in every room. Which means, I think, that whoever did this isn't living in the house — don't you think?"

"I don't know," Miranda said, still intrigued by the crude smear on the wall. Even though it was just a shape, there was something so familiar about it.

"Don't you even want to look into the tunnel?" Rob asked. He was sitting on the stairs. "Or did you just come down here for the art?"

"I've seen it before," Miranda said slowly. "It was . . ."

On the ghost's hand.

That was it! In a flash, Miranda could see it clearly. What had looked like a smear of blood on the ghost's hand was more or less this shape. The colors weren't as vivid as the paint on the cellar walls, but it was the same image, she was certain — just on a very different scale.

"It was what?" Rob prompted, looking puzzled. Miranda didn't reply. She didn't know *how* to reply. She couldn't tell him about the ghost, because he'd just scoff. And anyway, even if he believed her about the ghost, how could these pieces fit together?

Because — surely — ghosts couldn't paint walls. Miranda had seen the ghost stonemason at work in the Minster, but for all his activity, no changes were made to pillars and doors; there was no trace of his work when he disappeared. The palm of the ghost's left hand may have been painted *before* he died. Perhaps that was why the paint looked dark as blood and not bright like these swoops of color on the stone walls. A ghost couldn't buy cans of paint in the twenty-first century and use them to graffiti a wall, could he?

Unless someone else did it for him.

"WHAT?" said Rob again, now indignant.

"It looks a bit like a sunset, I thought," said Sally, wriggling into position next to Miranda. "Or maybe a big fire."

"A sky full of fire," Miranda whispered. A piece clicked into place in her head. It wasn't a picture, these livid streaks on the wall. It was part of a picture. An etching, actually, in black-and-white. She turned to the stairs, looking up at Rob with her mouth open.

"Okay, now you're just being annoying," he said.

"It's a detail . . . a detail from a picture," she said, stumbling over the words. "Something I saw — it's called *The Fall of Babylon*. It's a city under attack by God or the Persians or someone. It's on fire, and there's this big cloud of flame in the sky. And even though the picture's in black-and-white, I swear to you — the shape of it looks exactly like this."

"What are you *talking* about?"

"The picture I saw at Lord Poole's house."

"No way." Rob looked startled. "Lord Poole is the vandal?"

"No, idiot! But I think . . . I think I know someone else who's seen this picture."

"Who — Dad?"

"Okay, now *you're* the annoying one," Miranda

snapped. "I'm talking about someone who *knows* this picture really well."

Nick and his brother had practically grown up in Lambert House. They must have seen the John Martin print hundreds, thousands of times.

"Forget the police, Sal," Rob said sarcastically. "Miranda needs to get an art critic on the phone."

"Rob, shut up," she said, turning to Sally. "I have to go see the house on the Shambles. I think I know . . . I think I know . . ."

"KNOW WHAT?" he yelled.

"I think I know who's living in that house."

Rob opened his mouth to say something and then closed it again: He looked totally puzzled. Sally glanced from him to Miranda, clicking on the flashlight.

"I'll lead the way," she said.

Miranda followed Sally into the tunnel. It was no surprise that Rob couldn't cope with it: Miranda was stooped over, the moist stone ceiling brushing the back of her head. It was a passage so narrow that her shoulders were almost touching the walls. Underfoot, the stones were beyond slithery — so damp and mossy that Miranda seemed to be constantly slipping. She groped at the walls, willing herself to keep going. The only illumination was the pinpoint beam of Sally's flashlight, and the increasingly distant cellar light behind them. Sally was trying to move quickly, but it wasn't easy, especially with only one hand free to feel along the walls and keep herself steady.

"It's more or less a straight line," Sally called back; her voice sounded high and hollow. "Are you okay? You're not claustrophobic, too, are you?"

"I'm fine," Miranda shouted, though she didn't feel fine. This passage — an old road, or a Roman sewer, maybe? — was enough to induce a panic attack, even if you'd never had one before. She tried to steady her breathing. They'd been making their way along for ten minutes, maybe. It felt like the longest ten minutes of Miranda's life. They had to be almost there.

"I can see the other cellar, up ahead," Sally called at last. "I warn you — the entrance is small. It's easiest if you crawl."

Miranda crouched, hauling herself, with dirty hands, through the gap in the wall. They were standing in another cellar, this one even smaller than the White Boar's, and smelling of must.

"See?" Sally trained her light on the small trapdoor overhead. A lock that looked new, or at least recent, dangled down. "They could go in and out through there."

She flashed the light onto a rickety wooden staircase.

"This way up," she said. "We should be quiet, in case someone's come back to the house."

But nobody was in the house. Miranda and Sally clung together, taking careful steps and gasping in unison when the flashlight's beam picked up a mouse scuttling across the floor. It was a narrow building, dusty and empty. The ground floor was dark as pitch, and so were the two floors above. Every step made the stairs creak, but it couldn't be helped. Miranda was amazed that Sally had already made this trip once, alone. She had a lot of guts.

On the top landing, Sally paused to brush away a cobweb stuck to her hair. Miranda's grip tightened on Sally's arm. She wasn't sure what she was going to see up here, if the ghost would decide to make an appearance. Of course she wanted to see him, to talk to him at last, if that was possible. But the prospect of meeting him face-to-face, without the protection of the window, was scary as well. And what if he wasn't a ghost, after all? What if he was the cellar vandal? How would he react to two girls breaking into his house?

Whatever happened, Miranda told herself to keep calm, even if she felt jittery and weak-kneed right now. She and Sally walked slowly along the narrow hall to the sole doorway. It was ajar.

"As I left it," Sally whispered. They stopped in the doorway while Sally shone her light around the room. "Nobody here," Sally said, and Miranda could hear the relief in her voice. Miranda was relieved, too — relieved and disappointed at the same time. Where was the ghost? He'd shown himself to her so many times, through the window. Why not appear now, when she was here in his room?

As Sally had said, there were a few signs of life in the attic, and they were all on the side nearest the door, where the dormer window was boarded up. A dingy mattress lay pushed up to one wall, devoid of any bedding. In one corner, crowded onto the seat of a wooden chair, was a burner — the kind you'd take camping — and battered saucepan. Underneath the chair lay an empty can of baked beans and a discarded plastic spoon.

"No light," said Sally, flicking the switch back and forth. "But there's a candle over there."

She shone the flashlight over to the far wall, by the window Miranda could look into from her room. A stub of a white candle sat in a saucer, melted down to almost nothing. Miranda pulled on Sally's arm, the floorboards groaning and shifting as they crossed the attic. She crouched down to finger the candle. Could this be the one the ghost placed in the window? Or did he have some ghostly candle, pilfered in another lifetime, that he used to reveal himself whenever he wanted? Was he in the room right now, watching them?

"There's *your* window." Sally tapped on the glass. "I couldn't believe my eyes when I saw you there."

"I couldn't believe it either," Miranda began, swiveling on her heels so she could stand up. Sally helpfully pointed the flashlight down at the ground and, as the beam dipped, Miranda caught sight of something scrawled low on the wall, underneath the window.

"Hold the light still a second," she whispered. "Here — look."

Sally directed the flashlight at the wall, stepping back so she could see what Miranda was pointing at. The marks on the wall were words, smudged and black.

"Like someone was finger painting," Sally said, thinking aloud. "What does it say? 'Dark' something . . ."

" 'Dark soul and foul thoughts,' " said Miranda. Like the picture on the wall of the cellar, this was something she remembered, somehow. Dark soul and foul thoughts. Dark soul and foul thoughts.

"This place is so creepy." Sally shivered. "He must be a right nutjob, the bloke who's living here."

"Lord Poole," said Miranda, standing up. It had come to her in a flash.

"Lord Poole lives *here*?" Sally looked at her, mystified. "I thought he had some big house in the country."

"No, no," Miranda explained. "I don't mean Lord Poole lives here. I mean, I heard those words at his house — he said them. He was quoting someone, some poet."

"Well, how does it . . . how does it explain all this?" Sally waved the flashlight, arcing the beam around the room. "I don't get it."

"Hang on," said Miranda. "What was that?"

Sally's light had glanced over something out on the floor, in the far corner of the room. She scanned the peeling floorboard until the light picked out the object again.

"A piece of glass?" Sally said, walking toward it. "Or no — wait."

She bent down to pick up whatever it was, holding it up so Miranda could see. It was a clear glass button, as big as a quarter, trailing the frayed tail of a piece of black thread. Miranda reached out to touch it, her hand trembling. *No*, she thought. *No, no, no.*

Someone was living in this attic, and that someone was Nick.

CHAPTER SEVENTEEN

ally said they should get back to the pub cellar before Rob got frantic with worry, and Miranda agreed with a silent nod of the head. She didn't want to hang around in this attic a moment longer. Nick might come back. The ghost might appear. What the connection between them might be was starting to take shape in her mind, but it was still a gray cloud, like the ones that had loomed over York all week.

The journey back along the underground passage didn't feel any shorter, and Miranda managed to slip, halfway along, coming down hard on one of her knees. She was dirty, damp, and tired by the time she slithered back into the White Boar's cellar, the smell of mold rank in her nostrils. She had to explain things to Rob and Sally. They weren't going to believe her, but she had to try and explain.

"Where have you two been?" Rob was stamping his

feet with irritation. A redundant question, Miranda thought. "I've been going crazy in here. I was just about to call the police."

"We saw some other things," Sally said, stroking Rob's arm to calm him down. "Some words painted on a wall, and a glass button. I think . . ."

She turned to face Miranda, pinning her down with that blue-eyed gaze. Rob made one of his hurry-up-and-tell-me-already faces.

"I think they meant something to Miranda," Sally said slowly. Now was the time, Miranda thought. If only she could muzzle Rob, she might be able to get the story straight.

"Okay," she said, not sure where to begin. "Just don't start shouting at me, Rob. Let me speak, all right? I think . . . I think I know who's living in the attic. It's this guy I met. His name is Nick."

"The loser with the blankets and the attitude?" Rob glared at her. "I told you that guy was trouble. Of all the guys in this city, you have to meet a violent offender."

"We don't know he's a violent offender. He's *Lord Poole's grandson*." Miranda glared back at Rob. At least that particular piece of information seemed to shut him up. "And the thing is . . . Look, I know neither of you are going to believe this, but *please* let me say what I have to say before you jump all over me."

"Nobody's going to jump all over you." Sally sat down on a barrel that was lying on its side. Her voice was calm. "Really, Miranda. Just tell us everything."

Miranda swallowed. Everything in her head was a jumble.

"Well, *you* know, Sally, that I can see into the attic from my bedroom window. But I can't see the other side, where the window's boarded over. So I had no idea that Nick was sleeping up there. Living up there. He never told me."

"I bet he never told you that he liked to vandalize pub cellars or set fire to things either," muttered Rob, but a stern glance from Sally silenced him.

"The thing is, there *was* something I could see in that window. Some*one*, actually. Only at night. I've seen him many times since we arrived in York. I tried to tell you about it, Rob, but you wouldn't listen. He's a ghost. Sally, I can see ghosts."

"Miranda . . ." Rob began, in his most patronizing voice.

"Ssshh," said Sally. "Miranda, go on."

"You believe her?" Rob was incredulous. "You believe all this ghost stuff?"

"Well," said Sally matter-of-factly, "I've never seen a ghost, but that doesn't mean they don't exist. And didn't you ask me, Rob, if we had a cat at the White Boar? Remember, you said that Miranda had seen it that night your family came for dinner."

"What about it?"

"I told you we don't have a cat, and that was the truth. But Miranda's not the first person to see it. A black cat, wasn't it?"

"Yes," said Miranda, wondering if her guess had been right.

"About forty years ago, the previous owners had some building work done, because a room had damp in the walls or something. Their black cat disappeared, and some people said it had got itself bricked up alive in one of the new walls. Over the years it's been spotted, usually in one of the front rooms. And sometimes when people bring dogs in, the dogs go absolutely mental. Barking and jumping up at something that nobody else can see."

"So the black cat *was* a ghost," said Miranda, and Sally nodded.

"Why didn't you tell *me* all this?" Rob complained. "Why didn't you say, 'Dude, for real, your sister is a ghost whisperer'?"

"It was *her* business." Sally flashed Miranda a conspiratorial smile. "And I was going to ask her about it myself, when we had a quiet moment, but everything's been so . . ."

"Crazy," Miranda said. "I know."

"All right, then," declared Rob from his staircase podium. "I don't know if I buy all this, but go back to what you were saying. You saw some ghost in the window, *allegedly*."

"Yes." Miranda nodded, trying to ignore his suspicious tone. "And I knew that Nick had an older brother named Richard. Nick told me himself, and so did Lord Poole. Richard was a lot older than Nick, and he died in some kind of mental hospital seven years ago, when he was twenty-one. He committed suicide — hanged himself."

Sally grimaced.

"So you're thinking," she said, "that this ghost you saw in the window may be Nick's brother? That they're living together, in a way, up in the attic?"

"Well, mostly I thought he was the ghost of this murdered apprentice," admitted Miranda. "I read about him in my book. He's been seen in a house on the Shambles several times."

"Oh, I know about him!" Sally exclaimed. "I've heard the tour guides telling the story, and one of our customers claimed to have seen him ages ago. But that's not the house across from yours. It's right down at the end of the Shambles. Overlooking Whip-Ma-Whop-Ma-Gate."

"That street name is *another* thing I just don't believe," said Rob.

"He's just a kid," Sally added. "The apprentice, I mean. He was fourteen or something when he was murdered."

"Wow — okay." This was another new piece of information for Miranda to compute. So the ghost in the attic couldn't be the murdered apprentice. The house was wrong. The age was wrong. Pieces of the puzzle were sliding into place.

"Does this ghost look like Nick?" Sally asked.

"Kind of," Miranda replied. He was more handsome than Nick, she wanted to say. There was something much more charming about him. Debonair, her mother would say. "He has the same really dark hair and pale skin. And another thing — with ghosts, you know, you can often see how they died. You see the . . . the marks on them. He has a wound right here."

She drew her hand across the base of her throat to demonstrate. Rob flinched.

"And then there's that picture, *The Fall of Babylon*," she continued. "They grew up with it at Lord Poole's house. Nick and his brother stayed at that house all the time when they were growing up. And the other night, the ghost had a version of this fire cloud thing painted on the palm of his left hand. He showed it to me, in the window, but I didn't realize what it was until tonight, when I saw the paint on the walls here."

"I wish we'd brought you to look at the cellar sooner," said Sally ruefully.

"There's other stuff, too. Nick's been saying lots of weird things this week. . . ."

Rob snorted with derision, which brought him another cool look from Sally.

"Go on," she said to Miranda.

"Things about how he'd come back to York because he felt his brother calling him. Because it was seven years since Richard died — seven years today, actually. Nick said his brother needed him to do something for him, that ghosts reach out to us because they want our help. Sometimes we can help them, and sometimes we can't. But he said he'd do anything to help his brother."

"But why would his brother want him to break into our cellar and bust open all the barrels and paint on the walls?" Sally looked mystified. "And why would he want to set fire to our pub?"

"I don't know," Miranda said. She really had no clue.

"You said there were words painted on the wall in the attic," said Rob. He was sitting on the stairs, leaning forward. Not scoffing at her anymore, at least. "What did they say?"

"Dark soul something," Sally said.

"Dark soul and foul thoughts," Miranda reminded her.

"Sounds like Shakespeare," Rob said. "Dad would know."

"Yeah — why don't we text him and ask?" Miranda asked sarcastically. "Hey, Dad, we're not exactly at the concert right now, but we have a literary question that can't wait."

"Dark soul and foul thoughts," murmured Sally. "I should know this — I'm reading English at university."

"You've only been there one semester," Rob said. "Can you get onto the Internet on your phone?"

"Yes!" Sally tugged her phone out of her pocket and started tapping away. Miranda resisted the temptation to look over her shoulder.

"Any luck?" Rob asked.

"Hang on — sorry, the reception is awful down here.

Wait . . . here, it's loading. Yes! It's John Milton. A poem he wrote called . . ."

"*Comus!*" Miranda remembered where she'd heard the line before. "Lord Poole was talking about it the other day, when Dad and I went to his house. Reciting it. Something to do with the picture by John Martin. You know, *The Fall of Babylon*. Or . . . no! It wasn't about the picture. It was about John Martin himself."

"I'm confused," said Rob. "What do all these different Johns have to do with Nick's brother's ghost coming back to York after seven years or whatever — not that I necessarily believe all this."

"What's the connection?" Sally glanced up from her phone. "Miranda, do you know?"

"I think so." Miranda felt a rush of exhilaration. At last things were starting to make sense. "John Martin had a brother named — something. I can't remember. Anyway, this brother — he tried to burn down York Minster. And the lines from the poem had something to do with it. I don't remember exactly."

"I could look it up," Sally said, frowning at her phone. "But this thing is *really* slow right now."

"What about your book?" Rob pointed to *Tales of Old York*. It lay on one of the barrels, where Miranda had left it before venturing into the underground passage. "Maybe there'd be something about it in there?"

"There's a picture of the Minster burning," Miranda said. Sally handed her the book. "I remember the caption,

THE MADMAN'S FIRE, 1829. He was insane. Jonathan Martin — that was his name! Instead of hanging him, they sent him to Bedlam, the asylum. Lord Poole told us."

As she paged through the book, looking for any information on the 1829 fire, Miranda remembered something else. Lord Poole wasn't the only one who'd talked about that fire of 1829. Nick had mentioned it, too, the day they sat together in the Minster's Quire stalls. He knew all about the fire.

"Here," she said, finding the line drawing of York Minster, its wooden roof ablaze. "There's something here. . . .

"Jonathan Martin, a religious fanatic who had experienced religious visions as a child and had once been incarcerated in Gateshead Asylum, left a series of threatening letters on the Quire gates of York Minster. These letters foretold the destruction of the church as divine retribution for the wealth and decadence of the Church of England's establishment. On the first night of February, 1829, Martin secreted himself in the Minster after Evensong and, after it was locked for the night, slashed velvet from the pews in order to build a pyre, adding hymnbooks as the fire grew. By the time it was discovered the next morning, most of the Quire — including, sad to say, the great organ — lay in ruins. The terrible fire was not subdued for many hours. Only the collapse of the great Medieval roof above the Quire prevented the flames from spreading further, saving the Minster from complete destruction. Martin himself had escaped the burning cathedral by climbing scaffolding in the north transept, but he could not escape arrest."

"But that doesn't explain the Milton poem thing," Rob complained.

"Hang on, hang on." Miranda flipped the page. "Here — look. It gets mentioned here.

"At his trial, Martin was smiling, calm and unrepentant, behavior which enraged the citizens of York. He insisted that his act of arson was performed as a service to God, quoting at length from John Milton's A Masque Presented at Ludlow Castle, *also known as* Comus. *Martin contended that he himself had "light within his own clear breast" whereas the Dean of York Minster was a man who "hides a dark soul and foul thoughts." The services of a lawyer engaged by the defendant's brother, the acclaimed artist John Martin, were barely required, as Jonathan Martin concurred with every allegation of the prosecution. The jury took but minutes to find him not guilty on the grounds of insanity."*

"So why would these words have meaning for Nick and his brother?" Sally looked pensive. "Why would they be painting them on the wall?"

"Ghosts can't paint," Rob said matter-of-factly.

"Like you're the expert now on ghosts," said Miranda, though secretly she thought he was right. "You wouldn't even *listen* to me when I tried to tell you about them until Sally did."

"I wonder if they felt some kind of affinity with Jonathan Martin," Sally mused, ignoring Rob and Miranda's squabble. "Is Nick religious at all?"

"No." Miranda shook her head, thinking of her conversation with Nick in the Minster. He went there all the time but never, she suspected, to services. "Not religious. But he *is* quite bitter about the Church. When Richard died, he said, their mother wanted to have the funeral in York Minster. But someone — I don't know who — wouldn't give permission, and he was buried out in the country instead. That's what Nick said happened, anyway."

"So Nick could have a grievance against the Minster." Sally drummed her feet against the barrel. "And that means he and his brother could relate in some way to Jonathan Martin and *his* grievance. But hang on — there's something not quite right about this. I understand it from Nick's point of view. But what would Richard care about his funeral? He still had a church burial." .

"That's true," Miranda said. She remembered Nick's description of the funeral out in the country. It must have been the village near Lambert House.

"And," said Sally, warming to the subject, "obviously I don't know as much as you about the world of ghosts, but it stands to reason that ghosts haunt places because of things that happen *before* they died, or perhaps because of the *way* they died. Not something that happens *after* they died, like a funeral."

This made sense to Miranda as well. The pieces of the puzzle weren't falling into place quite so easily anymore.

Rob stretched his legs out on the stairs.

"And there's nothing else in that book to give us any clues?" he asked. "Because you two may be overthinking, or underthinking. This all seems kind of random to me."

Miranda turned the page, skimming the rest of the short chapter.

"There's some more stuff about Jonathan Martin going to Bedlam," she said, "where he died nine years later of natural causes. And there's something about his brother, the painter John Martin, and his . . . and his . . ."

"What?" asked Sally. Miranda frowned at the words swimming in front of her. It was just a coincidence, she told herself. That was all.

"Something about his son," Miranda said. "Jonathan Martin's son. His name was . . . his name was Richard. Listen, I'll read it to you.

"Like his uncle, Richard Martin was a talented artist. The young man went to live with John Martin after the trial, to enjoy both his protection and tutelage. He had some early success, exhibiting at the Royal Academy in London. But, sadly, he was also heir to the familial instability of temperament. Three months after his father's death in Bedlam, Richard Martin slit his own throat. He was twenty-five years old."

"Nice family," said Rob. "They make us seem normal."

"Same name as Nick's brother." Sally stood up — in fact, she practically bounced off the barrel. "Miranda, didn't you say that Nick's brother hanged himself?"

"Yes."

"And the ghost you've seen, the one we think is sharing the attic with Nick, he has a wound across his neck. Like a bruise."

"Yeah, I guess so. It looks dark and at first I thought it was clotted blood, but that's when I thought he was the ghost of the butcher's apprentice. It could easily be a bruise, from a rope or whatever."

"But you said the wound was here." Sally patted her throat. "Wouldn't the bruise from whatever kind of noose Nick's brother was using be farther up, under his chin? Think about it."

She used her hands, thumbs touching, to mimic a noose pulled taut around her neck.

"You're right," Rob said, scrambling to his feet. He towered above them from his perch up on the stairs. "It would be way higher up than if you used a knife or a razor, wouldn't it?"

He mimed a slash across the base of his throat.

"So you're thinking that . . . what? The ghost might not be Nick's brother?" Miranda remembered the ghost in the attic, that savage dark line across his white skin.

"But where it all falls apart, Sal," said Rob slowly, "is that Nick would know if this guy was his own brother or not. It's not as if he could wake up in the attic one night, see this ghost, say, 'Dude, are you Richard?' and the ghost nods, and then it's like, 'Okay, let's hate on York Minster and then go trash a pub if that's what you want, big brother.' He would *know* that this guy wasn't his brother."

"He hadn't seen him since he was nine," Miranda said quietly. She thought of the story Lord Poole had told her, everything Nick had said. "Nick hadn't seen his brother since he was nine. Even when he saw his brother's ghost for the first time, in the churchyard where Richard was buried, he only saw the back of him, not his face. He was sure it was the ghost of his brother, but . . ."

"Maybe it wasn't." Rob finished her sentence for her. "Maybe it was some other ghost. They're everywhere, right? Wandering around, attention-seeking, freaking out impressionable teenage girls?"

"That's true." Miranda decided not to rise to the bait. At least Rob seemed to be accepting the idea that ghosts existed. "It might have just been some other ghost in the churchyard, and Nick just really *wanted* him to be his brother."

"Or it might have been his brother there in the churchyard," Sally said. "But that was seven years ago. It doesn't mean that the ghost in the attic is Nick's brother. Or that Nick could even make a positive ID one way or the other."

"See?" Rob said admiringly. "I told you she was Miss Marple."

"Maybe," Sally continued, ignoring him, "as Miranda was saying, Nick really, really wanted to believe the ghost in the attic was his brother. Sometimes if we want something badly enough, we'll believe anything. You know, the way everyone here always believes that England will win the World Cup."

"Nick said he thought he'd been called back here for a reason," said Miranda. She felt sweaty now, and sick. A few days ago she'd thought that Nick was duping her, but now she was wondering if *he* was the one who'd been duped. "He was living in London, but he came back to York, where they grew up. It's the seventh anniversary of his brother's death. So if the ghost appeared to him, and said he was Richard . . ."

"And he only appeared at night, right?" Sally said, nodding at Miranda. "In a pitch-black attic where the only light is a candle. Nick wouldn't be able to see him that clearly."

"I guess," she said. She'd been able to see him pretty well, through his window and hers, even with snow falling. That handsome face, smiling at her. Something so charming about him. Of course Nick would *want* him to be his brother. And it would make sense to him — he comes home to York, and there's his brother appearing to him in the boarded-up house where Nick was sleeping. They'd found each other again, or so it might have seemed to Nick.

"Okay," said Rob, clapping his hands. "So poem, painting — what's up? Why is someone trashing this cellar? It's not like it belongs to the bad guys at York Minster."

"I don't know," Miranda admitted. "But go back a second. Say this ghost can't talk. Some of them can't, you know. Or don't choose to."

"Whatever," Rob said.

"Really, listen. If the ghost held up the palm of his hand," said Miranda, holding her own up to demonstrate, "then Nick would see the painting on it, the same way I did. But he wouldn't be confused like me. He'd recognize it as the fire cloud from *The Fall of Babylon* because he would remember it from their grandfather's house. He would think this was a sign. He would think this ghost, this Richard, was *his* Richard."

"Can I just say one more time — ghosts can't paint!"

"He could have painted it on his hand before he died," Miranda pointed out. "It looked dark, like blood, when I saw it. Not fresh and bright like the painting on this wall."

"And the words on the wall?" Sally asked. "Dark soul and foul thoughts?"

"Nick could have painted them. We know they had paint at some point, in order to do this." Miranda gestured at the wild swirls of red and orange on the cellar wall.

"But how would Nick know those words from the Milton poem?" Rob looked skeptical. "Unless Lord Poole quoted them on a daily basis. And even then — I mean, Mom and Dad are always quoting things, and I couldn't tell you a single line of a single poem. Or even the name of the poem. Or even if it *was* a poem."

"Not everyone revels in their stupidity like you," Miranda retorted, but Sally was waving her hands in the air, trying to get them to shut up.

"He had the book!" she said. "Remember? Miranda's book. I picked it up from next to his bed."

"His mother had a copy, too." Miranda remembered Nick telling her this — it felt like a year ago, when it was only days. "Maybe the exact same book. She might have given it to her father when she moved abroad."

"Did you lend it to him this week?" Rob asked. "I thought you'd just lost it."

"That's what I thought," Miranda said. She thought of her and Nick standing together in the snickelway on Thursday night, pressed together, Nick's arms around her. She'd thought he wanted to be close to her, but maybe all he wanted was to claim back lost property. "He could have taken it out of my pocket. I was carrying it around with me on Thursday and . . ."

She blushed. She didn't want to go into the details of how, exactly, Nick could have extracted the book from her coat pocket without her noticing.

"But if he read what we just read," said Rob, scratching his head, "then he might have figured out the whole Richard Martin thing, too."

"Not if he'd already convinced himself that this ghost was his brother," said Sally. "Back for the seventh anniversary of his death, asking Nick to help him. Isn't that what you said, Miranda? Ghosts reach out because they want someone to help them."

"But what would Richard Martin want weird Nick to do?" Rob was musing rather than asking, drumming his fists against his temples. "Take up where his crazy father left off and burn down York Minster?"

They all looked at each other. Figuring all this out had been exhilarating, but now all Miranda felt was a horrible sense of dread.

"No," she said, closing her eyes. "No, Nick. No."

As if in reply, something began banging and clanking on the painted side of the cellar wall.

CHAPTER EIGHTEEN

"What's that?" Miranda said sharply. "What's that noise?"

"I can't hear anything," said Rob, and Sally shook her head.

"Is there another cellar right next to yours?" Miranda asked. The banging was muffled, but still totally audible. She didn't understand why Rob and Sally couldn't hear it.

"I don't think so," said Sally. "Behind here is the yard, and then there's an alley that runs down the back of all the shops."

"You can't hear it?" Miranda made her way to the far wall, clambering over upturned barrels. She pressed her hands against the painted stones. "They're vibrating. Something . . . it sounds like something driving along a road. Really, you can't hear it?"

She moved her hands to another stone, which felt as though it was practically jiggling. This reminded her of sitting outside the Treasurer's House with Nick, feeling the ground vibrate as the Roman legion marched along deep below them. He'd said that if they were in the cellar, they'd be able to see them.

"Stonegate," she said, not turning around. "It was built on top of a Roman road, wasn't it?"

"Yes," Sally replied. "It ran to the river, I think. Where the river used to be, in St. Helen's Square."

"And up to where the Minster sits now," Miranda said, remembering what Nick had told her. She glanced back at Sally and Rob. "Part of the road's still here. I can hear them marching along it, or something."

"Who's marching?" Rob was wriggling his way over a stack of barrels.

"I don't know. Romans, maybe." She pushed on the stone, dead in the center of the painted fire cloud. It moved. "Help me!"

Rob reached in, pushing hard on the stone. Sally was leaning in from the other side, pressing the stone beneath.

"It's moving," said Rob, through gritted teeth. "Here — let me use a barrel."

Miranda stepped back so he could roll a barrel into place and use it to butt the stones at the center of the fire cloud. A large slab edged back and then, when Rob kicked it, rocked open like a narrow door. He dragged the barrel out of the way, and Miranda leaned into the gap in the wall.

Another underground passage stretched to her left

and her right. The cellar of the White Boar, Miranda realized, wasn't any ordinary pub cellar. In York's underground world, buried deep beneath the city streets, it was the crossroads.

Whatever ghosts had been marching or driving along the road had disappeared into the darkness, and the wall wasn't shaking anymore. But this passageway was even more musty and dank than the one that led to the house on the Shambles. Miranda wanted to gag. In the slice of tunnel illuminated by the cellar light, the stones were furry with moss. Water dribbled from the low ceiling.

"Here," said Sally, now crouched at Miranda's feet and peering down the passageway, too. She leaned in, steadying herself with one hand, and clicked on the flashlight. A beam of light, shone in the direction of the river, revealed the passage narrowing to almost a crawl space. In the other direction, toward the Minster, the passage looked low but still navigable.

"Ugh, it's stinky," said Rob, his head inches away from Miranda's. "What's that?"

Sally's flashlight had picked out a dark shape on the ground — too flat to be a body, thought Miranda; she was trying to keep calm. Too big to be a rat. And they didn't have snakes in England, did they? She wriggled into the passage, banging her head, and took a few uncertain steps toward it. Sally kept the light steady.

"It's okay," Miranda called back. "It's just . . . a blanket."

She gingerly reached out to grab it with the tips of her fingers and drag it back to the doorway. The blanket was sodden.

"Maybe the Romans dropped it," Rob said. He and Sally were squirming away so Miranda could squeeze back into the cellar. She pulled the blanket through the aperture and draped it over a barrel. The blanket was gray and a little worn, but its provenance was much more recent than Roman.

"What a stench!" Sally put down the flashlight. "It's soaking wet. Smells of alcohol."

Rob sniffed.

"Smells of beer," he said. He clicked his fingers. "Hey! That one time I saw Nick, when he was coming out of that store — he was carrying blankets, remember? A big heap of them."

"But there was no bedding at all up in the attic." Sally looked at Miranda. "Was there?"

Miranda thought of *Tales of Old York*, and its account of Jonathan Martin setting his fire. He'd ripped velvet from the pews and set them alight first.

She took a deep breath. "If the ghost is Richard Martin," she began, "and if he's talked Nick into finishing what his father started, then he'd need something to start the fire."

"Old bedding," said Rob. "You can thank me for the brain wave later."

"And you think he dragged it here?" Sally asked her. "Along the tunnel from the Shambles?"

"It makes sense, right? Here in the cellar, he could pull the tubes out of the wall and douse all the blankets with beer, so they'd be more flammable." Miranda couldn't believe how calm she sounded when talking about all this made her sick to her stomach.

"And he had to move all these barrels out of the way so he could get to the other door," Rob added. "He could use the paint to help start a fire as well."

"Paint, blankets." This really did make sense now, Miranda thought. Horrible, frightening sense. "He could drag them all along *this* tunnel until they were right under the Minster, ready to be used when the time was right."

"And when would that be?" asked Sally, but the look on her face, of mounting horror, suggested she knew the answer. "Not . . . not tonight?"

"I have to go NOW," Miranda said, turning around. Their parents were in the Minster. Sally's parents were there. They were all in terrible danger.

Rob grabbed her by the scruff of the neck.

"You're not going anywhere!" he shouted. "It's way too dangerous. You don't even know where this passage leads . . ."

". . . to the Minster!"

"And what if you get there and the whole thing's burning?"

"What if I get there and there's still time?" Miranda tried to wriggle free of his grip. "I can talk to Nick. He knows me. He trusts me. I can tell him that the ghost isn't his brother. I can get him to stop this."

"We should just call the police."

"And say what? There's an underground passage they don't know about, and a ghost, and some beer-soaked blankets, and a quote from Milton? . . . Just let me go, Rob! We've wasted enough time."

"Take the flashlight," Sally told her. "I'll follow you. Rob, if I'm not back in twenty minutes, call the police."

"Have you both gone nuts?" Rob was outraged. "I'm not letting you go off there to risk who knows what. . . ."

"He's right," Miranda told Sally, grabbing the flashlight. "You should stay. There's no point in two of us . . ."

"You may need help moving whatever's at the other end," Sally said firmly. "It took three of us to move this lot."

"Well, then you need *me*." Rob glared at Miranda. "Don't you? Come on, then. Let's go. Before that big old church burns down, with all our parents sitting in it."

"But *you* can't come," Miranda told him. "It might be even worse than the other tunnel."

"That's my problem, not yours. If you think I'm going to sit around while you two play Nancy Drew, you're mistaken. Come on!"

He almost shoved her toward the low doorway.

"Rob," Sally pleaded. "You know what happened last time."

"It wasn't life or death last time," he said. "And if that lunatic Goth can drag his sorry self along here with all his blankets and paint and God knows what else, then it can't be that narrow. Go!"

Rob was wrong, Miranda discovered very quickly. Her shoulders brushed the walls, and she was bent almost double in places. The only sounds were the dripping of water, the splashes of footsteps, and her own heavy breathing. She didn't know how Nick had managed to make his way along here, especially trying to carry a can of paint, or a heavy wet blanket. He must have made many, many trips. Maybe that's why he'd lit the fire in the pub, so the whole place would be sealed off for the final couple of days. He needed to go back and forth through the cellar without any interference. Thinking of Nick, and what he might be doing, made Miranda so worried and upset she wanted to scream. This was all a huge mistake. He was unhappy and lonely and adrift, and the ghost, whoever he was, had preyed on him. She had to find Nick and stop him, before it was too late. Before he damaged the Minster, and hurt people they loved. Before he hurt himself.

One hand gripped the flashlight; the other Miranda used to feel her way along the slimy walls. She had no sense of how long it would take to reach the Minster, or where this passage would lead, exactly. Walking along Stonegate itself, the journey would be ten minutes, probably less, but slipping along a dark underground tunnel was another story.

"Rob!" Sally cried out. Miranda slithered to a halt and trained the light back along the tunnel. Rob was on his knees, head down as though he was about to be sick. Sally crouched, her arms around him.

"Are you okay?" Miranda called, willing him not to black out. This passageway was vile, but for Rob it had to be utter hell.

"Yes." He raised his head. His voice sounded wobbly, but he was getting up. "Keep going."

Miranda pressed on, clawing at each stone, trying to ignore the dirt and slime. She skidded on something, bashing an elbow, and when she placed her free hand back on the wall, it felt different. Freezing cold.

Materializing through the wall on her right, like a mist taking human shape, was a man in an old-fashioned dark suit, his whiskers in huge bristling shanks down either side of his face. When he saw Miranda, he took off his hat and nodded. Cold rippled up her arm.

"Is this the way to the sewer?" he asked her in a low and solemn voice.

"I have no idea," she said. He stood staring at her as though he was waiting for her to say something else. Really, Miranda had just about had it with ghosts. It was all about them, all the time — and time was in short supply right now. She had to get to Nick. When the whiskery man didn't move out of the way, Miranda braced herself and took a big step right through him. Cold electrified her body: It was like walking through an ice shower. He was asking her the question about the sewer again, but Miranda ignored him.

She glanced back, but the man had disappeared —
either through the other wall or into the darkness. Rob
was behind her, staggering, and Sally was following him,
reaching out a steadying hand, urging him along. He was
making a superhuman effort, Miranda knew. The close-
ness of this space made her own head throb; she wanted to
smack the walls and claw her way out. The distance they'd
traveled and the distance that lay before them seemed
endless, immeasurable. If anything happened to them
down here, nobody would be able to hear them scream.

The beam of the flashlight caught a tumbled pile of
stones, like a cairn. The end of the tunnel.

"Here!" Miranda called, but her voice was strangled.
She hoped they wouldn't have to move all these stones.
Rob looked fit for nothing right now.

"Come on," Sally was urging Rob. "We're nearly
there. You can do it."

Miranda shone the light over the pile of stones: There
was no obvious door, or a slab that could be moved. Panic
washed through her, more potent than the chill of
the ghost. What if Nick had sealed off whatever portal he
was using?

Rob and Sally stumbled up, Rob grabbing at Miranda
to keep himself vaguely upright. Milky vomit stains
splotched the front of his sweater. Both of them were
breathing loudly. Sally's knuckles were scraped and
bleeding.

"Okay, it must be here somewhere," Miranda said,

shining the flashlight along each wall. "We should press on the stones."

"Listen," gasped Sally. "Listen!"

She pointed above their heads, and Miranda looked up. Sally was right: There was something, very faint, like a hum. In the distance, high above their heads. Rhythmic and droning. Music. The orchestra, with their mother conducting.

"Up here," Rob said. His voice sounded groggy. He twisted to lean his head back and reach his hands up onto the low, arched ceiling of the passageway. Miranda stuck the flashlight into the neckline of her sweater, ramming the handle into her tank top so the beam shone upward. With both hands, she felt along the stones above their heads. One slab looked a little bigger than the others, a little flatter. Sally was pushing one end of it, grunting with the effort, and it lifted — just a fraction, but it lifted.

"Okay," said Rob, who seemed to be recovering himself, "let me stand in the middle. We might have to push it up and then slide it."

He pressed his hands flat against the center of the stone and heaved. When it lifted a little, Rob leaned forward, letting it settle out of place, a gap of a few inches visible. The distant music sounded a little louder, a little clearer, though still foggy and far away.

"If Goth Boy could do this," Rob muttered, "then I sure as hell can."

He reached his fingers into the gap and pushed again. The stone slid back — just a few more inches, but it moved.

"Push me," said Miranda. She pulled the flashlight out of its sweater holster and handed it to Sally. The gap was still small, but if Rob hoisted her, she could slide it open more as she climbed through.

"I should go first," he said, but then he seemed to swoon, slumping back onto the wet cobbles.

"Rob!" Sally dropped to the ground, trying to cradle his head.

"I'm okay," he slurred. "Just . . . dizzy. I'll be okay in a second."

"Can you get through?" Sally asked Miranda, and Miranda reached up, pushing the slab as hard as she could, shoving it a few more inches along. Then she heaved herself up, her legs swinging, using her shoulders to push the stone again.

The air was different up here, almost fresh compared with the clamminess of the underground passageway. Miranda blinked, adjusting to the light of whatever room she was entering. It was dim, but nothing like the swampy darkness she was leaving. At first, all Miranda could see were flagstones, the base of a column, a vaulted ceiling. The slab they'd dislodged was right next to some kind of stone basin or trough. Propped against the next column was a huge slab of stone elaborately carved with ghoulish figures, their feet licked by pointy flames. The devils held up a giant pot crammed with dozens of contorted, howling skeleton-like people.

Miranda knew that stone. She'd seen it before, sketched in *Tales of Old York*. That was one of the drawings she and her father had noticed the day Lord Poole dropped the book through their front door, what seemed like a hundred years ago.

The carved slab was the Doomstone. The underground passage had led them straight into the crypt of York Minster.

CHAPTER NINETEEN

Miranda crawled away from the dislodged slab and stood, shakily, with one hand resting on the pillar. The stone floor of the crypt was dotted with candles flickering in the gloom. There was no other way for light to get in, Miranda realized, because the stairs up into the Minster, one on either side of the crypt, were blocked. So were the grates that would let someone in the crypt see the feet of people walking along the aisles. Miranda glanced behind her: a pair of sturdy locked gates. At this time of night, with the Minster locked up, the only way in or out of here was the underground passage.

She stepped slowly around the pillar, careful to avoid the candles. Her legs were still shaking from the journey here, and her hands felt dusty with drying mud. She was afraid of what was waiting for her on the other side of the pillar. Maybe nobody would be in here at all. Maybe they'd got this completely wrong, and Nick was out wandering the streets somewhere, looking for her. Rob always said Miranda had an overactive imagination, and tonight, possibly for the first time ever, she wanted him to be proved right.

But no. As soon as Miranda rounded the pillar, she saw him. Nick was standing, his back to her, on the raised stone altar platform. He was wearing his usual jeans and frayed gray sweater, the leather coat discarded in a heap nearby. If he'd heard the slab moving, he wasn't reacting to the arrival of an uninvited guest. He was totally focused on painting the bare stone wall with the same spiraling fire cloud Miranda had seen in the White Boar's cellar, though this one was even bigger and wilder. Nick slapped on paint in sweeping, crude strokes. Heaps of sodden blankets lay at the base of the altar, banked up against its rails. One of the paint pots, dripping a scarlet trail, sat perilously close to a lit candle.

Without his coat, Nick looked skinny and vulnerable. Miranda wanted to rush forward and grab him — hug him, maybe, or at least drag him away. But she had no idea about his state of mind. She stepped forward cautiously, conscious of the lamenting strains of music droning somewhere above their heads.

"Nick," she said. When he didn't turn, she raised her voice. "Nick! Nick — it's me. Miranda."

He swung around, staring at her without any sort of recognition, as though she were an apparition. His bloodshot eyes seemed to look right through her.

"Miranda," she said again, in case he hadn't heard her. He seemed to be in some kind of trance. She took another step forward.

The brush in Nick's shaking hand dropped with a thud onto the altar.

"No," he said. His voice was trembling as much as his hand. "You're not supposed to be here."

"Nick, I . . ."

"You're supposed to be at home. You're supposed to be safe."

"I *am* safe," Miranda told him, but even her voice was trembling now. The sight of him like this, so nervous and manic, was heartbreaking. "I don't believe you'd ever hurt me. All you have to do is come back with me now, through the tunnel. Forget all this. Let's just go."

Nick's deadened expression didn't change.

"You don't understand," he said. He groped around on the altar for the paintbrush.

"But I do." She took another step forward. Her heart pounded in time to the pulsing music upstairs. "I know what this picture is, the one you're painting. It's from *The Fall of Babylon*. You painted it on the cellar wall, too. At the White Boar. I saw it, you know. I saw it tonight. And the ghost — Richard. He has it painted on his hand, doesn't he?"

Nick looked startled, his eyes widening at the mention of Richard's name. His hand rested on the paintbrush, but he didn't try to pick it up.

"I've seen him, too," Miranda said quickly. She was trying to stay calm. She *had* to stay calm if she was going to persuade Nick to walk away. It wasn't too late, she kept telling herself. There was a lot of paint and mess down here, but nothing was on fire yet. "He's been . . . appearing to me, in the attic window. Almost every night. I saw him. He showed me his hand."

"You've seen him?" Nick said softly. His face crumpled like a child about to cry. "You never told me. *He* never told me. He said that nobody else could see him, only me."

"There are other things he hasn't told you," said Miranda, sliding her feet across another slab. If she could just reach Nick, take his hand, he'd come to his senses. "You think he's your brother, don't you?"

"He *is* my brother." Nick sounded defiant. Miranda shook her head.

"No, Nick. He isn't."

"He's my brother," Nick repeated stubbornly. "He found me and asked me to help him."

"Please, you have to listen!" Miranda pleaded. "His name is Richard, but he's not your brother. He's the ghost of someone named Richard Martin. His father tried to burn down York Minster all those years ago and he's been waiting for someone to help him . . . help him finish what his father started. He wants you to think he's your brother because he needs you to do this. Isn't that right? He needed you to carry the blankets and the paint here, to light the candles. To light the fire. You're the one who does all the dirty work. You're the one who'll have to go to prison."

"Oh, I'm not getting out of here," Nick said, and there was an eerie calm to his voice. "It all ends in here, tonight. You're the one who has to leave. Please, Miranda. I promised my brother that I'd do this, and I'm not going to let him down the way everybody else did."

"He's NOT your brother!" Miranda cried. Why wouldn't Nick believe her? "Think about it. The wound — it's all wrong. Richard Martin didn't hang himself, he cut his throat. You can see that on his neck!"

Nick picked up the paintbrush. He wasn't listening.

"And why would your brother want to bring harm to you? He wouldn't want you to put yourself in mortal danger. You were his little brother. He loved you."

"Living or dying," Nick mumbled. "What's the difference? It doesn't matter."

"It *does* matter." Miranda was crying with frustration now, smearing the tears away with the back of her hand. "When someone you love dies, it doesn't mean you give up. And I don't believe your brother would come back just to get you to kill yourself, too. Because that's what you're doing. That's what you're — ah!"

An intense blast of cold shot through her body. Directly in front of her, the ghost of Richard Martin had materialized, floating against part of the altar rail. His shirt was open so the bloodied slash across the base of his throat was clearly visible. His pale face was serene, the hint of a smile curling his upper lip. He was so hand-some, Miranda thought. She'd always thought that. But tonight she was seeing him differently. He'd lied to Nick — told him that nobody else could see him, when he knew that Miranda could. Lied when he'd persuaded Nick they were brothers. All week she'd been longing to meet him, longing to be in the same room with him. Now he was the last person Miranda wanted to see.

"Sorry, Richard," Nick said to the back of the ghost's head. His voice shook with nerves. He was afraid of him, Miranda realized: Nick was afraid of the ghost. She was a little afraid of him as well. How far would he go to get his own way? "I didn't tell her . . . You know I didn't tell her anything about tonight. She found the passageway."

The ghost slowly raised his thin white hand and pointed at Miranda. An icy jolt gripped her stomach, like a punch to the gut.

"Miranda," the ghost said. His voice was faint, and there was a soft burr to it. "O brave new world, that has such people in't!"

He was mocking her, Miranda thought, quoting her namesake in a Shakespeare play, *The Tempest*. How dare he? She'd thought his smile was seductive, alluring, but now she saw the cruelty in it. In his eyes, too — they glim-mered, steely and cold. He was a bully, she thought. A handsome, arrogant bully.

"You're not interested in a brave new world, are you, Richard?" she said, swallowing back her fear. She couldn't just stand there and let Nick ruin his life, ruin the lives of hundreds of other people. "You're obsessed with the old. With what happened in the past, to your father. You're just using Nick. Why don't you tell him the truth? Admit you're not his brother!"

The ghost smiled at her almost fondly, as though she were an amusing child entertaining him with a nursery rhyme. Miranda felt like slapping him, but she knew there was no point. How could she have been so taken in by someone so awful? How could she have daydreamed about talking to him, touching him, kissing him? The very thought of it disgusted her now. She'd been a fool — a silly girl with a crush.

Nick stood transfixed, staring at the ghost's hovering form. Some evil spell had been cast on him, Miranda thought, and she had no idea how to make it go away.

"And who," said the ghost, his smile fading, "is this?"

Miranda glanced over her shoulder. Rob and Sally had stepped out of the shadows and were standing a few feet behind her. Even in the dim light, she could see they both looked bewildered. They couldn't see the ghost, she realized. They couldn't hear him. To them, Miranda was talking to a flickering candle.

"All of you, get out," Nick said fiercely. There was a desperate look in his eyes that Miranda remembered from yesterday — the look of a trapped animal.

"No!" Miranda couldn't leave him here, not with this malevolent, lying ghost. Nick *had* to believe her. "Ask him, Nick. Ask him right now if he's your brother."

"It's too late, Miranda." Nick's eyes pleaded with her. "Get out of here while you still can."

"Or stay," said the ghost, surveying Miranda with gimlet eyes. How could she have thought they were so soulful? "You should stay, Miranda. Watch us complete my father's work."

Miranda gasped.

"Your . . . your father?" Nick stepped back, gripping the altar with one shaking hand. The ghost said nothing. He smiled at Miranda again, not even bothering to turn to look at Nick.

"What's wrong?" Rob's voice, behind her. "Miranda, what's going on?"

"He just admitted it," she said, not daring to turn around. She didn't want to take her eyes off the ghost. She didn't trust him at all. "The ghost. Richard Martin. Everything we pieced together — we were right. The ghost is sitting right in front of me. We're talking to him, Nick and I. He's just said *my father's work*. He wants Nick to finish HIS FATHER'S WORK. He's admitted it! Nick, you heard him!"

Nick said nothing. He looked utterly anguished, gazing around the crypt as though seeing it for the first time.

The ghost swept his arm through the air, and Miranda toppled over, knocked onto her butt by an icy wind. The candles near her teetered, and two fell over. He wouldn't need Nick to start the fire, she realized. It was too late. Everything was too late.

"The candles — out!" she shouted, grabbing the nearest one and extinguishing the flame with her fingers. She didn't care if it burned her. Rob darted past her, pulling his sweater over his head. He was trying to reach the ones near the beer-soaked blankets, she realized, beating at them with his sweater. The ghost regarded him coolly for a moment, and then whooshed his arm through the air again. Rob was blown back, slamming hard into the base of a column.

"Ow!" he shouted. "What the hell was that?"

"Help!" Sally ran up one of the staircases and started banging on the boards with the flashlight. "Help us! Someone!"

There was a thundering outside, like rain — applause, Miranda realized. The opera was over. *Please,* she thought, *everyone get out.* Her parents, Sally's parents, Lord Poole. They all had to get out before the fire started. What she and Rob and Sally would be able to do — that might be a different story.

Richard Martin rose into the air, floating high above the altar. Miranda, stamping candles out now, watched him warily. She couldn't fight him, but at least she could extinguish the flames. Nick, still standing at the altar, framed by his lurid fire-cloud painting, watched him, too. Maybe the ghost was leaving. Maybe he was —

Whhooooossssshhhhh.

This time he used his whole body, sailing the length of the altar like an attacking bird of prey. Nick and Miranda recoiled from the cold blast, Nick raising his arm to protect his face. The long line of candles fell, one after the other, onto the hedge of blankets, flames rippling and dancing in their wake. The ghost vanished, his work finished: The fire had begun.

Rob was back on his feet, beating at the flames with his sweater, without much effect.

"Get back!" he shouted at Miranda. "How did all those candles fall over?"

"The ghost," she told him, crawling toward the altar where Nick still stood, trapped behind a line of flames. "He can push things, blow them over the way he just did with you — like a hurricane. But he's gone now."

"Help!" Sally was banging with all her might, but nobody seemed to hear her. The concert was in the nave, a long way away. Hundreds of people were standing up, talking — they'd never hear her.

"It's no good!" Rob shouted. "We should just get out of here. Come on!"

Nick looked at her across the leaping flames, his face twisted with misery.

"Your coat!" Miranda shouted at Nick. No way was she leaving him here. "Throw it to me!"

Nick hesitated, as though he didn't understand what she was saying. Then he reached down for the leather coat and threw it high in the air. It soared over the fire line, and Miranda scrambled to catch it, using it to start bashing at the nearest pile of blankets, thwacking the coat onto the flames over and over. Sally was still banging and calling, drumming the flashlight against the wooden barricades so hard, Miranda thought the wood might splinter. Smoke was filling the crypt, billowing up from the altar rail.

"Miranda." Rob grabbed her shoulder, overtaken by a coughing fit. "Go!"

Miranda looked at her brother. The night of the accident, she'd sat there in the grassy ditch. Jenna dead in the car, Rob trapped for hours. Miranda dazed and stupid on the side of the road. Useless, useless, useless. Tonight she wasn't going to be useless, or passive, or confused. If she was getting out of here, so was Nick.

"Nick's trapped," she told Rob, choking on a mouthful of smoke. "We can't leave without him. We can't, okay?"

"Okay," Rob wheezed. He reached out a hand to Nick. "You're gonna have to jump!"

"Jump!" Miranda cried. "Nick — jump!"

Rob stepped back, but Miranda saw what he couldn't: The ghost was back. He soared through the air again, over Rob's head and back over the altar. The force of his ice-cold wind pushed Rob backward, thumping him hard into a pillar.

"The ghost!" Miranda shouted. Rob lay where he'd been thrown, his face contorted in pain. She glanced back at the altar to see that one of the paint pots on the altar had tipped over in the ghost's ferocious wake, red liquid seeping toward the flames.

"Jump!" Miranda screamed at Nick. He hesitated again, and then he was in the air, too — not flying, like the ghost, but hurtling over the altar rail just as the stream of paint caught fire. Flames leapt up the altar cloth and climbed the freshly painted wall. Nick rolled on the ground. He was on fire.

Miranda threw the leather coat over him, beating on it with her raw, singed hands. Her eyes stung. She was vaguely aware of Sally there next to her, helping her, a blurry shape in the smoke.

Nobody was going to die tonight, Miranda told herself. They had to get out of here, just like Rob had said. All of them, every single one. They'd have to lay Nick on his coat and drag him back along the tunnel.

"We have to get him out!" she shouted at Sally. Sally nodded, swaying as she stood up, reaching out to grab Rob. At least he was on his feet again, though his forehead was bleeding.

"Sal, you go," he said, bending over Nick. "Fast as you can. We'll bring —"

Whhoooooosssssshhhhh.

"Aaaahhh!" Sally screamed. The blast flung her across the crypt, skidding on her back all the way to the stone basin.

"Enough!" roared Miranda. She couldn't even see the ghost when she looked up — the air was dense with smoke now — but the arctic cold of his presence sliced through her. "You have your fire! Let us go!"

Rob had managed to roll Nick over onto the spread coat. Nick was limp — passed out, maybe. Miranda couldn't see him clearly. She felt weak and woozy, struggling to breathe in the thick smoke.

"I'll drag him over to the tunnel," Rob gasped. He grasped the collar of the leather coat and pulled Nick's prone form a few inches. It would take forever to get him along the underground passage. Hopefully, Sally was okay — Miranda couldn't even see her anymore. She couldn't see anything but flames and smoke and her brother struggling to drag Nick's body away. She had to help Rob.

Miranda staggered to her feet just in time to see the ghost materialize again, not high above her but inches from her face. He was smiling at her through the haze, his icy grip freezing her in place. He glanced over his shoulder at Rob still struggling with Nick on the make-shift stretcher, and the look alone had enough force, enough malevolence behind it, to wipe Rob out again. He lay on the stone floor of the crypt, as still and silent as Nick.

It was over, Miranda knew. She had no strength left. She'd tried, but she couldn't save her brother, or Nick, or Sally. She couldn't save herself. They were all going to die here, in this sealed-up tomb under the Minster.

She could hear distant shouts and knocks from some-where outside — or underneath — the crypt. More ghosts, she thought. Ghosts everywhere. Miranda felt a heaviness descend. She'd be joining them soon, joining their strange netherworld. She and Nick and Sally and Rob. They were all going to be ghosts.

Intense cold still froze her in place. The ghost of Richard Martin was leaning toward her. He closed his eyes and she realized that he was about to kiss her. With the last of her strength, Miranda reached a trembling hand toward his face. She wanted to push him away, but it was impossible: Her hand passed straight through him. The scar on his neck was clotted with blood. His lips looked thin and cold and papery.

All this week, Miranda had wanted to be close to him. She'd wanted to see him face-to-face, not through the window. Well, now her wish was going to come true. This surreal, perverted fairy tale would have its inevitable ending. The ghost in the attic — so beautiful, so evil — was going to be the last thing Miranda ever saw.

CHAPTER TWENTY

Miranda had read somewhere that the afterlife was all bright white lights and the faces of your loved ones smiling at you. So was the hospital. The lights hurt her eyes, which were still sore because of the smoke. Her throat was sore as well, and her head was thudding. Smoke inhalation, said the nurse in the blue uniform. Sister, the other people called her.

"We had to keep you overnight," Sister said, plumping up Miranda's pillow. "Make sure you didn't have any inhalation burns. Monitor your blood chemistry and your oxygen levels."

"And my brother?" Miranda managed to speak.

"Your hands will take a little while to heal, and he's got a cracked rib or two. But you're both going to be fine."

"And Sally . . . Sally Framington?" Miranda croaked. The sheriff's deputy had stood over her in the road through the cornfields, saying he was real sorry, telling her that her friend was dead.

"She's going to be fine as well."

"And . . ." Miranda started, wanting to know about Nick, but Sister shook her head.

"No — not another word! No more talking. You need to rest. You're a very lucky girl."

Lucky. That was the word her parents had used, too. When she first woke up, she saw the lights and then their faces looming over her, and even through her haze of medication, Miranda saw that people could look agonized and miserable and relieved and happy all at the same time. She was relieved, too: Her parents were safe.

"We've come so close to losing you both," her mother had sobbed. "Not once, but twice. In six months!"

"Everything's fine now," Jeff said, over and over. He'd also been crying. "We're lucky. Very, very lucky."

It was Monday, the day they were supposed to leave York. Miranda drifted into sleep again, and woke to find her parents back at her bedside. They were going to be released — like animals back into the wild, her father said, trying to joke — that afternoon. Sally would be discharged as well. Incredibly, she'd made it out of the crypt and all the way back to the pub. Crawling most of the way, Miranda's parents said, on her hands and knees. She was in a terrible state, but she'd managed to call the police as soon as she got back. By then they'd already broken through the boards and unlocked the gates. One of the ushers had heard a dog barking madly and had gone to investigate; he couldn't see the dog, but he *had* seen smoke and raised the alarm.

"I wish they'd found that dog," Jeff said. "I'd like to shake its paw."

The stonemason's dog, thought Miranda. Nick had said that dog never liked him. He always barked like crazy whenever he saw Nick. Thank goodness, she thought. At last — a useful ghost.

Her parents knew certain things now — that there was an underground passage, and that Lord Poole's grandson was somehow involved. Lord Poole's grandson, still alive, in another ward of the hospital. He'd regained consciousness, they told her. His burns would have been much, much worse, they said, if Miranda hadn't acted so quickly. Rob had told them that she'd beaten the flames out with Nick's coat. Nick didn't remember anything.

After lunch, when the detectives arrived to talk to Nick, Lord Poole came to visit Miranda. He'd been sitting with Nick all night.

"I lost my grandson once before," he told her, settling into the plastic chair beside her bed. "I'm not going to lose him again. When all this is over, he has a home at Lambert House. He knows that now, at least."

"Will he . . . will he have to go to jail?"

"It doesn't seem so. Probably some kind of hospital where he can get help and recover. What he did was terribly destructive and dangerous and reprehensible. But he wasn't in his right mind. You know that better than anyone."

"He's not a bad person," Miranda told him. Lord Poole looked so sad and so old, she wanted to reach out and pat him on the arm. But it was impossible. Her bandaged hands stuck out of the sleeves of her hospital gown like giant white paws, throbbing with a dull pain. "He thought the ghost of his brother was telling him to do all this. None of this was his idea. As soon as he realized that he'd been duped . . ."

Lord Poole's eyes were red. She hoped he wasn't going to cry.

"I feel terrible asking you this," he said, staring down at his hands. "But we might need your help, Miranda. It seems that . . . it seems that you knew Nick better than anyone in the days leading up to the fire. Anything you can tell the police and our barrister about Nick's state of mind — well, it would be very helpful."

"I don't know if they'd believe me." Miranda wasn't sure if her parents would believe it all, let alone the police. "If he's considered insane because he can see ghosts, then I'm insane as well. Because I could see the ghost just as clearly as Nick could. If I hadn't been able to, then I wouldn't have been able to figure out what was going on."

"Thank God you did," Lord Poole said, his smile unbearably sad.

"So you believe me?" Miranda struggled to sit up.

"There once was a time," said Lord Poole, "when I could see ghosts. When I was younger, much younger. Like you."

"Really?"

"Oh yes. There was one particular fellow — flayed alive and nailed by the Vikings to a church door. Saw him every time I passed. He was always shouting and carrying on. I couldn't stand the sight of him."

"Really?" Despite the lurid description, Miranda smiled. Nick had seen that ghost, too. He was planning to take Miranda the night she'd had to stand him up.

"St. Margaret Clitherow, too," said Lord Poole. "You've seen *her*, I think."

"I have." It was such a relief, finding an adult she could talk to about all this. "But how did you know that?"

"An inkling I had, that night on the Shambles," he said.

"But you couldn't see her?"

"No. Not anymore. I haven't seen ghosts for years."

"When did it stop?"

"Just before I married Mabel," said Lord Poole. "I can tell you the precise year — 1960. I was so happy that I think I couldn't *see* unhappiness anymore."

"You think you have to be sad to see ghosts?"

"Perhaps there has to be some great sadness in your life to make you open to the unhappy currents of the spirit world. My parents died when I was quite young, and I think I was an unhappy, lonely sort of lad until I met Mabel."

"I wish I could have met her," said Miranda.

"She was a wonderful woman. No sightings of her as a

ghost, I'm pleased to report. She's resting in peace, the way we all hope to when the time comes."

"I'm sorry . . ." Miranda began, and stopped. There was so much she was sorry for. She didn't know where to begin. "I'm sorry for not telling you that I'd seen Nick. He asked me to keep it a secret, and . . ."

"You were a true and loyal friend," Lord Poole said. He didn't seem angry with her. "You tried to stop him from lighting that terrible fire. You did all you could."

"But if there's anything I can do *now*," she said. Lord Poole's kindness made her feel even more guilty. "For you or for Nick. Tell me. I'll talk to the police — give them a statement — whatever you want."

"There's one thing you can do," Lord Poole said, reaching out to squeeze her shoulder. "Nick would like to see you. Before you leave the hospital. Would that be possible?"

Nick was in a room by himself, his back turned to the view of a parking lot. A policeman sat outside the room. Nick lay in bed, wearing a pale green gown, his arms and head bandaged. He looked like someone else altogether. Miranda told herself not to cry.

He lay very still. His eyes were the only things that moved, following Miranda into the room. She nudged an orange plastic chair close to the bed, knocking it into position with her knee, and sat down. Nick looked at her and said nothing. He was on a lot of pain medication, the nurse in his ward had told Miranda. He needed to rest. She could only stay five minutes.

"Can you speak?" she whispered. They had to leave the door open.

Nick blinked at her. His eyes were dark and liquid, like ink.

"The last thing I remember," he murmured, "is you telling me to jump. I think I knocked my head."

"I'm glad you're okay," Miranda said softly.

"And . . . your brother?" Nick rasped, swallowing with effort. "And the other girl?"

"Rob and Sally. They're fine. Everyone's okay."

Nick closed his eyes, and Miranda wondered if he was falling asleep. He opened them again and they were red. He was blinking back tears.

"Your hands," he said.

"*Your* hands." The bandages on his were even more impressive.

"No more painting," he said, with an almost smile.

"Good," Miranda said, smiling back, though she wanted to cry. It was relief, more than anything. This wasn't like the accident with Jenna. They were all alive.

"Can you come back and see me again?" he asked. Miranda shook her head.

"We leave today," she told him. He adjusted his position in the bed, wincing with pain. "Are you okay? Can I . . . do anything?"

"You saved my life," he whispered. "They told me."

Miranda dropped her head.

"You should be thanking the stonemason's dog," she murmured, and Nick's mouth twitched again, as though he wanted to smile but it was too much effort.

"They're going to put me away for a while," he said. "Till I get my head straight. Will you write to me?"

"Of course," she told him. "When my hands work again. Okay?"

Nick smiled at her — a sad, sweet smile.

"I didn't know you could see him." He didn't have to say "Richard" or "the ghost": Miranda knew exactly who he was talking about. "I thought I was the only one. I had no idea he was . . . lying about that. Lying about everything."

"And I didn't know you were living up there," Miranda said. "Right across the street from my room."

"We both had our secrets," said Nick, rolling back a little and wincing with pain.

"No more secrets now," she said. She wished he could touch her hand again, the way he did that day in the Minster.

"Time to say your good-byes," the nurse called from the doorway. Miranda slowly stood up. She leaned over the bed, careful not to brush against his bandaged arms, and kissed him. Although Miranda meant to kiss his cheek, Nick twisted his head — in a way that must have hurt — so his lips touched hers, tender and cool.

Walking back to her ward, walking out to the taxi with

Rob and her parents, Miranda could still feel the kiss. She would always remember it, she thought. Long when she'd forgotten what it was like to be skewered by the freezing grip of a ghost, she'd remember that sad, soft kiss good-bye.

"Yeah, don't worry about folding anything. Just stuff it all in."

Rob was sitting on his bed, supervising Sally, who was packing his bag. She was the only one of the three of them who'd avoided burns, though she was badly scraped and bruised from getting hurled across the crypt, not to mention the trip back along the underground passage. She held up Rob's vomit-stained sweater.

"Don't you want to throw this away?"

"No," he said, grinning at her. "Sentimental value. Ow!"

"What?" Miranda was standing in the door, trying to cross her arms and failing; the bandages got in the way.

"Everything hurts," he complained. "Next time you see a ghost, could you make it one that doesn't want to toss me around like an enraged bull?"

"Sally got thrown around as well. I don't hear her complaining. Though I think she'll be glad when we leave town."

"Don't say that!" Sally protested. "I don't want Rob to leave. I wish you could all stay."

"Mainly me, though." Rob shot her his smuggest smile. Miranda didn't know how Sally could bear it. Maybe it was hard to tell if guys were idiots when they had a foreign accent. Rob's accent wasn't as cool as Nick's, of course, but she guessed he sounded vaguely exotic to Sally.

"The summer's so far away." Sally tucked a pair of socks into Rob's duffel.

"What's happening this summer?" Miranda asked.

"I'm coming over," Rob told her, acting as though it was no big deal. "Plan cleared with the Parental Unit, before you start accusing me of anything."

"Yeah, well, you hate to fly."

"Over it."

"What — just like that?"

"Okay, well, in case you've forgotten, I've crawled my way through ten miles of underground tunnel. You know, to save the day."

"Historical revisionism aside," said Miranda, rolling her eyes, "I don't think you can overcome claustrophobia just like that."

"No," Rob agreed. "I guess not. But it's a start."

Sally zipped up Rob's duffel and patted it.

"What's going on across the street?" she asked. The boarded-up house had been swaddled in police tape all day.

"They took the boards off the front door," Miranda reported. "And they're swarming all over the place. I can see them through my window."

"Oh! That reminds me. I have something for you." Sally rummaged in the big silver purse she'd thrown under Rob's chair. The suede jacket he'd bought her at the secondhand store hung on the chair back. "Here it is — your book. We left it in the cellar."

Sally handed her *Tales of Old York*, Miranda grasping it as best she could with her bandage mittens. It looked slightly more tattered and falling-apart than it had just over a week ago, when Lord Poole dropped it off. Miranda was going to mail it to him when she got back to the States. It belonged to him, to his family. It should be sitting on the shelves at Lambert House when Nick got home, whenever that might be.

Miranda retreated to her own room to set the book on top of her carry-on bag. Her mother would have to pack it, just as she'd packed the rest of Miranda's things. A policeman stood in the window across the street, in the same spot where the ghost had once watched her. He was apparently dusting the frame for fingerprints. Miranda resisted the urge to wave to him. The Christmas lights of the Shambles sparkled in the fading light of the afternoon. It was dusk — not a real time, Miranda thought, smiling. But the time of day when ghosts started coming out.

Her mother, complaining that the attic rooms were too stuffy, had left the window open. Miranda leaned out, gazing down into the street. A group of tourists, all wearing Minnesota Vikings jackets, posed for a picture outside a tea shop. A ghost-tour guide strode up and down waving his black cape in a melodramatic way, shouting that the only "true and authentic" walk around York's haunted sights would begin at seven, outside the Roman Bathhouse. Two young girls, giggling and grabbing each other, were walking out of the photography store. Miranda wondered what they'd chosen as costumes. Cleopatra, Maid Marian, Victorian misses in crinolines and bonnets?

Behind them, stepping straight through the window and into the street, was someone Miranda had seen before. The ghost of Margaret Clitherow floated over the cobbled pavement for a moment, her long hair almost black against her white, blood-streaked shift. She looked up at Miranda's window and smiled. Gentle fingers of cold traced their way across Miranda's scalp, tingling against her skin.

Miranda smiled down at the ghost, not confused or afraid this time. She could see Margaret Clitherow today, but if she ever returned to York — *when* she returned to York — it might not be possible. Like Lord Poole, she might lose the power to connect with the dark currents of the spirit world. One day, maybe very soon, she would only see happiness.

EPILOGUE

At night, cornfields looked like the ocean, but during the day, at the height of a baking-hot summer, they were a swishing forest of green, stretching toward the sun.

Miranda hadn't been back to the crossroads for months, but today she said she'd go. Alejandro, the exchange student, was here from Spain again, and he'd called Miranda, sounding diffident and shy. He remembered Jenna from that party in the farmhouse, one long year ago. He wanted Miranda to take him to the place, he said. The last place.

There was nothing to see there, Miranda warned him. Nobody had stuck a little white cross into the grassy verge; nobody had left fake flowers, or candles in jars, or ribbons. If Alejandro wanted to see Jenna's grave, in the cemetery on the east side of town, Miranda could take him. There were always flowers there. Kids from school left notes for Jenna in a Mason jar. Miranda went there sometimes to tidy it all up, and wash the gravestone down with water from the rusty tap, so Jenna's parents wouldn't have to. But at the crossroads, there was nothing but the rippling song of insects — like radio interference, humming across the cornfields.

Rob said he would drive them. He was driving again now — not far, not often, but he was trying. They pulled over so Alejandro could walk around. Rob stood by the car, leaning against the hood. He kept his sunglasses on and his arms folded.

"You saw her, yes?" Alejandro asked, and Miranda gave him the bare bones of the story. This was the place the car landed. This was the path Jenna's ghost took, padding across the grass and into the cornfield. This was the place Miranda sat watching her. Feeling Jenna's cold fingers brush across her hair.

The last place she saw Jenna.

Miranda could still see ghosts — or, at least, she saw them occasionally, trying not to think about it too much. But she'd never seen Jenna again, and for that she was grateful. Nick had said that maybe Jenna had no unfinished business, that she'd only wanted to say good-bye. Miranda didn't want to think of her hanging around in a cornfield like that farmer with the shotgun wound three miles down the road. Jenna was somewhere else, somewhere better. Somewhere with excellent New Wave music, not insects, as a soundtrack.

Alejandro looked at the corn, and he looked at the road, and he looked at the wide blue sky. This place reminded him of where his grandparents lived, he said, near Córdoba in southern Spain, except there the fields were planted with sunflowers.

On the drive back into town, Alejandro thanked Rob and Miranda for taking him. He'd thought about bringing something from Spain to leave there for Jenna — a soccer team pennant, some sand from the beach at Barcelona — but he'd decided against it, and now he was glad. It should be left alone, that beautiful place where Jenna disappeared, he said, and then he apologized for his poor English. He invited them to come and visit him in Spain, any time they liked.

Miranda thought about the fields of sunflowers, their faces raised to the sky. One day she'd go over to Spain and find them. There was so much in this world to see and do. Every new day — bright with sunshine or swirling with snow — was a gift.

ACKNOWLEDGMENTS

Huge thanks to my patient and wise editor, Aimee Friedman, the team at Point/Scholastic, and the irrepressible Richard Abate at 3Arts. My husband, Tom Moody, was — as ever — a sounding board, first reader, and co-conspirator.

There would be many more factual errors in this book were it not for the advice of various well-informed friends — Gallaudet Howard (medical), Deborah Keyser (musical), and Andrew Keyser (legal and literary). I'm also indebted to one of the Pitkin Guides, *The Fires of York Minster*, and to *Ghosts and Gravestones of York* by Philip Lister. A special shout-out to the Haunted Walk of York for the winter's-night tour that gave me many insights into the city's stories; to my friend Trev Broughton, who reminded me of happy student days in York, when I went to Bettys every week and first learned the difference between a bar and a gate; and to Trev's daughter, Ellen Hart, with the hope that she enjoys this novel and forgives me for the many artistic liberties taken with her beautiful hometown.